THE WINDS BLEW

BY

S R KAY

The Winds Blew

Copyright © 1889 Books 2024

All rights reserved. The moral rights
of the author have been asserted..

Cover artwork © 1889books 2024
Paragaph dividers designed by Freepik
Cover font: Eduardo Recife / Misprinted Type ©
[http://www.misprintedtype.com]

www.1889books.co.uk

ISBN: 978-1-915045-30-0

Author's Note

This is, in a way, a sort of sequel to *Built on Sand,* but the thought I had was that the two novels could perhaps be read at the same time. I often like to have two books on the go at once, and love it when they complement each other in unexpected ways, through similar themes or opposing moods enhancing each other. My hope is that both books together provide a wide-angle view on life and inheritance. If that is too high-faluting, then I hope they at least entertain separately.

– S R Kay 2024

JOSEPHINE. I don't ever remember liking the name. Not from the very first consciousness I had of that being what people called me. Perhaps it was just too long and complicated a name, perhaps too hard to pronounce for a little mite, and then too hard to spell once I was made to sit it and dip a scratchy nib in an inkwell. I never could grasp why it didn't actually have an "f" in it. I called myself Jojo at my tea parties with my toys and dolls; Maisie called me that when we were on our own. Mother and father would get cross with me and insisted on chewing their way through the whole Josephine, or when I misbehaved: Josephine Mary.

'No. Not Jo-feff-seen Mary. Jojo!'

'But it is a lovely name, very refined, and Mary is our Queen's name and a princess's name you know.'

But I knew who I was. Later on, at school, I hated discovering it was a female version of a boy's name. And I hated Napoleon. I hated self-appointed cards and renowned hilarious grown-ups singing *Come Josephine in my flying machine.* All the time. Every time.

Little Jojo was born in a place called Eckington. I remember things from back then even though I must have been very young. They are like scenes from a moving picture – you know, like sometimes when the projector goes wrong and the images slow down and sometimes stop before the celluloid burns. I know I can't be getting confused with later life because we moved to Darnall after my third birthday. I thought all the flags and bunting were there to welcome me, not the royal visit – my mother told me that in an off-target jest. I now realise just how much she must have been putting a brave face on everything. She'd had to move house all by herself with a small child – my father having had to go away for work, she said, and not joining us for quite some time after. I was a little scared of him when he came back.

We had had a large garden in Eckington where my father grew things that we needed – that was what it was for: it served a purpose and any question of aesthetics or getting pleasure from being in the place was wholly incidental. But I remember walking through tunnels of plants as big as trees and the warm feeling that came from the praise I got for filling a little jam pot with the caterpillars

I'd collect from his plants: bright green juicy ones and funny small stripy ones.

'Those marvellous little fingers of yours, Josephine.' It was a story he'd tell later in life. He looked back fondly on that garden. It is what he missed the most. 'You were also just the right height to see the little blighters hiding under the leaves.'

I remember those tea parties in my nursery, patches of sunlight on the polished boards through the big window that came almost down to the floor, and Maisie, our servant, who often used to play with me. I don't think mother or father ever did. They always towered above me at the table or standing in the hall. But Maisie came down to my level on the smooth wooden floor with its little roads, railways and pathways, its islands and seas, and made my toys come to life.

I think I loved Maisie best of all. I cried so much when we had to say goodbye to her. I suppose my mother must have been jealous, perhaps that is why she chided me and made me sit in the back of the van amongst the boxes. I cried again when we got to our new home – my room was tiny and dirty and I had so few of my things: only a single tea chest containing a few toys and books. No rocking horse, no perambulator for my dolls, not even the oriental rug that Maisie said was magic. It took me to places far away when Maisie read to me. I'd hang on tight to its edges so as not to tumble into the sea, down a sand dune, or a snowy mountainside.

'But we couldn't bring everything, Josephine.'

'Why?'

'Because it won't all fit, will it?'

'It will.'

'There'd be no room to move. Besides it will be cosy once we settle in, just you see.'

'I want Maisie.'

My mother left me to calm down and I sat and looked around the horrid little room. The bed was black metal. It was like a hospital bed with a mattress on it – cream coloured with thin blue stripes and brown, stained patches in the middle. I listened to the clattering noises my mother made downstairs.

I imagine how difficult it was for my mother. She had been used to her comforts and to managing a household. That makes it sound grander than it was, but as well as Maisie, who kept everything clean, and me happy, there was a lady who ran the kitchen and organised the meals. I remember sitting at a huge table balancing on a cushion opposite mother, father at the end, and a plate being put in front of me and someone chopping it all up small.

'You were sent to us by heaven, Josephine,' my mother would say. 'Isn't that right, Ernest?'

'Indeed she was, dear. A blessing to us.'

So they must have loved me, but I have no memories of hugs. And kisses were only things to be dutifully delivered to downy, powdered cheeks. Did I ever sit on my mother's knee when I was little to hear stories? Or was that just Maisie? Anyway, from the time we came to Darnall I don't remember more than her patting me on the head or cooling my brow with a wet cloth when I had chicken pox or measles. They were firm believers in not spoiling a child. Praise was given when due, but affection... ? My father, especially, adhered to the "spare the rod and spoil the child" school of thought. All the men on our streets seemed to. They all wore the same broad leather belts with a big buckle whose main purpose did not seem to be to combat the effects of gravity on coarse serge.

'When can we go home?' I'd ask.

'This is our home, Josephine.'

'I want to go home.'

'That's enough now. I've told you. I'll hear no more of it.'

'But my horsey.'

'We had to sell it. Another little girl is looking after horsey now.'

'Why? It's not fair.'

'We've had to economise. Now, why don't you go and play outside. But don't go beyond the gate. And no playing with those rough boys.'

I kept asking for Maisie. In the end my mother must have relented. Maisie came round once and sat and drank tea from a blue and white cup balanced on a saucer and smiled at me.

'Leave Maisie alone, Josephine, dearest. You'll spoil her lovely frock if you're not careful.'

'Oh, don't worry, Mrs Cartwright.'

'No. I won't be responsible. She has to learn some manners. Sit down, Josephine, there's a good girl.'

I sulked and cried when Maisie went away again. I had made a show of myself and tried to try to hold on to her, but was sent to my room.

No more talk about our old house was allowed after that. Mention of Maisie just brought a: "That's enough" or the invisible, inaudible-girl treatment.

Then my father came back and added a masculine, brooding, rather threatening presence in the house. I was never told why we had gone down in the world. It was obviously a source of great shame to them both. They must have hated our new residence as much as I did. That might have been why they argued a lot. Did they know how much their voices travelled up through those floors?

The memory of Maisie's cuddles faded. It was years before I saw her again.

SOMETIMES, I don't know what it is, maybe a vowel a fraction too flat or an elongated syllable, or my tongue not quite closing on my teeth when I say *this* or *that*, but people sometimes ask me where I'm from. It is very difficult question for me. Even if I felt I could trust them, even if they had the wherewithal for the long and necessary explanation, I lack the energy or the patience for someone who simply wants to put me in a pigeonhole in order to frame their own identity more clearly. So I usually say something like: 'I have lived in several places but I am a Sheffielder.' It is my home, it is the place I miss most when I am somewhere else. I have a deep taproot here.

People like to know where you are *from* – it creates a sense of order, it puts people in their place. 'He is a born and bred Yorkshireman, therefore I know what he is like.' 'She is Irish – I know her sort.' 'A Jew? We all know what they're like.' 'West Indian: hard-working, prone to mood swings.'

They don't usually mean any harm by it. Some people are genuinely interested – they want to know about people and are happy to sit on a bus and tell a complete stranger about their women's trouble or their son-in-law's misdemeanours – that is one of the things I like about this place: its honesty and its openness. They take you for who you are and accept difference. Go just a few miles up the road and that changes; I don't know why. So when a Sheffielder asks about where you're from, if there is a hint of your being from somewhere else, it is often no more than a conversation starter – often they are simply genuinely curious and interested in what goes on elsewhere. They could find out by reading books or newspapers of course but that would not be so interesting. "On the way back from town today I got chatting to this lovely lady who... and she said... and I never would have guessed it... you never can tell can you... and she'd been to Friedrichs's, she was in the queue in front of me, so I recognised her on the bus and she bought a pork pie, too. That's a new one on me. I thought they were agin it."

And who can blame them? I'm not judging; I am no different. It's so very human after all. You define your own identity in relation to others and their experience. We all have a basic need to know our position in our tribe, to know who we are loved by and who we can trust, who we must be wary of. It is not just a question of survival, I don't suppose, but of happiness, of being at ease, feeling good in one's skin.

If I were to drop into the conversation with the woman on the bus that I was once a good little girl in the Bund deutscher Mädel she would, in all likelihood, look at me gone out. As if I had spoken Martian. I could explain it was like the Girl Guides in Germany – that's one way to see it. Or another way would be to say it was a form of indoctrination by a Nazi organisation – the girls' Hitler Youth. Then the chances are they would move seats. It is so easy to rush to judgement isn't it? "That Mrs Rose is a Nazi you know." "Well, did you ever? And her husband being one of them... How does that work?"

Because I was born there, some would regard me as German. In the streets around here the boys play games: they act out scenes and there are always goodies and baddies. Cowboys goodies, Indians baddies. The Indians have to die in the end. They rush in shrieking and hollering, oscillating their palms over their mouths as they do so, to create that mad sound, and are shot with cap guns by boys in cardboard hats and wearing star badges. Or it is the Germans who die – but no one ever wants to play the Germans: that is beyond the pale, no fun in that, unlike being a Red Indian. The Germans on the street are always imaginary and are huh-huh-huh-ed down by heroes with sticks slung at the hip. To those boys the German is pure evil, a thing to be feared, that screams things like: *Achtung! Gott in Himmel! Donner blitzen! Raus, schnell! Schweinehund!*

They read about it in their comics and have seen it at the pictures. It is ingrained in their boyhood culture. I have always worked so hard to obliterate any traces of accent for that reason; I also think it is lazy not to try to pronounce things properly. Most of the time, round here, they think I'm from down south because I still pronounce some things the way I was taught and how I have heard them on the BBC. I suppose my speech is like me – confused. An ineffective rejection of my past, an embracing of the country that has welcomed me and which I did my bit for, and attachment to the city that is home. I stress the "bin lid" not the "dust" of "dustbin lid," but I still take a *baar-th,* not a bath, and I hate it when my tongue and teeth let me down with a *ze* instead of a *the*. My name has changed with my sense of identity too. But, though I draw from my roots here, I cannot cut the ones that were put down in what used to be my *heimat.*

WE HAD CHICKEN soup for tea. It was nice but they always put too much salt in it. Then apple Charlotte and custard. Lovely. The food is good on the whole. The fish is always overcooked and they never have the best cuts of steak, but I mustn't grumble. I'm very lucky to be here; there's many who are worse off. I can sit by this window and look out at the garden and see the birds come and hop around, and they share a little bit of their freedom with me.

I had a bird table at Mr Broadhead's and would cut off all the bacon rind and leave it for them. Mr Broadhead was something of a Jack Sprat and insisted on his rind being trimmed off. They had pretty thin pickings off me, though – them birds. It's how I was brought up I suppose: to understand the value of food on the table. That memory of famine was handed down by my mother from my granny and never went away – scars like that are deep: the injustice, not just the sense of it but the effects, running down through the family. Mr Broadhead would never understand that of course. He had an appreciation of the finer things in life and had only ever experienced the making-do that rationing brought in the wars – even then I think he found ways around the worst of it. People like that usually do, don't they?

Once the nicer weather comes I'll be able to sit outside. I remember people sitting out on the front door step when it was nice – well, you couldn't sit so comfortably in the yard, what with the washing and the outdoor privies. And at the front you could have a little natter with people coming and going. That was most often the men folk after they got home and washed, in the warmer months, while they waited for their teas. The women were always too busy to sit and chat during the day.

There was that time, though, in the Great War when I was on my own – when I only had myself to look after and wondered what the point of anything was. Always better to be too busy than not busy enough.

AT FIRST I only played in our yard – we shared it with other houses and on Mondays you could run up and down between the lines of washing, or find a little room in a palace to hold a tea party. A big girl from somewhere in the yard said hello to me. She told me she was going to start school and had a lovely dolly called Florence, or Florrie for short. There was also a nasty boy in my yard who'd show off and run around and fling his ball at the walls and not watch where he was going and upset the tea parties. One of my real china plates got broken and mother had to glue it, but it kept breaking so went in the bin.

As my little legs lost their chubbiness and gained in strength, and as my surroundings became less alien to me I ventured out into the street past the forbidden front iron gate with its swirls and arrowheads. It was quite easy to open, so out I went. Other children were out there having fun and they also had a black dog, so my mother's battle to maintain a social aloofness was always doomed to failure. They made me laugh. Some of the boys had string to hold their short trousers up, and not everyone wore shoes – it was summer after all, and everyone's hair got all sticky up. Whatever "woe betide" was I never saw or heard it.

The big kids didn't make fun of my nice shoes and clothes. I watched the girls doing skipping and they tried to show me what to do, but I kept getting tangled up. Then they said they were going to play at Ivy's and did I want to come. Ivy was a big girl who lived right at the end of the street – their end house had a quite a big garden. Not like my old garden: full of secrets and magic, but a patch of grass, a bush and a few things that passed as flowers. Still, it was posh compared to our yard and the small patch of muck at the front.

After a while they all got bored in Ivy's garden and decided to climb over the back wall into I-didn't-know-where.

'Are you coming? It's fun.'

I looked back down the street to check for anyone warning me not to. 'Yes please.'

Like they'd done it loads of times before, one boy bobbed down and another curled up in a ball next to him. A big girl straddling the wall said: 'Hold my hand and climb up then.'

'Ooh! Ow!' they went. 'Too much pudding.' And I was hauled up and dangled and dropped down the other side. What a magical place! Boys digging a big hole with dirty fingers and bits of slate as shovels. Girls picking daisies and making chains for each other's hair.

I felt for the first time that this new house perhaps wasn't so bad. That summer and the ones after often found us in that field, before it later became a building site. I'd set up a little shop and sell bits of broken pot that our archaeology unearthed. Pretty blue and white and all sorts of other pastel colours. The prices ranged from penny pebbles up to buttercup sovereigns and dock leaf banknotes. We'd pick and eat bread and cheese from the early summers hawthorn bushes. Why the leaves were called that I never knew because they tasted nothing like, but I suppose they were "greens" we'd happily nibble on: it being a choice and not something served stinking and steaming on a plate. The boys would play at cowboys and Indians, and a found some old lorry tyres and we'd take turns to be rolled down the slope curled up inside them. On hot summer days we'd venture as far as Bowden Houstead Woods where we'd paddle in the brook. Then at harvest time we'd stray into the next field to ours: a farmer's field, and play at houses inside the stacks of wheat or barley, or whatever it was.

Playing out is what I remember most. As soon as we got home we'd meet up on the street, run back when shouted for our tea by mothers standing at front gates or rattling pans. We'd wolf it down – "please may I get down?" – then run back out, terrified we'd miss something, until called in at bedtime or for our baths on a Friday night. I can't really remember how we entertained ourselves in the winter months, when it was too dark and cold. There were the patches of light under the streetlights, and ropes suspended from the ladder rests at the top made excellent swings, but my memory is of it always being summer.

Once I was at Whitby Road School I learnt to read quite quickly, I think. I'd read anything, but best of all were the comics we'd swap – *Comic Cuts*, *Pip and Squeak*, and *Tiger Tim's Weekly*.

They were always very ragged by the time they got to me and I'd have to turn the pages extremely carefully.

My friend at school, Michael: his dad was like a baddie that Pat the Pirate might meet. He had a patch over his eye and only one leg – even a beard. He was always very quiet. He'd sit outside on the pavement in the summer with his crutch at his side and his trouser leg pinned up, and watch the world go by. We were all a bit scared of him – even Michael. He kept his cutlass under his bed, so Michael said. I mentioned it to my mother when I was helping her clean the oven out – getting in with my little arms and the flue brush to clean out the soot.

'There's no such thing as pirates any more.'

'But Michael...'

'Don't be foolish, and don't tell tales. He was at Salonika, that's all.'

Which sounded just like the kind of exotic place where you'd find a pirate hoisting the Jolly Roger and swinging alongside a galleon ready to board.

Michael's pirate-dad didn't work any more – he'd probably got doubloons and pieces of eight enough to live off. Most of the other fathers worked at Tinsley Colliery, like mine. They always looked scary when they were coming back off shift – all covered in black – like fierce, ragged minstrels: white eyes and red mouths standing out from their dark faces. In the milder months they always used to sit outside on their front steps once they'd got washed. I suppose you would, after having been in the dark and hemmed in all day. After hours of dust and the stink of sweat and muck you'd want to breathe God's fresh air. Just like the ponies my father looked after. Sometimes he'd take me to see them when they came up to the fields after their underground stints. Then, when I was older, I'd take him his supper in an old mess tin, round to the hut where he'd sometimes spend the night keeping watch over the ponies – by then there was only me and him. He didn't seem to mind being stuck on his own in the hut. He didn't crave company or feel a need to surround himself with mates at the pub. He always was something of an outsider. I suppose he came from a different background.

As I look back, I try to remember if there are tiny bits of the puzzle in my memories. Did I notice something different or was it only hindsight? I loved singing – but it wasn't really until I got to school that I became properly aware of how wonderful it was. There were prayers before school, but in assembly we'd also get to sing hymns. At church it hadn't been the same. I'd never been taught to sing or learnt the words and I'd often just sit on the floor while the grown-ups went through this joyless ritual. The difference was Miss Oughtershaw. She had a beautiful voice herself and was so enthusiastic about it. I just loved her from the start and tried my hardest to make lovely sounds come out of my mouth too. I'd also sing with a group of girls in the street. We'd sing "In my sweet little Alice blue gown, when I first wandered down into town" – trying to learn all the words from one of the dad's gramophone records. My mother would often tell me to pipe down – that I was giving her a headache. But that might have been about the time she wasn't well.

I'd often sing to myself in my bedroom. Sometimes to drown out the shouting that came from the kitchen below my bedroom. But sometimes as I lay in bed I could hear my mother weeping and couldn't help but listen. Every word came up through the bare floorboards.

'Oh, don't start that again, Edie. What good is it? I wish I could go back, but I can't. What's done is done. We have to make the most of it. At least I've got a job. That's better than many fellows have these days. I don't know where I'd be if old Fothergill hadn't stood by me: done me a favour.'

'But poor Josephine…'

'Oh, she's all right. Kids are resilient. They don't know any better.'

'But I'd wanted so much more for her. Have you heard how she speaks these days? And no matter how neat and tidy she is when I send her out, she comes back looking like an urchin. It wasn't supposed to be like this.'

'What do you want me to do? Are you always going to blame me.' There was quiet. 'Well? Oh, for Chrissakes! If it hadn't been for your constant wittering. Practically drove me to it. Your demands and expectations.'

'That's right, blame me for your wrongdoing!'

He gave us eyes to see them, and lips that we might tell, how great is God Almighty, who has made all things well.

I'd joined Miss Oughtershaw's school choir and that was one of the songs we were learning. She said she we should skip one of the verses though, because it was nonsense and wicked. How exciting! How could a hymn be wicked? But she was right. *The rich man in his castle, the poor man at his gate. God made the high and lowly and ordered their estate.*

'That is not the God that Jesus teaches us, is it? Jesus does not teach us that God made people to be rich and poor and that they should be happy with their lot. He taught us compassion. He sided with the poor. He taught us that a rich man could not make it into heaven. Jesus would say that the rich man in his castle should help the poor man at his gate.'

She later became my class teacher. She was very pretty and was calm and patient with us. She had no need to keep the cane ever-ready on her desk to get us to do our work. Most of us did it just because she asked us to.

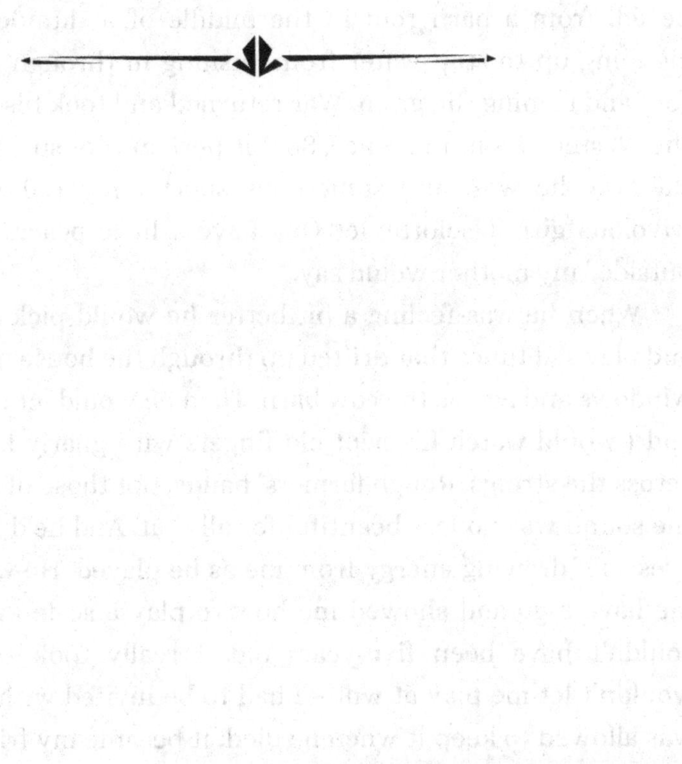

I don't have many memories of my grandfather. He was a serious, quite distant man and died when I was young. I have memories of him lying in his bed with his eyes shut, and of being quite scared of him. He carried a heavy burden. My mother told me that he had nearly died of typhoid in the war against France and returned with a musket injury that left him in great pain. It didn't stop him taking over the family farm and building it back up to a point where he could support a family. That wasn't happy ever after, though, for my grandmother died soon after my mother was born, leaving grandfather to raise her and her two brothers with help from a female relative. Then he lost one of his sons to an accident, when he fell from a barn roof in the middle of a thunderstorm after climbing up to stop water from gushing in through a hole in the roof and ruining the grain. War returned and took his other son on the Western Front in France. So it is perhaps not surprising he was the way he was, and sometimes short tempered with a small frivolous girl. 'Liselotte, let Opa have a little peace. Go and play outside,' my mother would say.

When he was feeling a bit better he would pick up his violin and play sad tunes that drifted up through the house and out of the windows and across the cow barn. Then he would let me sit by him and I would watch his bent old fingers with gnarly knuckles play across the strings. Rough farmers' hands, not those of an artist, but the sound was no less beautiful for all that. And he'd look into my eyes as if drawing energy from me as he played. He would also let me have a go and showed me how to play a scale even though I couldn't have been five-years old. I really took to it, but he wouldn't let me play at will – I had to be invited without asking. I was allowed to keep it when he died; it became my friend, I'd seek solace in its company, and I believe that later on it saved my life.

After my grandfather got sick, all the work on the farm was done by my mother with help brought in from the village, now and then. I helped her too. What child could not be happy growing up on a farm? I was free to roam over the purple moors in the summer, and I breathed clean air. When times came thick, we were sheltered. Many endured starvation in the war, and after, but we were self-supporting and did not have to subsist on the inadequacies of the ration book. Our chickens didn't take into account how many millions of marks there were to the dollar before they laid an egg. I wasn't surrounded by other children, being an only child, but I had lots of friends on the farm. There were the cows who I especially loved: beautiful, creamy white beasts that I loved to snuggle up to when I milked them. The milk was delicious when warm and the butter and cheese that my mother taught me to make were unlike anything I have ever tasted since – you see, even though it was so long ago that part of me is still there, even though that small girl often doesn't seem like she could have been me.

It was then that I first met Jakub, or James as he was known as later. He used to come to the farm with his father who was a cattle dealer, to buy calves from us, or if we needed money to buy a new cart or something. My mother became quite friendly with Jakub's dad, and while they were drinking coffee at the table or discussing business, Jakub would torment me and try to show off. The trouble was he rarely pulled it off. Even though he was several years older than me, I was better at climbing and better at hiding, and he couldn't outrun me either. I also had the advantage that he would get into trouble if he scuffed his polished shoes. I remember collecting shiny black beetles with him and staging beetle derbies on an elaborate track we built in the yard using stones and bits of wood. 'You were the only girl I knew who liked beetles, never mind the only one who didn't squeal when one crawled on her hand,' he told me. Such flattery! Such romanticism! Most girls used their charms – their eyes, smile or flowing locks, or melodious voice. For me it was beetles.

When the farm got too much for mother she reluctantly decided to sell the business, and Jakub's father helped her manage the sale and the move.

We travelled to the town on a cart and I cried when the time came to say goodbye to my beautiful cows. I went round and kissed them all one by one and spoke their names one last time.

'It is not fair, why have we got to leave them?'

'We have to, Liselotte. It is too much.'

'But I promise I'll help more, Mama.'

'No. You cannot – you must concentrate more on your schoolwork, and we need to get you into a better school: especially when you go to big school.'

'But I don't want to go to school. I want to stay here with the animals – I don't need school.'

'Trust me Lottie Liebling. You need school – there is so much to know about in this world. Things you need to know so that you can decide things. So that you don't just get told what to do by others. One day you will understand.'

We were both crying. It made little sense to me, back then.

Her words were rather ironic since the main purpose of school seemed to be to get us to accept what we were told to do by others. The double irony being that by nature, the more I am told what to do the less inclined I have always felt to do something. I don't know where I get this character trait from – certainly not from my German side. I know so little about my other inheritance.

School taught us to be good, obedient Germans. We learnt about the Greeks and Romans and the greatness of their civilizations. One of our teachers, Frau Müller, also taught us that the Greeks were a rather backward race of peasants until the arrival there of the Doric Invaders – an Aryan people like us – and thereafter the Greek civilisation exploded. I believed it at the time. Why would I not? Frau Müller was a magnificent woman: tall, blonde and pretty, with a Gretchen hairdo – you know where your plaits are twisted round on the back of your head – typical German.

So that is how I started wearing my plaits too. She was also the *Ringführerin* for the *Bund Deutscher Mädel* in our town and the main reason I joined – although a sort of fever overtook us all when the Nazis came to power, and most girls I knew joined. I soon realised what was really going on, though. Jakub called them the *Bund Deutscher Matrezen* – the League of German mattresses, because of the things that went on when they got together with the boys from the Hitler Youth and at the midsummer bonfires. But I get ahead of myself – I only joined after I left school, that's when all the craziness really took off.

In addition to the classics we learnt about Immanuel Kant and were taught to believe in the Rechsstat: a state established in law that gave everyone rights. It gave us an unwavering faith in our country. There was also the Holy Roman Empire, Frederick the Great, Napoleon and Bismarck. We learnt about the importance of *ordnung*. It is a stereotype of the German, but true none the less. *Ordnung* is more than just order – it is a concept of organisation and discipline and rejection of chaos or disorder. But this was all very dangerous. It created fertile territory for what followed. *Ordnung* was a rejection of sloppiness but also of unconventionality, a repulsion of the eccentric – something which is celebrated here. In England, and especially in Sheffield, as long as you don't cause harm to others, folks leave you alone. But back then in Germany there was developing a right and a wrong way to behave, to dress, to speak and think. I knew nothing about the economic troubles after the Great War. Our cows and crops knew nothing about the purchasing power of paper Marks. But by the time of the Great Depression and the unemployment and fights that followed, I could see with my own eyes what it did, and it offended my learnt ideals of *ordnung*. Then along came Hitler to put it all right, and everyone was excited. Actually, not everyone. My mother's gaze was wider, despite her having to work so hard to put bread on the table and pay my tuition fees. She always said that

"Hitler would never fill his gullet." Then there were the views of Jakub and his family, which I initially dismissed as over-reacting.

Mother still found time to read – she spurned the Goethe or Fontane that we read at school. Instead she favoured English writers like Agatha Christie or P G Wodehouse; both of whom I too have come to rely on to take me away from darker places. She read them in English, though not very quickly. I have her to thank for insisting that I learnt the language and for paying for extra tuition for me.

'Must I learn English, Mama? It serves no purpose.'

'Please be patient, Lottie. You might not see the importance of these things right now. The English are good people. I would like you to be able to visit there some day.'

'But everything I need is here in Germany. Why waste my time?'

'It is not wasted – you are so impatient right now, but you will come to see time differently.'

I resented it back then and didn't understand her eccentricity – it seemed unpatriotic. Thankfully that phase of youthful exuberance in my life didn't last long. I suppose most people reach a point in their young lives when they become certain they know best – when they condemn their elders as fools who have messed everything up. The future belongs to them, so the old folks should simply move aside. Sadly many people never get beyond that certainty – they never question that they are right, it is the others who are wrong. They retain their fifteen-year-old brains. That was one of the reasons things went wrong – too many people who were so convinced they knew the single answer that they would never contemplate there being an alternative. That is the cause of the fanaticism that proved so dangerous to my mother in the end.

I have her and my father to thank for my escape from my conviction of thought. Maybe it comes down to intelligence: not book learning, but real intelligence – the ability to actually think and process information, not just spit stuff back out. I think that perhaps the most undervalued character trait in the world is self-doubt. Most of the bad things that have happened in history have been carried out by people certain of their own perception of the world – people who see others as so wrong that they need to be eliminated, metaphorically or literally. That was certainly the case with Hitler – right up to the end. But perhaps, when he sat weeping in his bunker, he realised he had not been right after all – or more likely, he just blamed the international Jewish conspiracy or traitors in his midst for the defeat and took the cowards' way out. Churchill, on the other hand, always strikes me as someone who was wracked with self-doubt: so worried about every one of his decisions that he probably knows precisely what a flawed human being he is. Not a bad man, nor a good one. Just a human being, burdened with a lifetime of trial and error, stuffed with preconceptions and conceit. But he knew it, and that was the difference in the end: what made the better leader.

I keep departing from my subject, but the trouble is that none of this is linear. Lottie Rose did not start at 'A' and go to, where I am now? P, Q, R or S, via B, C and D. Life is more like three-dimensional chess: with ups and downs, and forwards and backs, and sideways leaps. It is not even just about me. I am linked to others through time: to people I have never met – their decisions are my fate. I sometimes wonder if I pass close to them in their trajectory as I go round in loops and spirals – others on different tracks in different times, but there being an influence, like gravity acting, albeit weakly, on distant celestial bodies.

I was still on the subject of my schooldays, I think. One of the main purposes of our education was to prepare us for our role in life as German wives and mothers. *Kinder, Küche, Kirche* – children, kitchen and church. We spent much time on domestic science – learning how to cook and sew, and run a house efficiently in order that we would please a husband.

I OFTEN THINK about all my children; it gives me great satisfaction. They used to write to me every now and then. Some of them anyway. Though not so much these days. Well, they've all moved on haven't they? Everyone has such busy lives these days. Some have even gone to Canada and South Africa. It's very kind of them to think of me and to say thank you for what I did for them. It is recognition isn't it? That I did a good job. I always tried to anyway.

I often wonder about them. I still remember their names – I suppose that comes of reading them out every day on that… that list thing, that we did at the start of class. All grown up they'll be with children of their own. Except for those that didn't make it through – boys, I suppose. I have much to look back on, good times as well as not so good.

I did my best to set them on the right path. That's what life's about isn't it? Fulfilling a purpose, improving things, getting rid of unfairness. Life is not easy. It's not as if justice and fairness are laid on like hot and cold water in a fancy hotel. You have to fight for them. It's not meant to be easy. Look what we achieved after the last war – we made a better stab at it this time than after the Great War. I can't help feeling that so much was wasted that first time – all the best men were lost, and that those who made it back were so dreadfully scarred by it, like he was. It was never the same. All those long, black lists of casualties pinned up on walls and in the *Independent*. All the talent. All the wisdom thrown on the pyre. It was all messed up. Even those who hadn't had the stuffing knocked out – they raged, were ignored and gave up. But in forty-five brought a resetting, at least for a while, something that we should have done that first time round – a consensus around providing for people when they were ill or just old – a determination to build a fairer way.

There is something cringing and snivelling in this country, though. Only a small bold step is taken before they get scared and go back to their feudal masters to take control again – it is a deep-set servility. We are sorry for stepping out of line and getting beyond ourselves, Sir. We know we had the audacity to nationalise a few things and create a welfare state and we are sorry. We'll let you tell us what to do again. You know best. We'll just do as we are told now. Thank you, Sir. We know we've never had it so good.

Perhaps it is more a case of two steps forward and one step back. It's remarkable what can be achieved if only people put their minds to it – a Russian has just gone into space in a rocket so they say – it just goes to show.

'It's only me, Mrs B. Can I come in?'

'Should I get my hat and coat on? Has Mr Broadhead come to take me for a drive?'

'No Mrs B. Not today. Is it all right if I change your linen? *As you sail across the sea, All my love is there beside you, In Capri or Amsterdam, Honolulu or Siam*'

'Someone's in a cheery mood.'

'Yes, my husband bought me a Dansette... a record player for my... my birthday, and I've been playing one of my favourites on it.'

'I had one of those you used to wind up, you know. We sometimes danced around the kitchen.'

'I can imagine you cutting a bit of a dash across the kitchen floor.'

'Oh, I don't know about that.'

'We used to dance in our kitchen too, before the war. To the swing bands on the wireless. *To the harbour of my heart, I will send my love to guide you, As I call across the sea.* There. That's done then.'

'You have a nice voice.'

'Thank you.'

'I used to like to sing, too.'

'Don't you still?'

'I don't get the chance now, dear. Not since I stopped going to All Saints. When is dinner? It's always late.'

'You've had your dinner already. It was steak and kidney and rhubarb and custard, remember?'

'Oh, yes. I...'

'I'll catch you later, Mrs B. *Sailor stop your roaming, Sailor, leave the sea, Sailor, when the tide turns, Come home safe to me.*'

IT WAS AROUND that time that my mother took ill. I'd come back from school and find her lying on that horrible scratchy old settee looking very pale.

'I'll have to let you get your own tea, and for father. There's some money on the side there – pop down for a bit of mince and you can fry it with some onions, and go round to get a bowl of steeped peas from the Hudson's to go with it.'

She then had to go away for a bit and it fell to me to do everything about the house – breakfast and tea. It is strange that some of those happiest memories came at a time of great hardship. Perhaps you just appreciate the good things more when they come along, and that made them special and memorable. Like when I fell asleep in class when I was supposed to be reading scripture. Instead of smacking me and humiliating me, Miss Oughtershaw kept me in at playtime. I burst into tears and told her everything. She was so kind it made me cry even more.

Sometimes when I came home from school I'd find my mother lying in bed, either asleep or propped up on a pillow with her arms down by her side, staring at the wall opposite. When father wasn't on shift he would sit with her, but sometimes we had to leave her on her own, with only Mrs Dunstan from next door popping in to give her her dinner. I'd then take up some tea when I got home from school and sit and tell her about what I'd done in class and sometimes read to her from books that Miss Oughtershaw lent me or that I'd borrowed from the library.

One day I got home and found Mrs Dunstan waiting for me in the yard.

'You're to come to ours for tea, Josephine, dear. Your mother is really very poorly.'

'Can I go and see her?'

'No, dear. The doctor is with her and mustn't be disturbed. You can play with Ellen after tea.'

I slept on a camp bed on the floor of the room that belonged to Mrs Dunstan's two daughters: Ellen, who was in the year below me and her little sister, Evie. It felt like an adventure – the two of them and me in that small back bedroom.

It was only few days later when I came back from school that Mrs Dunstan sat me down with a slice of cake and a cup of tea. There were only us two in the kitchen – the girls having been sent out.

'I wanted to talk to you about your mother, Jo. She really was ever so poorly, but she is no longer suffering.'

'Has the doctor made her better?'

'No. I'm afraid not. There was nothing he could do except make her comfortable. She was very peaceful, Josephine. She wasn't in any pain in the end.'

I just looked at her, waiting for the words.

'She's gone to a better place now.'

I knew this was how grown-ups spoke to avoid actually saying it. Why don't people just say it: dead. Dead. Dead. Dead. Not passed over, or at rest, at peace, with Our Lord, or in a better place. Just dead.

I went upstairs and cried for her, but also, if truth be told, for my father, and, if not more so, for me. I was now motherless. I would have to come home to an empty house and make my own tea and do all the jobs around the house. I was only a half-orphan, not like Jane Eyre, but still I wondered if I would I get sent away.

I barely saw my father over the following days. I'm not sure why. He carried on working. I suppose he had to. Perhaps he didn't want me to see him upset.

Mrs Dunstan dressed me in a horrid black dress that smelt of mothballs and did my hair for me and polished the borrowed shoes I was to wear. I had the day off school. Lots of people gathered at our house and shook my father's hand.

'Perhaps it was for the best. At least she didn't suffer too much in the end.'

They smiled down at me.

'Haven't you grown? Hasn't she grown, Eric?' said a lady in a hat decorated in black lace to a weasely, nodding man with hair slicked over his head and who looked uncomfortable in his starched collar. 'We've not seen you since you were tiny. You won't remember us: Aunty Maud and Uncle Eric. I'm your mother's younger sister. It's such a shame we couldn't see you in happier times. But it's not easy to get here is it, Eric?'

The man called Eric shook his head.

Then someone would say: 'You do look smart, Josephine. Your mother would be proud of you. She's like her mother don't you think, Maud?'

Another of those smiles. She was a rather skinny woman was Aunty Maud, no hips and a flat chest, similar to my mother. I could tell they were sisters. They also had the same thin nose, not like mine. But perhaps noses were something that changed as you grew?

Had I known my mother had a sister? I didn't remember her being mentioned.

Someone else said they thought I had my father's eyes. I looked over at my father who was standing with his back to the kitchen window, looking lost. His eyes were brown like mine, but I'd never thought of any resemblance. I didn't know what they meant. I'd also been more aware of my difference to my parents than any similarity. I was just *me*.

I got confused by all the people I met. Aunty this, from Congleton, your father's cousin, and Uncle that, from Leek, your grandmother's brother; and an Aunty and an Uncle who were sister and brother to my father, I think. Another surprise to me.

It was all very serious, everyone speaking in quiet voices as if they would get told off – *get done* or *get wrong* as we used to say. Some went out into the yard when it started to get crowded and they didn't want to smoke in the house. Some went through into the front room and came back again looking strange and sad. I wasn't allowed.

I went to stand next to my father and he put his hand on my shoulder. Then a scary-looking man holding a top hat arrived and nodded to my father who followed him through to the front room. Some of the uncles went too. I heard a banging noise followed by silence again. Aunt Maud stuck her head round the door and waited.

'Right, you come with us, Josephine,' said Aunt Maud.

We went through to the front room which was all dark with the curtains drawn and out the front door, which was something we didn't usually do. In the street was a sort of carriage, painted black, harnessed to a single black horse with a black feather on its head. It then struck me that my mother was in the coffin on the back and I felt panic rise in my chest and tears welling up in my eyes.

The driver set the horse going and we followed. All the houses in the street had their curtains closed and some of the neighbours were out in the streets standing, not talking. Then, as we made our way on to Prince of Wales Road and over the railway, everyone else in the street stopped what they were doing and removed their hats as we passed.

We went to a little church in the graveyard – not to St. Albans, where we went on a Sunday, and there the vicar talked about mother, and mentioned my father and me.

We sang a hymn I'd never sung before, but I had the words in front of me and soon picked it up. I tried to do my best singing for my mother, but I couldn't get through the last verse: "Then, when on earth I breathe no more, The prayer, oft mixed with tears before, I'll sing upon a happier shore, Thy Will be done".'

Father and some of the uncles carried the coffin outside afterwards. It had started to drizzle and the grass wet my shoes. We watched the coffin being lowered into the ground – I knew mother would hate it in there and that made me cry again.

Back at the house, the men drank bottles of beer, and after I'd had a piece of sponge cake I was allowed to escape round to Mrs Dunstan's and went to sit in the front parlour with Ellen and we read comics. Ellen tried to be nice to me because I'd not got a mother any more.

WHEN I LEFT school it was at that time of the great unemployment. There were not many jobs, especially for girls. I could have helped mother in the shop – did I say she had a grocery shop? When she sold the farm, Jakub's father helped her buy our shop. It had a kitchen and storeroom at the back, and two bedrooms and a bathroom upstairs. She worked really hard – she made her own cheese and *bregenwurst* to sell in the shop: only what she had always done but more of it. So she was working even when the shop closed in the evening. She wouldn't let me work in the shop after I had left school. 'There is nothing to do,' she said. 'Not enough money coming in for two.' But I think she also wanted me to learn independence so she made me take up a post at a doctor's house as an apprentice cook, earning only seven marks a month for working my socks off. The house belonged to someone that Jakub's father knew: Herr Doktor Menchel. He was a very popular and successful doctor and looked after all the wealthiest clients in the town. I helped the cook and set the table for the family and progressed to special tasks within the kitchen, such as being in charge of bread-making – providing the family with crisp fresh rolls for their breakfast and again for tea.

I had my own bedroom in the house but I saw a lot of my mother at the weekends and helped her with the cheese making and the bookkeeping. I fondly remember, during my last days there, sitting listening to the wireless – her prized possession – she'd tune into the BBC in London and ask me what certain words meant, even though she often knew better than I. She was almost obsessive in her thirst for Englishness.

I also made cheese for the Menchels. It was something that Cook could not match. It gave me a special status in the household – and from starting on a mere seven marks a week I doubled it, and got greater reward in praise. I was paraded before guests like some kind of prized possession when I brought dishes through.

'Here is our wonderful cheese-maker, Liselotte. You will never in your lifetime taste a finer *Handkäse*, Herr von Rehlingen, of that I assure you. It is beautiful and fragrant with a soft white rind.'

'Then beware, Herr Doktor, for one day you will wake up and find her kidnapped.'

One evening before Christmas, I was invited to sit at the table when the Rosenbaums were invited over to dinner. Since we had moved I had not seen much of Jakub. He was busy studying at the secondary school and, well, what girl is interested in an adolescent boy? Best left well alone until they and their bodies work things out for themselves, that's what I thought – which bit goes where and in what proportion, and which strategy of natural selection their minds chooses: greed and possession, or respect and understanding – to be a master and a taker, or a companion and protector. Like caterpillars, moths and butterflies. You can't tell what they're going to turn into – whether they'll emerge gracious beings or beasts.

The family weren't particularly strict. They celebrated the main holidays: Pesach and Yom Kippur. There was no ham or pork in the house but they put up a tree at Christmas, which sort of blended into Hanukkah. The tree was bigger than anything my mother would allow, and was decorated with garlands, nuts, little presents and the gingerbread hearts that I had baked.

I had been helping cook all day and rushed to spruce myself up and get changed at the last minute. My cheeks were rosy when I gave myself one last check in the little mirror above my chest of drawers before going down. I felt nervous heading into the dining room. It looked lovely that night. The fire was blazing in the hearth, and the table was beautifully lit with candles. The doctor was laughing loudly at some joke or other.

Jakub's father was the first to see me and stopped what he was saying to hurry over.

'Liselotte, *mein liebes Kind*. How you have grown! You are quite the young lady. You will be sure to fetch your violin and play Tannebaum for us after dinner. That would be good. *Ja*, Herr

Doktor? You let her play in the house? Of course, of course. She must practise. A talent for music needs nourishment.'

Jakub was hanging back, shuffling his feet on the carpet.

'Come, come, Jakub. Do they teach you no manners at that prestigious school?'

Jakub stepped forward and offered his hand and bowed slightly. He was no longer the boy I had known. He had changed so much since I had last seen him – he was tall and had broadened out. He looked very German, very Berliner, in his double-breasted jacket which seemed to pinch in at the waist, matching well-pressed, baggy trousers and rather bold necktie. His light brown hair was slicked back, his eyebrows so perfectly bow-shaped above his big brown eyes, like a girl's. I was completely tongue-tied. The adults drifted back to their conversation.

'I suppose you have been on your feet all day. Shall we sit down?'

We went to sit by the window away from the heat of the fire. The piney scent of the Christmas tree wafted round as we passed.

'Caught any nice beetles recently?' he said.

'Only the one I baked inside your bread roll.'

'Ah, I do like a surprise gift.'

We both stared at our feet.

'How is your work here? Do they treat you well?'

'Yes. They are kind, but it is hard work and I am doing my apprenticeship too. How is it at the *Aufbauschule*?'

'Hard too – but I should pass my Abitur. Then I hope to go on to study engineering.'

I sat between Jakub and his mother at dinner. His sister opposite, next to Mrs Menchel, the two young Menchel children having been sent to bed.

Jakub's mother talked so much and asked me so many questions I was surprised she managed to eat anything at all. She wanted to know all about the recipes, the ingredients, how long we left things in the oven. Looking back on it I believe that she was trying to hide her nerves, to drown out the conversation of the men. I could only half-hear what they were saying.

'But we must have faith in the good sense of our countrymen. These hot heads will not prevail. The people are too sensible to be taken in by –'

'What stock do you use in your French onion soup?'

'We always make it from beef.'

'All my clients, for example, they would not countenance any –'

'Just beef?'

'Well we use cook's own recipe and boil the bones with carrot and bay.'

' – and yours, Izaak, what would the farmers around here do without you? Nothing is eaten as hot as it is cooked you see. It will blow over.'

'But I saw them in Berlin in thirty-one. Thousands of them. Such hatred in their eyes. The police did nothing to stop them rampaging down the Kurfurstendamm.'

'And how long do you cook the onions for?'

'I was stirring the pan for a good hour or so.'

'You poor thing. No wonder you have such lovely rosy cheeks.'

'They beat people up just for looking Jewish. Luckily they did not know me, and it is not so obvious is it? Or I would have been attacked too.'

'And wine?'

'Yes, a French Riesling.'

'But that is German, surely?'

'They smashed the windows of Jewish cafes and restaurants.'

'That was a one off.'

'You know it wasn't. The German people, your sensible moderate German *volk*: they stood and watched as Nazi thugs in black arm bands beat old people and destroyed businesses. They are not going away. You see them round here too, now.'

'And did you make the toasts, too?'

'Yes. From my own bread.'

'But they lost ground in the last election did they not? And anyway, what is the alternative? Surely there is more to fear from the communists. They would destroy our livelihoods.'

'*Nein, nein.* We will see, we will see.'

'Darling? Is Riesling German?'

'You ask a very philosophical question there, my dear.'

I hardly got chance to speak to Jakub. Even if I had, I wouldn't have quite known what to say.

The Menchels' beautiful house was on the edge of the town, set back from the road and surrounded by a white picket fence set atop a stone wall. There were linden trees in the garden, sheltering the house from the worst of the winds in winter and keeping it cooler in the summer. Jakub took to passing by on his way to and from school, and from the kitchen window at the back of the house I could hear him whistle from road that went down the side of the house. If cook wasn't around, or if we weren't too busy, I could sneak out and chat to him from behind a tree from where I couldn't easily be seen from the windows of the house. Sometimes he'd be waiting in the road to walk me round to my mother's on a Sunday, or he'd come with us for a walk in the afternoon. My mother liked him – you're not supposed to have boyfriends your mother approves of are you?

There was huge enthusiasm in the town when Hitler became Chancellor. There was a parade in the square that evening; the brownshirts had been out all afternoon organising things, making their presence felt. We all had red paper flags with swastikas on and a band played as they came marching, carrying burning torches, led by a booming drum marking out time as their studded boots rang out on the paving. Looking very serious in the steel helmets, dark shadows flickered across their faces as they kept their eyes fixed on the man in front; boom, boom, boom. The smoke from the torches curled up into the night sky as the singing began and everyone raised their arms.

Die Fahne hoch! Raise the flag.

Die Reihen fest geschlossen! Ranks tightly closed.

SA marschient mit ruhig festen Shchritt. The SA marches with calm steady step.

We were now sure to see an end to the rot that had set into our country. Herr Doctor Menchel and Herr Rosenbaum were overreacting. There was nothing to fear, I thought. There was nothing against good Jewish Germans. That was just a fringe element, no more than that.

How wrong that naive little girl was!

The next day Hitler dissolved the Reichstag and called new elections; not for him the position of a figurehead for the government. His gullet was open wide.

Jakub wasn't the only boy who sought my attention back then. Girls of that age don't really need to try too hard to attract attention from boys, and I already had curves, my hair was blonde – add in the navy blue skirt, white blouse and black tie of the BdM, or my favourite dirndl, and I suppose I caused a bit of turbulence in the breasts of boys whose hormones were like the spring tide.

Kurt Maier was a boy whose father ran the butcher's near to my mother's shop. He was my age, a good-looking boy, not very bright, but nice enough – polite and friendly. He was really into the Hitler Jugend and clearly saw in me some sort of ideal. I probably shouldn't have been as friendly to him as I was, in hindsight, but I'd seen no reason not to talk to him when he came round to our shop or when I went round to theirs on an errand.

I loved being in the BdM, though the Menchels started to get a bit annoyed with all the time I was taking off. But what could they do about it? They would draw unwanted attention if they tried to stop me, so they had to be diplomatic – I was a young and flighty fifteen-year old and quite enjoyed the power that the swastika gave me over them. Don't all teenagers play such games of power and guilt with their elders to test the strength of their constraints? Isn't it part of growing up? Though admittedly my trump card was stronger than any teenager has a right to hold – one full of brooding evil, as all around people lost sense of right and wrong and what was required to avoid crossing the line. There were rumours of people disappearing, never to be seen again, or of bodies being found in the woods. Some said they were just communists, like the one who set fire to the Reichstag, subversives or criminals, so it didn't really matter that much. People were being taken away for their own good: the workshy, drunks, rapists and thieves. That's what it said in the *Zeitung*. Taken away for re-educating and getting off their old filthy habits and degenerate ways of life. People couldn't object to being rid of them and feeling safer on the streets at night. The law-abiding had nothing to fear. But after the arson attack they limited freedom of expression, and many feared saying anything even vaguely critical of the National Socialists, and the fear only got stronger in the following years. But it didn't affect me. I was a good German girl and the state was just, or so I thought, naively.

I wonder how many people would actually like their teenage selves if they could meet them. I think I could probably make allowances. That world was a strange place, and the majority were swept along one way or another. I'm not asking anyone to like that blue-eyed girl in Gretchen braids; the most you can do is try to understand and to reflect on what you would have done if it had been you.

The BdM was a highlight of the week. We'd do gymnastics, which I was quite good at, having been brought up on a farm climbing trees and ladders and getting a good diet. Then there was the storytelling, sitting in a ring around Frau Muller. She wove pictures in our heads: the tall Knight of Bergen in his black armour enchanting the queen with his dancing at the masked ball,

Siegfried bathing in dragon's blood to make himself invincible, or so he thought, and Arminius destroying three legions of the Romans and preserving the German blood line. We'd do handicrafts and sing folk songs in addition to more patriotic ones. I don't suppose many of us really thought about the meaning of some of them:

Denn heute gehört uns deutschland, Und morgen die ganze welt. Today Germany belongs to us, tomorrow the whole world.

For us it was more about friendship and doing fun things – it wasn't overly political.

The Hitler Jugend boys, in their shorts, polished shoes, and always with neatly combed hair, would hang around after our meetings and offer to walk us home, trying but largely failing to impress us with what they've been up to – assault courses and handling real guns. I don't know what it was with Nazis – I came to realise that there was something perverse about them almost in a sexual way – the way they preened and worshipped physique – not just female – their love of black leather. Women too were attracted to the display of power – the cult around Hitler was strange and had a sexual element, though god only knows why. But the inevitable hypocrisy that comes from repression always carries a darker side. They adored and were disgusted, in equal measure. To them, the licentiousness that the end of the First World War released in bars and cabarets in cities like Berlin was everywhere; I suspect that those who were most repulsed feared something in themselves, some kind of attraction. They despised the nature of humans and wanted to be apart from that. Feelings themselves became crimes. Take your adoration of the Aryan ideal too far into physical or even figurative expression and they would kill you for it.

I AM SITTING out on the verandah today. A lovely afternoon. I've got the warmth of the sun on my face and arms and there is a soft breeze, so it isn't too hot. Very pleasant. The lawn is being mowed by that man... bother... the one who does the roses and the lawn and outside things. I can smell the mown grass, and the sound it makes: *whirr whirr whirr,* like a giant cat, is just lovely, and I can see him, the outside-chappy, walking up and down.

Mr Broadhead loves his lawn. Not a weed allowed to grow on it. I love daisies and even dandelions but if it wasn't grass it had no place on his lawn: perfectly rectangular with stripes. I thought I'd get into trouble just for walking on it. Fancy living in a place like Totley. That's going up in the world. Not just a backyard but a proper garden, front and back. He'd have hated what happened to it. Well, I can't look after it like he did, can I? Mr Hargreaves, who helps out with the parish magazine pops round every now and then and cuts the grass. He chops things back willy-nilly – not precise pruning according to season and method like Mr Broadhead, and the grass isn't raked and forked any more, and sprinkled with that fish, bone, what-is-it? He scattered it so precisely, his sleeves rolled up and his hat, always a hat outdoors, so many ounces to the square yard, according to the calendar and the weather. His garden is just another thing I feel guilty about. Let him down a bit, I suppose, didn't I?

I was very lucky to meet him of course – he was married to Mrs Broadhead. Was she... Evelyn? Or was that someone else? He worked at Laycocks after the war – the Great War – the one that was to end all wars. I used to chat to her at the Soroptimist lunches and met Harold one time when he collected her in his brand new Rover and they offered to give me a lift back to Artisan View on the way. It was sad what happened to her: Mrs Broadhead.

I don't suppose I ever really loved Mr Broadhead, but we suited each other. We rubbed along quite nicely. I was tired of living on my own. Just having someone around who you can interact with, who doesn't bother you too much. He always had my respect and my friendship. That's surely enough. Being comfortable. He was glad to have someone to replace Mrs Broadhead, someone to look after him, to look after the house and spend his money. I sometimes wondered if he ever noticed much, just a replacement for the one that was damaged, like replacing a settee. So long as the settee doesn't mind.

I wouldn't say any of the other ladies here are my friends, but they don't trouble me – I much prefer young people anyway. Not the old people in here – poor dears. Some of them barely leave their rooms and others just stare at the wall all day or listen to the wireless without saying anything. I wonder if they are lost in their heads or if actually there's nothing there.

'Would you like to have tea out here, Mrs B?'
'That will be very nice. Are you coming to sit down too, Mary?'
'I'm not Mary, Mrs B.'
'There's no need to speak down at me. I'm not a child, and I'm not deaf.'
'I know you're not Mrs B. I wouldn't dare. I'll be back in a minute.'

WHAT A HARD time that was for my father. No sooner had he buried his wife than the great strike started.

During a strike or lockout all the ponies were brought up to the surface and had to be looked after, so my father carried on working whilst all the others were idle. However, he was expected to pay what he earned into the strike fund and only draw strike pay like everyone else. It was something he'd lecture me on in later years: how the whole thing was a set-up and how the miners and the trade unions ran full pelt right into the bosses' fist. The bosses had planned it for years. They'd taken government money to head off a strike the previous year and had used the time to stockpile and prepare a plan to take on the miners and win. The Mine Workers' Union had no such plans and their funds only allowed a couple of weeks' of strike pay.

He seethed, and resented working for nothing – to hand his money over to a bunch of fools and charlatans. It didn't help that the other men looked down at him: they were the lords of the pit – the hewers, earning three shillings a shift more than my father, even though he was far cleverer and more educated than them. They were suspicious of him. He thought they were no better than sheep.

Miss Oughtershaw explained a lot of it to us – answered the questions we were too scared to ask our fathers or mothers.

'Why have our dads been locked out, Miss?'

'Yeah, Miss. Why have the bosses stop them working?'

'Settle down. Open your Testament at Matthew 20, and if the headmaster comes in that's what we are discussing. Understood? The vineyard owner in the parable chooses to pay some people more, not cut the pay of anyone. Not like the mine-owners.'

'My Dad calls the bosses rude words, Miss, and says they want to steal ours money, Miss.'

'In a way that is true, Billy. Who are the bosses? The mine owners and the rich landowners, who want more than their fair share of the money made by the miners. The whole industry needs modernising – it is inefficient and dangerous, with one-and-a-half thousand men being killed every year. But that would mean the owners having less money in order to pay for improvements. So they want to pay the miners less and work them for longer instead. Therefore they are holding the miners to ransom until they agree to less money and more work.'

'But why is it just the miners now, Miss? Why didn't everyone else stay on strike too? Have we been betrayed?'

'It certainly seems that way, John. The strike was called off by the TUC without having got any promises. It was perhaps a missed opportunity for real change.'

My father stuck it out on strike pay for a while. Then I noticed a change. He came home with some extra money one week and a piece of steak for our tea. We had been living off dry bread and thin soup for weeks.

'Can you manage to do something nice with this for our tea, lass?'

'Of course, father. Would you like it frying with onions?'

'That'd be just the ticket. And here's a shilling. You can run down to the shop for some butter too.'

A week and another pay day went by – all my friends complained about how hungry they were. If they saw another kid eating an apple they'd hang about and ask to have the cowk – that's what we called the core – and they'd eat them pips and all. I'd slip a few biscuits into my pockets and share them out. My father didn't admit where our extra money had come from but I soon found out.

One evening a *deppytation* arrived at our back door.

'Is thi father in, love?'

'Dad, there's some mesters at the door.'

I went and sat in my mother's chair and picked up my book.

'Good evening, Cartwright. We've heard a rumour.'

'Have you now. You shouldn't listen to rumour and tittle-tattle. I'm not interested.'

'Tha's not denying it then?'

'I've not said anything. What are you on about?'

'Tha's going agin t'union, then?'

'No. I'm not against them.'

'If tha's not wi' us tha's agin us. Tha's tekkin thi money, in't tha?'

'Yes. It is my money. Can't you see there's no point any more? You – we – are bound to lose. The only question is when. They can starve you out but you can't hurt them.'

'Some of us have got principles.'

'You can't eat principles. What's the good of principle when your wives and kids are starving? Where does that get anyone?'

'So tha's going to carry on scabbing then?'

'Call it what you will. I've already lost my wife. I'm not going to see her fade away before my eyes too.' Over the top of my book I saw my father jerk a thumb to where I was trying to be invisible.

'Well, on thy head be it, Cartwright. On thy head be it.'

'Aye. Reckon it will.'

After that everyone crossed the street when my father was coming. When he bought tobacco or a newspaper, the transaction passed without any exchange of words. The shopkeepers had to keep on the side of the community or face a boycott. One local shop refused to serve him, so he had to walk further.

Even some of my friends started avoiding me. Backs turned on me in the playground and I heard the word "scab" being used. But Miss Oughtershaw got wind of it and spoke to our class.

She had sent me out with Michael to do the ink monitors' job: mixing powder and water in a big jug to the right recipe. When we came back from the stock room, carefully balancing all the inkwells on a big tray, something had clearly happened in the classroom. Everyone was subdued and afterwards in the playground I was allowed to join in again. She kept me back after school.

'I heard what has happened, Jo. If you have any more trouble from the children you must come and tell me. All right? The squabbles of grown ups have no place in school. You have no say over your father.'

I started crying. She put her arm round me.

'Don't cry. Come on, wipe your eyes.'

'I wish my father was like everyone else's.'

'He has to be his own man; everyone has to make their own choices, Jo. Your father has been through a very difficult time. No one has a right to judge him.'

'Thank you, miss. I'm sorry, miss.'

'No need to apologise. And if you just need a chat you know where I am.'

In that summer of the miners' lock-out she would take us on a picnic up to High Hazel's park and we were given bread cakes and cheese or ham, and apples and cakes to eat. I don't know where she got them from. Then she'd read stories to us, we'd sing songs or play rounders. We also started work on a play: a version of Peter Pan that she'd turned into a script. I played the part of one of the lost boys – or "lost boys and girls" as we were.

If you've not lived in a mining community you won't appreciate the strength of that word *scab*. They say elephants never forget, but they've got nothing on miners. It lives with someone forever, and they take it to the grave. Sons continue to pay for the sins of their fathers and grandfathers.

Had my father not already been set apart – independent and self-reliant, it would have broken him sooner. The fact that he was ultimately proved right didn't make things better – if anything it was worse. The miners were routed, they saw the sunken eye sockets of their women and the protruding ribcages of their kids. Their usually strong muscles wasted away. They crept back to work with their tails between their legs – no matter what they said about heads held high, no matter whether their bands played Jerusalem. They returned to work on less pay for longer hours. Their moral high ground was a barren rocky peak in an arid desert, miles from reality. For some of them it was as if one man drawing his seven and six pence ha'penny a shift tending a few miserable-looking ponies in a field full of dock, had brought about their downfall.

He never went out much before, but afterwards he rarely went out at all. He used to come home and sit and read or listen to the wireless: it was his prized possession – and I believe the loss of that had the biggest impact on him when he was made to give it up. He occasionally would put on his best suit and catch the tram into town to go to a lecture or a meeting at the Central Library or the Victoria Hall on things like Practical Psychology or Ancient Rome, but I'm not sure he had anyone he could call a friend. It made me realise how much he had leaned on my mother and then on me. His closest friends all had four legs and manes.

Despite being the daughter of a scab, my life carried on relatively unperturbed – my classmates at least stayed my friends and most of the kids on the street soon came round. On Saturdays we'd go to the Lyric to see the cowboy films – serials which left you hanging and desperate to rustle up thre'pence for the next week. We called it the "bug hut": they said you walked in and rode out. It was all part of our sense of community before the war. We shared everything. Us kids shared: head lice, scarlet fever, tiger nuts and acid drops; and the grown-ups: gossip, cups of sugar and tea, and kindness – unless you were a scab.

And so it went on year by year. Father's cough grew worse and his face became drawn. He would sit hunched over in the evening as if breathing itself was something he could only achieve by conscious effort. In. Out. In. Out. And his anger would well up inside him and burst out every now and then when I did or said something wrong, often to subside in a fit of coughing. He'd get out of breath walking in the fresh air to the end of the road, never mind the miles they had to do underground, breathing in dust; although the air in Darnall was never really fresh – even on a Sunday when all the factories were at rest – not like on the moors or at Skegness, but still a hundred times better than that underground. He tried to go back to work several times when he was feeling a bit better but it didn't come to much. He kept saying he'd get a different job – one that wouldn't trouble his chest, but the fact was, by then, work was hard to come by. More and more men were to be seen hanging around on street corners. Fit men, healthy men, not broken ones like Father.

He was sitting in his chair when I came in from running an errand for Mrs Dunstan.

'What's the matter with you? Look like you've seen a ghost.'

To be honest I thought I had – or, if not, my father's corpse. He was sitting with his hands gripping the arms of his chair, knuckles white, head tipped back, his face like tallow, ancient, not that of a man in his mid forties.

'I'm sorry, father you just startled me. I didn't expect to see you.' I did my best to sound bright and unruffled.

'Where the bloody hell did you expect me to be?'

He wasn't one for swearing. It shocked me.

'I'll make us some tea, Father. Shall I switch the wireless on for you? It'll be the afternoon concert on soon. I've got some oxtail to make some soup. There you go: it's just starting. I'll go and get the milk from the pantry.'

They made him pay for nineteen twenty-six. The community didn't rally round to help when he had to face the shame of going on the relief. No one asked after him – except Mrs Dunstan that is. She'd see me out in the yard, pegging something out, or crossing back from the lavatory and she'd call me over.

'Why don't you just come in for two minutes, come and have a sit down.'

Her kindness would sometimes make my eyes water.

'How's he doing? I heard him shouting.'

'He doesn't mean to Mrs D. He's just stuck in, with nothing to do and it all comes out when I get back from school.'

'I've got some tea in the pot. You just sit there and I'll pour you some.'

She never just gave me tea. Something else would always appear next to it, unmentioned – a piece of fruitcake or a buttered pikelet, or a slice of cold steak and kidney pie. She knew I was making do on ten shillings of groceries that we got from Gallons with the relief coupon.

It was when they came round to do their means test that he had to sell his wireless, and just about everything else we had that wasn't essential, in order to qualify for relief. He was then cut off from the world and just sat for hours staring at the wall.

I continued to do well at school despite everything, and got my matriculation certificate. But what was I to do with it? What could I do but look after my father? I managed to earn a few pence extra – I ran errands for everyone, fetching shopping, minding babies, taking in washing and ironing. I made myself useful and was busy, and that kept me happy in a strange sort of way. People forgot I was the daughter of a scab, and were grateful to me and I made them smile.

'Eee, tha's a good lass,' they'd say. 'And bonny too. One of these days tha'll break a young man's heart.'

'I shan't have anything to do with boys, Mrs Connaught. They're nothing but trouble.'

'They all say that. Then one day you find yourself up to the elbows in nappies and wonder where it all went wrong.'

I'd tried to get a look at myself in my mother's dressing table mirror before my father got home. I mistrusted that word bonny. People often used it when they were calling someone plump. I was certainly not skinny any more – my hips were filling out. I noticed how boys' eyes drifted towards my no longer flat chest. My mother's brassieres that I had stolen from her untouched drawer no longer fitted me – but what could I do? I couldn't exactly ask my father for money.

THE EVENTS that spring took many of us by surprise, even Jakub. He hadn't shared his father's pessimism; he was young, he believed in progress and had none of his father's experience of the world and of the darkness of men's souls – things his father had seen but didn't speak of, when he'd fought on the Eastern Front.

One Sunday towards the end of March, Herr Rosenbaum called round to advise my mother on repayment of a business loan or something – anyway they had account books and pieces of paper with numbers on spread out on the table between the coffee cups and a plate of Mother's *butterkuchen*, which is more than payment for an hour of anyone's time.

I was sitting in the empty shop at the front reading, but earwigging in on their conversation.

'They only narrowly won a majority but they will not stop until they crush all opposition. They create fear so that people do not dare to speak out – acquiescence is as good as support to them. The *Mitläufer* are equally as bad as the most rabid Nazis.'

'Surely not, Herr Rosenbaum, not everyone can be equally guilty.'

'But they don't want to see what is going on. They only pretend they can't see.'

'Yes, I suppose. But people are frightened, or just want so much to believe everything will turn out for the better. You can't blame them. It is a human reaction after all.'

'But the Nazis actually despise human beings, they treat people like herds, to be manipulated and they have all the tools, overwhelming might, control of the newspapers and radio; and now seem to be set on taking over the machinery of government. Do you think the judiciary will stand up to them?'

'I don't know... I know if they caught us speaking like this openly we'd be in trouble. They use fear and despair to make people turn in on themselves – turn our backs on what is going on, give up on any belief that we can change anything.'

'And evil steps in when hope moves aside. They are playing a very clever game, that is true – they send out their simple but stupid messages, but hardly anyone recognises them for what they are – blaming others for everything that is wrong – the communists, the Worker's Party, or the Jews, leaving themselves as the only solution.'

'It's that Goebbels…'

"*Ja, der nachgendunkelte Schrumpfergermane.*'

I always remembered that phrase and thought of it whenever his name was mentioned – the darkened shrunken Teuton.

'He and his master are now returning to their Jew-hating theme with this boycott.'

'Will it happen?'

'Oh, yes. The thugs will make sure of it. I fear for my business. I have already lost customers. You hear the term cattle-Jew more and more often now. I'm now Rosenbaum, the cattle-Jew, not Herr Rosenbaum, cattle dealer.'

'But you are as German as the next man.'

'And I don't even regard myself as a Jew – I don't go to synagogue – God is of no interest to me. The whole world would be better off if it weren't for Gods and superstition.'

They were sitting quietly when I went through for another piece of cake.

'Ach, this gets us nowhere, Frau Heitmann. Perhaps everything will turn out for the better after all. Perhaps it is as Herr Doktor Menchel believes – that the good sense of our countrymen will prevail. There is a big difference between the German Jew who is so integrated and the Eastern Jew with their strange clothing and customs. We are Germans first, second and third, after all. Many of us don't practise the faith – some of us go to church for goodness sake! We are more German than that Austrian dog. It's our fatherland. We mustn't be morose. We press our thumbs.'

'Indeed, Herr Rosenbaum. And thank you for your help.'

'You know I can never say no to your baking.'

I dismissed all their fatalistic talk – always worrying about something these grown-ups. Never happy unless they had something to moan about. We had been given hope for a better Germany and all they could do was see the worst in everything.

I didn't have to wait long before I realised exactly how different the way I saw the world was from the World Outlook, *der Weltanschauung*.

It was Saturday morning and I was to go to the shops as I often did with Frau Menchel. She liked to shop for frivolities, and she had to work hard to always be so immaculately dressed, always needing a new scarf, belt or lipstick to finish off her look – more like a woman from Berlin or Frankfurt than from a provincial town. She needed someone to carry all her shopping for her, and I was a very useful symbol of her status.

She used to like to drop by this lovely little cafe, owned by a friend of hers from the synagogue, for coffee and *apfelkuchen*, and, in return for accompanying her, she liked to treat me and we would sit awkwardly trying to think of things to talk about: hats, jewellery or fashion. I think she was basically quite lonely, and would have preferred to be talking to someone closer to her own age, but I tried my best to live up to her expectations, and I suppose I was closer to her age than her husband was, so perhaps she identified with me in some way. She was a good employer and a decent human being. The cafe also sold dainty little cakes and sweets that she'd buy on our way out, to take home.

That Saturday morning, the first of April it was, after breakfast, as we we're getting ready to go shopping, there was a commotion in the household – a brownshirt was standing outside the house and a few people were gathered round looking on. Herr Doktor Menchel went out to see what was going on. I heard raised voices outside. As the doctor came back inside I caught sight of a sign on the door: "Germans beware. Avoid all Jews. Do not be defiled."

He slammed it behind him.

'I won't have this, Mathilde,' he said to his wife.

'Please, Gerhard, do not make a scene. It will not help.'

'But that young thug is turning people away from my surgery. I will not have it.'

He went upstairs, and could be heard cursing and slamming drawers. He came back down.

'I will embarrass him into leaving us alone. This shows my loyalty to the fatherland,' he said, tapping the medal pinned to his jacket. 'I'll ask him if he knows what it is, that I earned that being injured three times in defence of my country. More than that young pup outside has ever done for the greater good.'

The doctor stood outside next to the SA man. We could hear him speaking to the people in the street, only being able to make out the odd word: Verdun...   by my own hand... ... outrage... ... this young man... ... respect... ... shameful... .

It worked, whatever it was he said. Soon we heard jeers aimed at the Nazi. Several more people joined the small gathering outside, including patients of the doctor. The nazi cut his losses and left. The sign was taken down and we resumed our Saturday.

'Come on, Liselotte,' said Frau Menchel, 'let us go to the shops. We have wasted enough time.'

We turned the corner into the high street, past the house on the corner with the cherry tree that would soon be coming into bloom. The first shop on our way was the butcher's. Outside, Kurt was standing in his Hitler Youth uniform – he had moved on from shorts and shoes and looked taller in black trousers and shiny new boots.

Over the road, old Herr Dressler, the haberdasher, was defying the sentries posted outside. They were helmeted with guns strapped to their belts, carrying signs on poles reading: *"Deutsche! Wehr Euch! Kauft nicht bei Juden!"* – Germans, defend yourselves, do not buy from Jews.

He had a bucket and sponge and was trying to get to his shop front to clean off the whitewash: a star of David, dripping at the corners had been daubed on his window and the words "Jews will be our downfall" underneath – the whitewash trickling down the glass and onto the beautifully maintained shop front.

'Leave our artwork alone, *Judenlümmel.*'

They shoved him, grabbed his bucket and tipped it over him.

'That will clean you up, a bit. Filthy Jew.'

Kurt laughed out loud, then saw us approaching. He stopped laughing. He smiled at me. '*Heil Hitler, Fraulein Heitmann.*'

I ignored him and walked on. Frau Menchel's eyes were alert, looking left and right, her senses on edge.

'Perhaps we will just go to the café, then go home,' she said, as she caught my eye. 'To show them we are not to be cowed.'

There were two SA men, strangers from out of town, posing in their highly polished boots, standing outside our usual cafe. Their poles across the door barring entry carrying the same "Do not buy from Jews" signs.

'This is our country, too. We mustn't be put off.' But still she stopped and hesitated before moving on.

The brownshirts looked at us and smiled, but not in a nice way, under the brims of their kepis. 'Can't you read?' one of them said. 'Go somewhere else.'

'I have every right,' said Frau Menchel, her voice breaking as she spoke.

'She's one of them.'

'In that case, *meiner Dame*, since you are not German, do proceed,' said the other one with a mock gesture of deference. 'But before you enter, I will be happy to relieve you of your money.'

Frau Menchel turned to me. 'You go home, Liselotte. There's no need for you to stay.'

'You heard her, Fraulein. What are you waiting for? Run along, *Jew*-lover.'

I stood and looked at my feet, away from their horrid eyes. I've already said I am inclined by nature to do the opposite of what I'm told. It was not an act of political defiance or anything noble that made me push my way through – more that I wouldn't be ordered about by uncouth individuals, and the thought of being denied my *apfelkuchen* was a deep injustice that overcame any fear I had.

Frau Schiener served us in silence, her eyes red and puffy from crying.

Frau Menchel sipped at her coffee and pushed her apple cake around her plate with her fork. I was not going to deny myself this treat. When we got up to leave, the two women spoke briefly to each other in hushed voices as Frau Menchel paid for our cake and coffee and a small box of chocolates to take home. I took my opportunity to cram Frau Menchel's untouched cake into my mouth.

'Filthy Jewess,' the brownshirts muttered as we left.

'Disgusting betrayal.'

'Traitor.'

When we got home we found one of the windows on the front of the house was smashed. I fetched a dustpan and brush to clear up the broken glass inside.

Not long after Herr Doktor Menchel lost his German patients. Oh, you see! This is what I hate: this imposition of identity on people that Hitler brought about. German, non-German, Aryan, Jewish, *Mischling, Ostjuden, Reichsbürger, Volljuden*, converted Jew, Catholic Jew, quarter Jew. All to be determined scientifically by the length of one's ear lobes or the angle of one's nose or whatever. Of course all Doktor Menchel's patients were German – he was forced to reduce his patient list to those they classed as Jews. It meant they could no longer afford to keep the house, or a cook, or a cook's apprentice. Frau Menchel had to keep house herself, thereafter; but at least the house they moved to was not such a big house to keep tidy.

They were only biding their time until they made arrangements to leave for America. The doctor's faith in his *Rechtsstat* was worn away bit by bit. The Nazis banned other political parties and trades unions. Then anyone who still thought that Hitler was a *Gleichschaltung*, a mayfly – and would disappear as soon, was forced to change their minds after the night of the long knives. It was clear nothing would get in his way. Any remaining shreds of hope that Herr Doktor Menchel might have had ended when old Hindenburg died and Hitler became Chancellor and President. Up until that point, Jews had who had fought in the Great War – the *Frontkampfers* – had been protected from the worst of the laws against Jews in positions of responsibility. It completely shattered the remaining traces of faith he might have had. He lost all sense of who he was and felt he had to start again in a new country. Frau Menchel certainly lost all her confidence after the *boykotten*. Until that point she had regarded herself as one of the leading women in the town, so her fall to that of *untermenschen* was particularly hard felt.

In the meantime I had finished my apprenticeship, and taken my final exam. I begged my mother to let me help out in the shop when the Menchels left but she wouldn't let me. She wanted me to learn to handle difficult situations and to negotiate my way through life's troubles. Looking back she was right. Had it not been for those hard lessons, things might have turned out very differently for me.

There was not much work going so I took a position in the house of a proper German family, the Wertheims. They were one of those families who aspired to be something that they were not, who believed they were owed a debt by everyone else, never happy with what they had got and intensely jealous of everyone who had more than them. They had a sense of injustice that they could not afford a cook, housekeeper, a governess, maid and a footman. But they had me instead – a "*Haustocher*": preparing their meals, looking after their brats, skivvying around, and all for just eight marks a week with only Sunday afternoons off.

Herr Wertheim had no brain, not that he could call his own. He was one of the vilest sorts of Nazis – the ones who don't question anything they are told, who just soak up all the hatred and spit it all back out. Whatever he was told he believed – if Hitler had told him to despise anything that was made of porcelain, he would have cleaned out his cupboards and made the household manage without plates, cups and bowls. He would have denounced his wife to the Gestapo for even yawning during a speech by Göring. I had to be careful not to upset him because he was so short tempered. He was a nasty, ugly little man, a bank clerk who, it was said, only ever got on in life, not by talent or the use of his wits, but by toadying up to party officials and reporting as many people as he could to the Gestapo. His lack of scruples or a conscience gave him an edge – if others fell around him he could be noticed just by being left standing.

I worked for up to ten or twelve hours a day, so I had hardly any time to myself – except what I could contrive. I met up with Jakub when I could, often by pretending to go to BdM meetings. Herr Bank Clerk couldn't exactly object to that, could he? His being stupid did have some advantages too: he was easy enough to fool so long as he thought you were a patriot.

But what do you do when you have no money and the evenings are cold and dark? Jakub had no money either. Their business was suffering and rumours spread about the cattle-Jew Rosenbaum being an exploiter of hard-working German farmers, and he was accused of *Händler* tactics – being very clever in business and so, swindling people.

'For an Aryan, it would be regarded as no more than sound business sense,' complained Jakub. 'Paying the market rate and trying to turn a profit, but in a Jew it is sly and underhand. As if we are somehow tricking people into accepting less than something is worth. They see us as parasites now, not partners in making farming successful.'

'Your father was always fair with my mother. I hope she was fair too.'

'Of course. She was happy to pay a fair price for a heifer. Everyone has a living to make. But now they expect you to make no profit at all. Of course sometimes, more profit is made than at other times. That is just business, and if a farmer is too stupid or is boorish – you know, those who exploit their estate workers – why should you go out of your way for them?'

'You have a special price for the nasty ones?'

'Well, so what? It gives you a certain leeway to give a much fairer price to those who are nice, or who refused to make their own labourers take all the pain when the depression was hitting hardest.'

We laughed. Such tiny victories became very important.

I did most of the food shopping for the Wertheims which meant I saw Kurt a great deal.

'My favourite customer. What is on the menu tonight? We've just cut up some nice lamb.'

'Thank you, Kurt. But I was thinking some brisket for a pot roast.'

He wrapped the meat in paper. 'Anything else?'

'No, thank you.'

'That's four marks eighty, or four marks fifty plus a smile.'

I handed over four marks and eighty pfennings.

'Aw, Liselotte. You're no sport. Why no smile?'

'I'm not in the mood, Kurt.'

'Aw, go on. To make me happy. I'll tell you what, can I take you to the *Lichtspiele* to see a film to cheer you up?'

'I've no money, Kurt.'

'Come off it. It's only a mark. I'll pay.'

'No. I'm rather tired. I'd fall asleep in the dark.'

'Then what about a quick drink after work?'

'There is no "after work" for me. It's straight to bed when I'm done.'

'Please. Just ten minutes, then. A little nightcap?'

'I'm sorry, Kurt.'

'Another time maybe?'

He didn't give in easily. He kept up with his attempts to draw me into conversation and to get to see me. But he was, to be honest, a bit dull. He was perhaps more classically good-looking than Jakub, but he did not attract me – I could not have imagined him putting his arm around me or his mouth coming anywhere near mine – a rather repulsive thought – a bit like kissing one of his cuts of pork belly. Jakub on the other hand was more like dark chocolate and cherries.

Jakub was hit very hard by everything that was going on. And, when I saw what happened to him, I lost my remaining belief that things would turn out for the better. First he was told not to return to school. He had studied so hard and was so close to his exams, but they were for Aryans only. Then he was dropped from the town's football team. They had no other goalkeeper like him – he was quick and brave – I'd seen them play a few times – but they would rather lose than have a Jew stopping shots for them. It's only football, I thought – only a game, but then I saw just how much it hurt him when in July that year a big festival took place in the region and all the local churches, political parties and clubs joined in a parade. Jakub had to look on as his former team-mates marched in their football kits, their scrawny, inexperienced, useless, but Aryan, goalkeeper leading them through the streets. They didn't even look at Jakub. He no longer existed.

His friends gradually abandoned him – some of his former Aryan friends said they could no longer see him, others never even spoke to him again. His good friend Heini had showed up on the doorstep one evening, after dark, with some books he was returning. He wouldn't even enter the house, never mind sit with the family as their guest, as he had done since they were in the same class at school. He said he was extremely sorry but could no longer be friends. That was it. No explanation given. None needed. It wasn't the first or last time. There were not many Jewish families in our small town, so other than me he had no one of a similar age to talk to.

It got harder to see him, our meetings more and more clandestine so as not to attract any attention. There was no point making life any more difficult for ourselves.

HE WAS NICE enough too, was Mr Broadhead. He always potted me up some hyacinths ready for Christmas and he knew just how long to leave them in the pantry before bringing them out. Oh, and he'd bring me things he'd spontaneously bought when out and about or ordered from a catalogue, or magazine. He'd come back with a sunlamp or an egg-slicer. We had a television before most others. We got an electric clothes dryer – a cabinet thing – what luxury – no messy washing hanging up in the kitchen in the winter.

Strange that such a meticulous man could be so afflicted by spontaneity. He once wrote off to America for a Charles Atlas booklet having seen an advert. Just fifteen minutes a day and Harold Broadhead could be transformed into the complete specimen of manhood, who would no longer be ashamed to strip for a swim! It didn't last long. Poor Mr Broadhead.

A kind man. A funny man. He was happy to go to Blackpool for his holidays, but would only admit to staying at Lytham. We never went to Bridlington, but to a boarding house in Sewerby. Relaxing on the beach he'd maybe go as far as removing his jacket and rolling his sleeves up. He might even take his shoes and socks off to reveal his pale bunions, but he always kept his tie on outdoors. He'd even mow the lawn with a tie on. You see, he was funny. That made me laugh. He'd always put on a pinafore when he did the washing up, and hold his sleeves up with those springy, sleeve things. It was a job of precision for him, like everything. There's a word for it. Ridiculous. Matriculate. No, met– something.

It was through the Brincliffe Operatic Society that we met again. He had a nice tenor voice – it was very funny. You wouldn't expect a voice like that to come out of a man like Mr Broadhead would you? He was an unconvincing Nanky-poo to my old-maidish Yum Yum, and it all just seemed as if one thing led to another. No fluttering hearts, no mad passion, no tears, no stolen moments by moonlight. Just an "I've been thinking…" and "it strikes me that... if you're of a mind and don't think it too forward…" kind of thing. I took retirement then, but he carried on working until he turned sixty-five. Did the whole gold watch thing. Then was soon gone from me. I often thought it was stopping work that finished him.

Very fond of his motorcar he was, Mr Broadhead. It was cleaned every week and polished. Never left out in the rain but put away in the small garage built at the side of the house. It doubled up as his workshop for sharpening his tools and making things on the little wooden bench at the end. He was always very good with his hands. A proud member of the Automobile Association – and prominently displayed the badge on the front so they would recognise you and salute as you went past. I teased him by calling him Mr Toad when he put on his driving gloves: "Nothing like the call of the open road. The only way to travel." I did rather enjoy those little runs out into the Peaks, though – out to Castleton for a stroll and lunch at the hotel. I miss that.

As WINTER came on, father's chest got worse. He spent a lot of time in bed. He said he was tired and would maybe come downstairs later. I kept a fire going in the little fireplace in his room to try to keep him comfortable, but it was devilish to keep going, being so small; there was never enough of it left in the morning to get it going again so I had to relight it and the cursed thing pothered into the room and needed a newspaper holding over it to try to get it to draw. I was worried about all the smoke in the room affecting his chest, but I also worried if it was too cold. Mrs D leant me an ornate, little brass bell, with what looked like the Virgin Mary as the handle, which I put by his bedside for him to ring when he needed something and I was downstairs.

One morning I'd made him a cup of tea and took it to his room and opened the curtains a bit.

'It is cold but bright today, father. I've brought you your tea.'

I put it on the bedside table but he didn't stir. He was lying on his side with his mouth open. I put my hand on his shoulder and gave him a gentle shake. Still he didn't wake up. I touched his cheek. It was cold. I took his hand, which lay outside the bedspread. Cold also.

I stood and looked at him, not knowing what I should do. There was nothing I could do. He didn't look much different to usual. In books they always say that colour had left their face, and things like that, but he didn't look a lot different to how he had. His eyes were shut and he just looked asleep. I wasn't crying. I was supposed to. I went over to the window. Outside in the street Mrs Holcombe was carrying a bundle of something wrapped up in a blanket. Probably off to Fieldsends to pawn something to tide her over the week. Behind me was something horrific, but it was the outside I was drawn to. Out there everything was the same. No one even knew. No one really cared. A scruffy tabby cat sculked along the edge of the wall and dashed across the road as a cart turned the end of our street. *Rag i'n and bo'* the man shouted. *Rag i'n and bo'.* His dappled pony stopped in front of our house and flicked its mane. Mrs Johnson from across the way came out with a pile of old clothes and Martha, my friend Muriel's big sister, dragged a broken pram over to him which he lifted onto his cart. They were given donkey stones in return – you know those rubbing stones for steps. *Rag i'n and bo'* he shouted and again, waited a few minutes while he fished in his jacket pocket for his snuff, then turned the cart around and went back up the road.

I turned round off expecting my father to tell me off for idling at the window. But he hadn't moved. Still hadn't touched his cup of tea. I took it away and threw it down the kitchen sink. I put on my boots, hat and coat and went to tell Mrs Dunstan. She'd know what to do. She came round to ours and went upstairs, returning with a sad look on her face. She sent me first for the doctor and then to fetch Mrs Burton who lived on Station Road. She was an old dame who was often called on to help with nursing and babies – I don't think she was a proper nurse or midwife or anything but she probably knew a lot more.

She had a headscarf and her housecoat on. 'I'll just get our Annie to take over and then I'll pop round,' she said. By the time I'd got back, the doctor had been and gone. Mrs D was sitting downstairs waiting for me.

'Sit down and have a cup of tea, Jo. You look all hot and bothered... and I'm not surprised. He looks very peaceful, at least. I don't think he suffered. Probably passed in his sleep, Dr Jowitt said.'

When Mrs Burton came round, carrying with her a little bag like a doctor, they set to, laying him out and asked if I wanted to help.

'Can you fetch his razor and soap? We'll just smarten you up a bit, Mr Cartwright.'

I mostly stood and watched as they efficiently went about their business. I worked up the shaving soap and brushed it on his chin, like I had seen him do, and, as I did so, tears fought their way out and I had to blink them away. This was not my father, just a shell. I was now an orphan.

'Can you get his best suit out for us, Jo? And a nice shirt and clean collar?'

I stood and couldn't move.

'Shall I get them then? Where are they?' She looked at me, waiting for me to speak.

'He hasn't got them any more.' I stared at the bare floor. 'We sold everything. That's all he's got on the back of the chair.'

'Never mind. I'll fetch a nice collar from ours – it's amazing what just a starched collar does. We'll get you smart looking, Mr Cartwright, don't worry.'

'We'll get you undressed now Mr Cartwright,' said Mrs Burton. 'Why don't you go and bring us some more water.'

When I returned with a jug and bowl, Mrs D was blocking the doorway. 'Just pop it down there, love. You go and tidy up a bit and we'll call you in a bit.' As I turned I caught a glimpse of father's pale body lying on top of the bed and Mrs Burton moving around over him. He would have hated this – he'd not even let me help him get washed or shaved.

When I was called up again he was dressed. Mrs Burton brushed some powder onto his face and made him look more like he used to – less grey-looking.

'Where is his comb, love? Would you like to straighten his hair out? There Mr Cartwright, you're looking so much better now.'

We saw Mrs Burton out and Mrs D gave her a few shillings for her trouble.

'Shall we go and look for his papers now? We need to work out what to do next. Do you know where he kept them? And where did he keep addresses? We'll need to write to any relatives.'

'There's an old biscuit tin under the bed that I'm not allowed to touch. That might be it. Should I fetch it? Am I allowed?'

'Of course. You're the boss now. We need to know. I'll put the kettle on again.'

I pushed the bedroom door open and crept towards the bed, half expecting him to sit up and shout at me for creeping about. The old Jacob's biscuit tin was pushed up against the wall so I had to reach right under – I shuddered as I thought of my father's body directly above me. I slid the biscuit tin towards me with my fingertips and quietly removed it like a thief.

'Right then, let's see if he had any insurance or anything? Receipt for the wireless. Letters from the colliery.' She took things out one by one. 'Ah, this looks like addresses.'

'That's my mother's writing.' I ran my finger over delicate curves and loops on the paper.

'She had lovely writing.'

'Yes.'

'Do you know whose addresses they are?'

I recognised some of the names from my mother's funeral. 'Maud and Eric Winstanley. That's my aunt, I think.'

'Perhaps you could write to them and let them know, but first we need – ah, this looks promising.'

She went quiet while she read slowly her lips moving, like she was half reading aloud. 'I think this is it... and it looks like it's fully paid-up. Do you remember the insurance man coming round?'

'No, I don't.'

'He must have paid it up a while back then.'

'What does that mean?'

'It means we have got the money for a decent funeral at least. The first thing you need to do is go round to the funeral directors and sort that out for as soon as possible. They'll come and move him to the front room. Then you need to write to everyone and tell them when it will be.'

'I'm not going to have to stay here am I? With him?'

'Not if you don't want to. You can always come round to ours.'

I took the old, red biscuit tin with me. They made up a bed for me on the settee in the front room. Everyone had gone upstairs, and I only had an oil lamp to read by. I picked up *The Old Curiosity Shop* from where I'd left off, but I couldn't face it. It felt too much like real life – I knew that Nell's grandfather's fate was sealed and couldn't face the thought of what might happen to her on her own. Every book has its time and place – I felt my existence to be too Dickensian to continue reading.

I picked up the battered, old biscuit tin and took out the papers to see if it contained anything else of interest. There were more receipts. Our tenancy agreement – I supposed I'd have to tell the landlord, and we were behind with the rent too. Would I still get the relief money? There were so many things I didn't know. Then there was an old photograph – of a baby – boy or girl it was hard to tell in a christening dress. Curly fair hair – so not me. This tin contained secrets. I found my parents' marriage certificate – 1909 in Staveley Parish in the County of Derbyshire, complete with a stamp with King George's head on it. Then I found my birth certificate. Josephine Cartwright. Born 25th of February 1916. Name of father Ernest Cartwright, occupation: law clerk. Law clerk? That wasn't what I'd expected. I continued searching. I found my mother's death certificate and my father's grandfather: nineteen-nineteen, when I was three. I didn't remember a grandfather.

So, there was another gathering of relatives I didn't know. Not as many this time. Aunt Maud and Uncle Eric arrived first, the day before the funeral, and took over the front bedroom. They slept in the same bed my father had died in. I didn't like to tell them. Perhaps they didn't mind. I had to join them back in the house and helped my aunt make cottage pie for tea.

'I suppose she will have to come to live with us now, Eric,' said Aunt Maud, as we sat down to eat. Uncle Eric just shrugged.

'Why will I? I'd rather stay here.'

'We'll be your guardians now, I suppose. Since your mother was my sister. We're your closest relatives. You'll like Gateshead, it's not very different from here, is it, Eric? We'll find you a nice little job, that way you can pay your keep, and you can help look after your cousins.'

Gateshead? Had she said Gateshead? Where Jane Eyre was locked up in the red room and cruelly treated by Mrs Reed? I shuddered.

'Cousins?'

'Yes, our William, Alice and George. They're all a bit younger than you.'

I didn't want to move away, to leave everything I knew and my friends. And I didn't want to end up being less than a servant, scivvying after her children, being locked in the red room for showing spirit. What could I do? I was not yet even fifteen. Old enough to get a job but not old enough to have any say over my life.

We returned to the chapel at the cemetery, about a dozen of us all told. This time the street did not close their curtains or stand at the edge of the causeway, heads bowed. Why would they mark the passing of a scab? Miss Oughtershaw was there at the chapel – sitting at the back on her own. That made me cry – she didn't need to be there, she wasn't family. She had come just to be there for me. We lowered my father's coffin into the same grave as my mother. I couldn't bear to think about it – what was in there.

A few people came to the house for a cup of tea and a piece of cake, but soon dispersed leaving me with my aunt and uncle.

Later we had a horrid cold tea – soggy cold potatoes, a slice of ox tongue and some piccalilli.

'Well, Josephine, pet, it's the start of a new chapter for you. You'll need to pack a small suitcase – we can't be taking very much – not that I suppose you have many things, but we can't take things with us on the train. We'll set off in the morning.'

'So soon?'

'Well you can't stay here. Eric has to get back to his work – he's already lost two days. He's going to go and see the landlord and hand over the keys to him. What little there is to sell might just clear the money owed.'

'But what about my friends?'

'You can write to them and tell them about your new home.'

I pushed my chair back and went to grab my coat and hat.

'Josephine where are you going? Come back you can't just...'

I was away across the yard. Tears rolling down my cheeks. "Unjust! – Unjust!" said my reason.

I reached the end of the passage and stopped. The street was dark and the air was thick with dampness – somewhere between a drizzle and fog, swirling round, mixing with smoke from the chimneys, wetting my face and making haloes around the gas lamps. Lights were on in some of the upstairs windows, a shadow moved across the curtains of the Woodhouse's opposite. It was too late to call round at any of my friends.

It was nothing special, our street: better than some, worse than many, but I didn't want to leave it. And I didn't want to leave the city. I'd never been out of it – not since I was three. Not once.

I started to shiver, so crept back up the passage and went back in the house, removed my hat and coat and sat back down. The plates had been cleared away and they both had a slice of parkin and a cup of tea in front of them. They slurped and chewed without acknowledging me, without speaking. Uncle Eric was clearly having trouble with his dentures and his top teeth getting stuck. I weighed the teapot to see how much was in it, then took it to top it up from the kettle. My aunt gave me a look. This was my house and I wasn't going to ask permission for anything. I poured some tea in my cup and sat back down.

'Well. I'm waiting, young lady.'

'What for?'

'An apology – for your petulance.'

'I have nothing to apologise about.'

'After all our kindness to you, and our willingness to take you in. You treat us like that!'

'But I didn't say nothing.'

'You didn't need to, young madam. Your manner said it all. Stomping out like that.'

'I didn't stomp.'

'Don't you answer back.'

'I don't want to leave, that's all.'

'What you *want* is of no consequence; you're just a child. You'll do as you're told.'

'I shan't come with you.'

'Eric? What have you got to say?'

He looked up from the crumbs on his plate. 'Be reasonable, Josephine. Your aunt is only wanting what's best for you.'

Aunt Maud nodded. A triumphant, told-you-so look on her face.

'Oh, what's the use. I'm going to bed.'

'And get your suitcase ready. We'll head to the station, first thing.'

'No, I won't.'

'You little vixen! I always said there was bad blood in you. If only little Joseph– '

I looked at her from the doorway. She checked herself and didn't finish the sentence. I ran up the stairs. I cried into my pillow. I wasn't going to let them hear me. All their horridness was out in the open now. She was nasty and didn't care what was best for me at all. And that toad of a husband didn't give a stuff. All he was bothered about was an easy life. I couldn't sleep. It was going round and round in my head. And what was she about to say? *Bad blood? If only little Joseph– ? If only little Joseph– ?* How could that sentence end? *"If only little Joseph-ine"* couldn't go anywhere and still mean anything. If only little Josephine... hadn't lost her parents? But she wasn't saying it to someone else. It was just an uncontrolled emotional spewing forth of words in her head. If only little Joseph– .

What if? A thought then hit me, setting my heart racing. I got out of bed and picked up the red biscuit tin off the floor and quietly opened it on the bed. Only a dim light came in through the curtains from the houses over the back. Where was it? I tiptoed across to the window to see if I could read it, but it was too dark. I'd have to put on the light, but I didn't want them to know I was awake. I flipped the switch on for a brief second. *25th of February 1916.* Darkness again. I flipped the switch – *Josephine.* Did the 'h' flow into the 'i'? I heard a noise and switched off the light and waited until it went quiet again. I flicked the switch and put the document right up to my nose. There was definitely a join between the two letters. Had I had a brother? Joseph? I switched the light off and took out the photograph of the baby and held it up in the dim light at the window. Who was it?

They wouldn't make a mistake on an official document like a birth certificate. That couldn't be it. Why change it? The explanation was more obvious: I wasn't their child. It was so obvious that I should have thought it before. I didn't really look like them, or think like them. But who was I? Where did I come from? Why change the birth certificate – why didn't I have my own one, or adoption papers? I was shivering on the edge of the bed, so crept under the covers.

Wild thoughts swirled around my head. Then she wasn't my aunt. So had no claim over me. But she knew. She'd said *If only Joseph–* had survived? Then they must have got me from somewhere and just added an 'ine' on the end. Then, did that mean that my birthday wasn't the twenty-fifth of February at all? Were all those birthdays a deceit?

I felt I had hardly slept when the first light filtered through the thin curtains. I got dressed and took out my mother's suitcase and folded the few clothes I had, to go in it. At the bottom of the suitcase I placed some of the papers from the biscuit tin, my hairbrush, a small mirror that had also been my mother's. *Mother's?* Did that even mean anything, any more?

I needed to pick my moment. Perhaps I'd just put my suitcase near the back door and then run for it when they weren't looking. Or I could take off when we got to the end of the road and go through the tunnel. I'd be faster than them and I knew all the shortcuts and jennels. Perhaps they'd just call the police. Or could I give them the slip in the big station in town?

THAT YEAR, my world fell apart. I ended up back at mother's and was so broken I wouldn't even leave the house.

It had been a hot summer. I'd have been eighteen years old by then, so considered myself very grown up. I'd meet up with Jakub on the edge of town and we'd walk along the country lanes or through the woods. The woods were popular at the weekends for walkers. They all flocked to an inn near where many of the footpaths started and which always had a ready supply of beer and lemonade, cake and coffee. Many never made it beyond the pretty little garden, where they'd get merry listening to one of the local bands playing.

In the evenings we could be on our own and could walk hand in hand or cool our feet in the river. Then if we had more time we would walk up to the heath where you could swim in the lake, or we'd lie down and cuddle on his jacket among the heather with only the setting sun as our witness. Mother wouldn't have liked it if she had known we went up there. It had somewhat of a reputation with the older generation; we'd often see young couples emerging from the undergrowth. In those days there were not so many opportunities to be in love.

One morning I went into the butcher's and Kurt was not his usual self. No cajoling or drooling. He was serving another customer. He waited until she'd left.

'There's something you need to know.'

'Oh, what's that? – that pork loin is half price for a kiss?'

'Don't fool around. I'm being serious.'

'That makes a change then.'

'That *dreckjude*...'

'What?'

'Someone's seen you with him.'

'What are you talking about?'

'I can help you.'

'I don't need help from you.'

'Can you not see the seriousness of this? I stuck up for you. Said you were not like that.'

'Like what?'

'A... a Jew-whore.'

'How dare you!'

'Those aren't my words. I defended you, said they must be mistaken. You must stop seeing him or there will be trouble. Come out with me. Please. For your own sake. If you're seen with me I can sort everything out. They won't mess with me.'

'Who?'

'People. Everyone. There's talk about what's going on.'

'There's nothing going on. Please pass me that bacon and I'll be going.'

I never mentioned it to Jakub. Perhaps I should have done. But it wouldn't have made any difference. In that respect Kurt was right. The only thing that would have prevented it would have been to end it with Jakub and put on a show by being seen on the arm of Kurt Maier.

Jakub and I talked little about what was going on in the world. When we were together nothing else really mattered. No, that's not quite true: it was more that we were so powerless. We could change nothing, do nothing; we weren't even old enough to vote. What would talk achieve? Why make yourself ill with worry? Human beings have to construct barriers around their souls to protect themselves from just how awful their species is. For many their strongest, most unbreakable barrier is their faith in a God: no matter how awful this life is the next one will be paradise. It works for many despite their only evidence bring muddled sentimentality. There are fools who took comfort from angels they believed were looking after them, and they continued their faithful blindness right up to the point that their misfortune and suffering ended their lives. But laziness and stupidity seem equally effective:

never troubling yourselves with the world because it is simply too complicated and not worth the effort, and what better protection from fear than ignorance of it. Deny any evidence that points to fear, never enquire into the reality and you feel better. Put your faith in gods, in kings, kaisers, fuhrers and politicians who say they know the way: all you need to do is follow sheep-like and all will be well. Don't bother thinking, because the object of your ideology will do it for you, and so much better.

Others just don't have time to stop and think: too concerned with survival, working to put bread on the table, with only a few hours sleep before having to do it all again. No time or energy to ponder life's meaning, or what it should be like; or so full of hatred for everyone that they can never make things better, only spit venom and scratch and fight and kill.

The more of these protective shells you have, the saner you are deemed to be. If they crumble or wear thin, so that you start to seriously question, they will come and get you, apply electrodes to your temples, inject you, sterilise you or exterminate you like rats, for the sake of the *Volk*, to preserve everyone else's concept of sanity, for racial purity.

For Jakub and me, we knew all this, but we sought shelter and comfort in each other. We were walking arm in arm back across the heath with a view down to the town below. I lent towards him so that he had no doubts.

'No matter what, you have me.'

'And you have me too. No one can ever take that away.'

'We just have to endure and hope that good people prevail, and one day we can be ourselves, that people can live their lives.'

'I would like to live on a farm again, like we used to, mother and I. We could have a big dairy herd.'

'The best: and produce the finest milk in Germany. And sweet butter and cheese to sell in the market. You can run the dairy and I'll be the herdsman.'

'Or we could employ people, and mama could help us.'

'Or we could supply her shop.' He turned to look at me. 'Lottchen... '

'Yes, Jakub?'

'Will we... ...? Will we really be together?'

'Why do you not... ?'

'I want nothing more. But how... ? We have no money.'

'I don't care. It doesn't matter.'

'Then... Would you... Do you think?'

I stopped and took both his hands. 'Are you asking me... ?'

'Yes. I think so... I'm rather making a hash of it, aren't I?'

'No.'

'So will you... will you marry me? Maybe not soon, but some day, when we can. When we can afford to rent a room?'

'Yes, Jakub. Not some day. But as soon as we can.'

'Oh, Lottchen – '

But he never finished his witterings because I reached up and pulled his lips to mine.

It was not long after that; it was a busy Saturday morning and I was doing my usual trip for the weekend's shopping. They must have been lying in wait for me, knew what time I usually called in at the butcher's shop.

Both Kurt and Herr Maier were behind the counter. His father sharpening his knives for cutting a flank of beef. Kurt cut some sausages with his scissors then twisted them and wrapped them for a customer. She paid and left.

Kurt then looked up at me. 'I'm sorry. I tried.'

I was grabbed from behind and heavy hands dragged me back and forced me down onto the wooden chair that waiting customers used. I turned my head. There were two of them, in SA uniforms. I swore and tried to get up, one of them came round to face me – flabby-faced with red patches, his face marked by acne scars and dark stubble.

'Shut your mouth, Jew-whore or I'll shut it for you!'

'You've no... '

He smacked me hard across the face with his big ugly hands. I felt a trickle of blood across my upper lip and a searing pain across my cheekbone. I think I went into shock and closed down. I don't remember much that happened afterwards. It is more that a number of images remain seared on my brain: the butcher's broad back and the schnip-schnip sound of knives being sharpened, the ugly face close to mine, his breath, the scissors used for meat coming towards me, my plaits being waived in my face then thrown on the floor, Kurt's impassive face as he looked on.

'This is what you get for betraying your country.'

I was unable to lash out, unable to speak. I wish I could have. So many times since I have thought about what I could have done and said.

'Right! Now the whole town will see your shame.'

I was forced to my feet and kicked on the back of the legs. I fell onto the sickly smelling sawdust.

'Get up, *schlampe*. We have a necklace for you.'

A sign made of cardboard threaded with string was hung around my neck. It read: "I consort with Jews." They used their rifle butts to keep me moving out into the street. The sight that awaited me was even worse than anything I'd already seen. Jakub was on his knees in the middle of the road with two thugs stood over him. His face was battered and bruised. He had obviously shown more spirit than me.

'Come on let's get the parade going.'

I was flung out onto the road and fell again.

'Lottchen, what have they done to you?'

He got up and lunged towards the man who had done it to me. Before he had got far he was struck right between the shoulder blades and staggered back down onto his knees. I saw the sign he had round is neck: the Swastika, the Star of David, and the words:

"I have defiled the German race." I saw that one of his trouser legs had been cut off at the knees. Like they had butchered my hair, they had made him look comical. De-humanising us.

No one intervened. No one said anything. The street was busy on Saturday morning with shoppers and horse-drawn carts from out of town. But no one came to help. We were shoved ahead of the thugs and made to walk down the main street past all the blank faces of people who stopped their business to stand and stare. Some at least had scared eyes; others ignored it as if nothing out of the ordinary was going on. Not their business. Of no concern.

I saw my mother rush forward but she was dragged back and held by some people – probably for her own good. I would not have been able to stand her being beaten too.

When we got to the Hindenburgplatz the brownshirts turned around and left, leaving us alone in the middle of the square. Jakub looked at me and stroked my bruised cheek with such sorrow in his tearful eyes.

'I'm so sorry, Lottchen. I have done this to you.' He removed the sign from around my neck, tore it up and scattered the pieces, took a handkerchief from his pocket and wiped my face. He removed his own sign and cast it to the floor.

'No. It is me who has done this to you. I ignored their warnings.'

He took me by the arm and guided me to the pavement and we walked back to my mother, avoiding the gaze of everyone, heads lowered.

My mother wept afresh at the sight of us close up.'

'I'd better go and get cleaned up, Frau Heitmann.' He had blood on his collar and one of his eyes was swelling up. 'And I don't want my father to do anything rash – I might have to stop him. There is nothing to be gained.' He turned to leave. 'I'm so sorry.'

'Don't be, Jakub, she said. 'None of this madness is of your doing. You are a good lad. A thousand times better than them.'

They knew how to shame me. What they did to my hair was so humiliating – I was very proud of it and how it made me look so German; they were not only cutting off my hair but my identity – denying my belonging.

'Don't worry, liebling. We can make it look lovely.'

'No, we can't!' I tore at what was left with my hands.

'Liselotte, don't. Come. Where is that postcard of Luise Ullrich. I'll get my scissors and tidy it up, shape it properly – you'll look just like her, you'll see.'

'It won't work, mother. I'm not going out again ever again. Not until it's grown.'

'Don't be a silly. I'll get some lotion and we'll put a finger wave in it. It will look lovely; I always thought you should do it. You know what they say: *alte Zöpfe abschreiden* – it will be a new you.'

'Well, I'm not going back to work. I can't work for Nazis again.'

The next day Mother told me that Jakub had been taken away. Little did I know that I had seen him for the last time in Germany; I would see him again long after, but at the time I convinced myself that I would never see him again. I cried even more that second day. It no longer mattered how awful my hair was or how ugly the bruises on my face looked.

WOULD YOU LIKE to come down to the day room Mrs Broadhead? There's a lady from the Soroptimists coming to give a talk on the wild flowers of the Peak District – she's got some slides to show. And I think she said she would bring some spring flowers in, that she has picked – although, does summer start tomorrow? I never quite know. It sounds right up your street? Mrs B – is everything all right?'

'Do stop prattling on. I'm fine. Just leave me alone.'

'Wouldn't it be nice to get out of your room?'

'Will you leave me alone. I'm all right. I don't want to sit with a load of old ladies.'

'Shall you come down for your tea later, then?'

'No, I'm staying here.'

'Then we'll bring you up your tea on a tray.'

'Thank you, dear. Would you pass me my biscuit tin from the bottom of my wardrobe before you go.'

'Yes, of course. Did you not eat all your lunch? If you're still hungry I can bring you up some fruit or something.'

'No, don't be silly. There aren't biscuits in it.'

'Is it this one? The Peak Freans tin? It's heavy. What have you got in here? Old love letters?'

'Don't be so nosy. If you could put it on my table. Thank you.'

He had such lovely eyes. Such fine limbs. A good man. A kind man. There are so many *if onlys*. So many forks in the road where you have no choice but to follow one, where you are repelled by pitchfork-wielding devils or by death itself. It sometimes seems remarkable that any of us survive, even more so that anyone is happy. When choices present themselves: straight ahead or turn back, or take that narrow stony path up to the right or the one that slopes down through the bracken on the other side. How can you know you made the right choice? To carry on is easy – keeping doing what you do, being pushed and prodded on the way from one day to the next. Will the stony path up be hard? Will opening the lungs feel satisfying and provide reward at the top: views of great prospects or cloud or deeply furrowed peat bogs. Does any of it even matter? Is it all irrelevant which paths you choose and which are denied to you? Perhaps happiness didn't lie in the other direction; perhaps that is simple illusion. And yet...

If there is a God, he is not just. And yet somehow I persevere in my faith. Some people have no choices and the only paths lead to pain and despair. I have done my best. Tried to do the right things, and not just for me. I have been one of the lucky ones. Everyone who survives is a lucky one. I wonder if she is still out there? If she is she'll be forty-five…

THAT ESCAPE PLAN only ever happened in my head. I sat on that train, taking me towards my fate – the red room and Mrs Reed – with a sullen face stuck in a book. I had to share a room with their daughter, sleeping on a pull-out mattress. My meals were taken with the children: delicacies such as stewed cow's heel, boiled sheep's head, sloppy milky puddings, yesterday's bread and cheap and runny jam. I was not allowed the nicer crockery or cutlery reserved for my aunt and uncle, just the nasty ones used by the children, and had to drink, not from a glass or a china cup, but a revolting, stained earthenware beaker. I was treated as if I too were no bigger than seven by an aunt and uncle who I knew were not related to me. Perhaps they had a sense of Christian duty. I know I should be more charitable, but I cannot find it in myself. They said nothing more about who I was. After her little outburst on that last evening back home my Aunt watched her tongue and I opted to bend with the wind.

Their children were simpering, obedient little fools who seemed to be constantly dripping from nose and wet lips and had pink splodges as a result of their skin being soaked. They repulsed me. They even smelt funny. Aunt Maud tried punishing me, locking me in the bedroom, but that wasn't much of a punishment – it meant I was away from them and their offspring. When I got the chance I'd get away and spend hours wandering around Saltwell Park. She didn't dare send me on errands, and the children didn't want to be with me.

In the end I was so sullen and unresponsive that they got rid of me as quickly as they could, for which I was grateful – though none of that gratitude they saw, nor deserved. It was not an escape route I had planned. I could take no credit for having thought through and implemented a strategy. The best my imagination had come up with was a fairy godmother, but the real life outcome was just as magical to me.

I was sent to a family in Tynemouth to be a nanny and home-help. Fake Aunt Maud must have lied about how nice and polite I was, to get rid of me.

Mr Forbes was a newspaperman at the local newspaper. He came across as being very rough and serious but he wasn't in reality. He was really quite kind and gentle once you'd got used to him – to my fifteen-year old mind he was a bit like Mr Rochester. His wife was elegant, though rather frail of health, which is why they lived on the coast. They paid me five shillings a week at first. I think my aunt had expected me to give some of that to her, but I never even went to visit them, never mind stay with them. I wrote to them for a week or two, then stopped. They didn't write back more than once. They didn't like me and I didn't much care for them either.

I was given aprons to wear: a coarse linen one for the mornings, for my cleaning jobs and helping in the kitchen, and a lacy one for the afternoons. There was another girl there too: Gertrude, or Gertie as she was known. We shared the attic room in the house. It had sloping ceilings and window which you could look out of if you balanced on the chair arm. We were just off the seafront and I could feel the sea air on my face and see the stars; and if I craned my neck, the moon reflecting on the sea, and white crested waves rolling in. I used to spend hours at that window. In summer, holidaymakers came and wandered down our street, arm in arm on their way from their lodgings or from the station to the beach.

I helped Mrs Forbes look after the children – above all else they did not drip and drool, nor did they smell unpleasant. I'd push little Millicent around in her perambulator on the seafront and play cricket on the beach with the two boys. I read to them – and told them stories: things I made up from other stories, or drawing inspiration from things I'd seen at the pictures. I got time off on a Wednesday afternoon and every other Sunday evening. I'd go up to Whitley Bay to the Coliseum or to the Albion in North Shields, sometimes with Gertie if she was free, or sometimes on my own – Gertie was from Newcastle, so often went home on her days off. For just sixpence I was transported to a different life, where Norma Shearer was my mother and Clark Gable my father, or I frightened myself silly watching Frankenstein. My version of Frankenstein became one of the children's favourites – in which a small boy called Frank mended his teddy bear after it was destroyed by a dog and it came to life after his tree house was struck by lightning.

I was made to feel part of the family and counted my blessings. Gertie and I often ate with the family rather than in the kitchen and they would let me listen to the wireless with them in the evenings, and there was always a ready supply of newspapers.

I was sixteen when Stan and Ollie came to the town. It was a lovely hot summer day in thirty-two, in the middle of a heat wave – although it never got as hot on the coast as I remember it getting in Sheffield. There was nearly always a breeze off the North Sea, whereas Sheffield's hills often trapped the heat of the sun as well as the heat from the forges and rolling mills. Sometimes where we were, a cooling sea fret spilled in – you could walk mo more than a few hundred yards inland and you were out of the chill sea air and into blazing sunshine. That day though, when Stan and Ollie came, the sea was reflecting the bright blue of the sky.

Loads of people turned out for what was the biggest thing that had happened for ages in our sleepy seaside town. Stan Laurel must be the most famous local-boy-made-good, and all the bigwigs were out including various chief constables and the mayor. The verandas and steps of the Plaza were packed, as was the beach, not that they could really see much from down there. We, however, got a really good view up on the top veranda because of Mr Forbes working for the newspaper.

A horrid bi-plane buzzed overhead as we waited for them to arrive onto the little wooden stage. They handed out presents to all the local orphans and Stan pretended to fall over and then had to have his tie straightened by Ollie so he tried to repay the favour only to get into trouble and start crying – you've seen it all before, but we got to see it for real, not in a film. Stan waved to the crowds and sat down by mistake on Ollie's knee. It was very funny.

Afterwards me and Gertie walked arm in arm along the seafront while Mr and Mrs Forbes and the children joined the guests of the newspaper for afternoon tea.

Gertie didn't stay much longer. She went back to Newcastle to look after her mother and got married soon after to a boy she had known since childhood – I didn't see her much after that.

I had no such plans – and what other course was there but to carry on as I was? I was happy, and appreciated in the household, and I was, by then, earning seven shillings, most of which I didn't spend. I gave my savings back to Mr Forbes to look after for me – he put it in the bank and kept a little book for me.

Like with all the best-made plans, Fate often has other ideas and everything was to change two years later.

In the summer holidays I spent a lot of time with the children on the beach – it suited them that they could meet up with their friends and play all sorts of games and keep themselves entertained for hours; and it suited me – I could immerse myself in a book with just the occasional glance up to make sure that no one had drowned. Millie was old enough to be sufficiently sensible not to wander too far off and didn't pester me often, being content to play with the bigger kids.

It was a hot day and I wandered down to the sea to cool my feet and to watch the children, who had gone for a paddle and a swim.

'Not too far, Millie. I'm not diving in to rescue you if a wave bowls you over. Come on, then. Hold my hand, there's a good lass.'

She turned and giggled at me and splashed some water in my direction.

'Got you, Joey!'

'Oi, gi'o'er!' Sometimes Sheffieldish just slipped out like that, when I didn't have time to think about it. Mostly everyone thought I was a posh southerner, the way I spoke, and I'd only picked up one or two of the Geordie inflections and the odd word or two. But getting splashed with water like that, I was right back at Bowden Houstead Woods with the gang off our road with my "gi'o'er."

There were two young gentlemen at the water's edge. I'd noticed them earlier when I went into the shallows – smartly dressed, still in their waistcoats, wearing ties and rounded collars, and their sharply pressed trousers at risk, from being turned up to below the knee, as well as from salt stains. One of them, with horn-rimmed glasses and dark hair, Brylcreemed in a film-star wave, was now looking over at me and prodding his mate. I turned away and tried to ignore them, talking to Millie about some nonsense.

'I'm thirsty, Joey.'

'Come on, then. Let's go and get a drink of pop shall we?'

As I turned, the young man in the glasses caught my eye and smiled at me. He opened his mouth as if about to speak, but I hurried past him to where our blanket was spread out on the sand. Millie sat with me for a bit then some of her friends came to find her – they needed a customer for their little shell and pebble shop – it didn't feel so long ago that I used to play that game – I was quite jealous.

As I picked up my book, someone plonked themselves next to me and made me jump.

'Which bit of Sheffield are you from?'

I turned to look at him: the young man with the glasses.

'Why? But...'

'I'm terribly sorry for being so forward. I'm not normally. But my friend there, Stan – ' he gestured over to where the other man was sitting grinning like an idiot. '– he wagered me to come and ask you. Anyway there, I've done it now, and made myself look a right chump, if but tuppence up. I feel exceedingly foolish. I'll go. Terribly sorry, miss.' He started to get up.

'Darnall,' I said, smiling. He had gone bright red and looked very sweet. 'You're not from here either, then?'

'Oh, no – terrific,' he said, sitting back down. 'I knew it. I thought I'd made a fool of myself for a minute. I'm from Hunter's Bar – Jack's the name,' he said holding out his hand.

'Josephine. Everyone calls me Jo.'

'Or Joey?'

'What? Oh, you heard Millie call me that? That's just Millie.'

'It's a bit like meeting a fellow Englishman in the middle of the Arabian Desert or something. Having someone who speaks properly, not all *Howay, bonny lad. Am gannin yam* and all that.'

'Way aye man, that's proper canny like, divvn't ya nar'

'Ha ha! You've got that off to a tee. Do you live here then?'

'Yes, for the last few years – I live with a family – Millie, she's one of the children I look after – a big house just up there. What about you?'

'I'm only here for a few weeks. I work for Vickers and have come up to help out on a project at the factory up here. I'm going back next week.'

We sat and chatted for so long that his friend came up and said he was going to head off.

'I'd best be off then,' said Jack.

But his friend placed his hand on Jack's cap and stopped him getting up, then kicked him in the side. 'No need. I'm going to drop by Geordie Thompson's on the way, see if I can cadge a pint out of him.'

Jack looked all embarrassed. 'Oh, very well then. If you don't mind the company.'

'No. You were about to going to tell me about the new library in town.'

We talked all afternoon, like we had known each other for a long time – about things we had in common, books and music: he had seen Louis Armstrong and his Harlem Hot Rhythm Band at the Empire a few months before, which I was most envious of.

'So what is it you do at Vickers?'

'I'm a draftsman.'

'I'm not sure I know what one of those is.'

'Basically I draw up designs of things in order that that we can make them with precision – down to tiny fractions of and inch.'

'You get paid to do drawing?'

'Hah! That's one way to look at it, I suppose. I'm lucky; I really enjoy it. You know Malcolm Campbell? Well, one of the things I was involved with was the design of the crankshaft for Bluebird.'

'That must make you proud to think that he's breaking records with your crank-thingy.'

'Crankshaft – it's part of the Rolls Royce engine. It's what turns piston motion into rotation. A lot of Sheffield steel in Bluebird. We do all sorts though: boilers for power stations, aircraft parts, guns and turrets for ships.'

I must have gone quiet because he said, 'What's the matter. Did I say something wrong?'

'It's just I hate aeroplanes and warships. They scare me. All this talk about bombing. You can't stop a bomber they say. Mr Forbes said if you build a better anti-aircraft gun, they will just fly higher – you won't even know the bomber's there until the bomb drops – you can't stop gravity.' I flattened little mounds of sand with my foot, as if to emphasise my point. 'Do you think a war is coming?'

'I don't know. I hope not. I'm a member of the League of United Nations Union and will be helping with the National Declaration – the Peace Ballot – you've heard of it?'

I nodded. 'We see the warships as they come and go out there,' I said, looking out to where the Tyne meets the sea. 'On their way to the docks or setting out to sea for the first time to create fear of death with those guns of yours. Huge monsters of death they are to me.'

'I agree, but we had to have aeroplanes and ships to defend ourselves from threats to our civilisation.'

'They say there won't be any civilisation left after another war. We can't defend civilisation by blowing it up.'

'No. But we have no choice but to stand up and fight fascism.'

'I don't know. I hate all this talk of fighting this and fighting that.'

'So do I, but the truth is that they don't think the same. Good people have to force themselves to fight sometimes because the other side has no such qualms. They revel in violence and spreading fear, and don't think twice about imposing their doctrine. That's why when Mosley came to Sheffield there were fifteen thousand of us outside the City Hall, letting them know they weren't welcome and sending a clear message to the Police that they should not be sanctioning their hate.'

'The Police have got to keep order though.'

'But they're creating conditions for fascism to thrive. If the fascists get in power they wouldn't allow anyone opposing them to hold rallies. They put them in concentration camps. They bleat freedom of speech only when it suits them. Look, I'm sorry, you've set me going now. You need to tell me to shut my mouth. Enough of this gloominess. Come on I'll buy you an ice cream.'

When it was time to head back for tea, he helped me carry our things to our front door. I ushered the children inside.

'I really enjoyed talking to you, Jo. Thank you.'

'I suppose...' I said. 'Would...' he said, at the same time.

'Sorry, you go first,' I said. 'I interrupted you.'

'No. I just... I wondered, do you get any time off?'

'Not until Wednesday.'

'I'll be gone by then.'

'But, I could ask.'

'Could you? That would be...'

'I'll ask about Monday evening.'

'In that case I'll call round, either way.'

He took me for afternoon tea in the lounge of the Dolphin Inn which had been recently done up all modern and we walked around by the castle and onto the pier and watched the last few fishing boats heading back into haven before he walked me home.

Schutzhaft they called it: protective custody. Taken away for your own good to stop the mob from killing you. He was sent without trial to a *konzentrationlager* out near the Dutch border. He never spoke much about what happened there. They slept in single storey huts laid out in rows, but there the similarity with Butlins ended. I know he was forced to work in the fenland digging drains and was beaten and abused regularly as part of his *re-education*.

When mother came back one evening with tears in her eyes, I feared the worst but was relieved, and ashamed, when she told me that the Rosenbaums had decided to leave. The business was doing badly and not worth trying to save they said. They were selling up and we're going to the Netherlands, to a town not far from the border. They had relatives there and could try to get help to Jakub.

I could see that mother, too, was worrying about her business. Things had gone quiet in the shop. That reassuring, friendly bell on the door used to go off all the time.

'It's always quiet in the holidays,' she said.

'It's not that though, is it mother? It's me. I've dragged you down haven't I?'

I went to sit on the floor in front of her.

'No you haven't, Lottie Liebling.'

I rested my head on her lap, like I used to do when I was little, and she stroked my hair. I closed my eyes and thought for a while. It seemed obvious what was to be done.

I looked up at her. 'There are two options open to us, mother. Either I stay here with you and help run the shop, or I go away. I will not get another job round here – everyone knows now, and they'll all be too scared to make a stand or to do the right thing. No matter how good they are, or how good I am as a cook, no matter how unfair it all is, they won't risk being ostracized because of me.'

'Oh, but I'm sure it's not that bad. It will blow over.'

'You don't really believe that any more than me.'

Her eyes gave their own answer.

'The same thing applies if I stay here with you. How long can the shop last without its customers? A month? Two?'

Her eyes filled with tears again. Mine had run dry after days of crying.

'We could try,' she said, without conclusion or conviction.

'I don't want to sit here and watch you go through it. Everything you've worked for, slowly collapsing because I fell in love. I'm right aren't I?'

She didn't resist. 'You are so grown up, Liebchen. You amaze me sometimes. I wonder where you get it from.'

We sat quietly for a while holding hands.

'There is your great aunt Auguste in Bremen . She wrote to me last week saying she was worried that she won't be able to cope on her own much longer – her legs are so bad, and she fell again and spent a few days in hospital. Perhaps she would take you in, to help her?'

'Then write to her and tell her I'm coming. It is for the best. You should then join the *Frauenschaft* and hang a swastika over your shop. You can tell Frau Hahn that you have disowned me, then everyone in town will know within hours – she crows louder than her namesake.'

'I can't put that flag up.'

'It's only a flag.'

'It's much more than that.'

'Anyway that will put things right again with your customers. They won't need to sneak in the back door like I've seen some of them do.'

'But would you be all right?'

'Yes, I have to be.'

'But poor, Jakub... '

'I don't think I will ever see him again.'

She broke into loud sobs.

'What is it mother?'

'You mustn't say that. It's just...   I know what you're going through. Your father... Now you're all grown up, I should tell you.'

'Not if it upsets you. I don't need to know. The war took him away. What else is there to know.'

'It's not that. There's more to it. Something you should know, especially if you're going away. I might never see you again.'

'Mother, don't – '

'I know what forbidden love is like. I don't blame you. I need you to know that. To understand. No one can help who they fall in love with. We will have a talk, but not now. I will write to Aunt Auguste.'

A few days later a reply was received and preparations were made for my leaving. One evening, after we had tidied away the plates, my mother said: 'Come on, we need tea. Put some water on to boil.'

The tea and the tea cups with roses on didn't come out often – only on special occasions or when we needed to cheer ourselves up.

As she busied herself getting teacups, sugar and cream, I could tell she was composing herself and her words.

We sat at the table in the back room and she took my hand.

'I wasn't married to your father.'

'I think I had guessed that. Opa never spoke of him. I knew there was something.'

'It wasn't only that...   He was the... was the enemy... He was an Englander.'

We put lumps of sugar – *kluntje* – into our cups, poured in the tea and trickled the cream down the side.

'So... you mean... I thought he died at the front... '

'I never lied to you. I never said that. I only ever said he was taken away by the war – that was true.'

'But how... ?'

'He worked on the farm. He was a prisoner of war – they used to make them work on the farms. They were the lucky ones. Many died in the salt mines at Soltau. He was terrified of being sent there. They were not treated well. When he came to us he was extremely thin. Very unhappy. It was wartime – many Germans were starving too. He got better when he was with us – he shared our food and the demons he had started to leave him. I fell in love with him, Lottchen. And then...   and then... He never came back. They took him from me.'

Tears rolled down her cheeks. She sipped from her cup.

'They took all the men from the lager in the village away – I don't know. To other farms... Back to the main lager.'

'Is he... ? Did you... ?'

She shook her head. 'I don't know. The war went on for another two years. You came along and became my focus. There was nothing else... my refuge. So many things happened.'

I stared into my cup and watched the *wulkje* – the creamy clouds – rising like my thoughts. I looked into her sad brown eyes.

'It starts to make some sense. Some things... What was he like?'

'Everything I have ever told you about him was true. You get your blonde hair and blue eyes from him. He was a brave and strong soldier. He was gentle. A freethinker – like you. Spirited – what he'd been through would have broken most men. Your grandfather was... well, you can imagine. Your Uncle Manfred was killed at the front. All the propaganda was that it was the English who were the devils. They caused the war – they were threatening Germany so we had to defend ourselves.'

'People still say that – their greed and lust for Empire, to dominate everything.'

'It is complicated. But the English were not horned devils. They were just men like our brothers and friends. But your Grandfather...   he was very traditional, very Prussian in his outlook. He didn't want an Englishman on the farm, but he was told he had to.'

'What... what was he called?'

'Smith, as in *Schmidt*'

'No, his first name.'

'That was it. It must be an English thing. His second name was Otter Shore – like in *otter ufer. Niedlich,* yes?'

'Tell me about him.'

'You have his eyes – expressive eyes. I take so much comfort from you. He is a part of you.'

I squeezed her hand.

'I didn't always understand his words, but I understood him in a different way – he had a very strong accent.'

'Why? Where was he from?'

'From the North – from Sheffield. It is famous for its cutlery – industrial, hardworking. Your grandfather sent him up onto the moors to cut heather for the byre, but he would not work here – said it was not his farm. Instead he often sat in the sunshine and slept. He liked it up there. Said it reminded him of home.'

'But didn't you say he came from an industrial town?'

'Yes, but not that big perhaps. Surrounded by moors. He said it was just a big village really – where people were connected and looked out for each other.

'Anyway, I went up to the moors to take him some dinner when he forgot it, and found him swimming in the stream. Not working. Not a single piece of heather had been cut.' She smiled a sad smile.

'Were you not cross?'

'Yes. But he smiled his cheeky smile and said: "It's not my heather. They're not my cows." It was his spirit you see... His resistance to the war, despite everything. He was a beautiful man. And...

'It could never be mentioned in the house. When it became obvious, that winter, Opa's first reaction was to throw me out. His temper, you know... But it was winter. Where could I go – and... he needed me on the farm, you know. He was grumpy, but he did have a heart, your grandfather.'

'Yes, I know. Poor Opa. You only had to hear his violin to know his heart. It can't have been easy.'

'No. So we agreed a story to tell the gossips – that my fiancé, Hans, who really was killed in France – was not dead after all, and had been found in a hospital, and that I had been to see him and it was his wish that we got married there. We spent a week or so together, but then he deteriorated and passed away. It sounded very noble and patriotic. So you might have heard something like that from other people. It was to protect you. There is such a stigma... and it was tenfold given who he was. I was always going to tell you when the time was right.'

I left on the Saturday morning. My trunk had already been sent to the station. I looked out of the front window of the shop. My train was due in half an hour.

'Shouldn't you get off?'

'I want to wait until it is busy in the street outside so that I can put on a little performance for them.'

'What do you mean, liebchen?'

'You'll see. But you mustn't be shocked. Promise?'

'Why? What... ?'

'I want to make it convincing, you know. Let's say our goodbyes inside the shop – then you'll know how much I love you. I covered her downy cheeks in kisses. I will write to you.' We hugged and cried together. 'Now you must come to the door. Get ready, mama dearest, for a film star's performance. This will be funny.'

She stood at the door and I turned, my audience ready.

'And I'm never coming back!' I yelled. 'You're as bad as all the rest.'

I saw her face. She was shocked, but then I saw the glimmer of realisation in her eyes.

'How dare you, speak to your mother like that,' she shouted back, rising to the game.

'Look at them!' I gestured around me. 'I hope they're worth it. You should all be ashamed of yourselves. Some of them reeled back in horror at someone actually daring to speak their mind. You've lost all sense of morality. You and your rotten party! And *you* – you've no right to call yourself mother!'

'Well, really!' she said. 'And good riddance!'

I turned and ran down the street towards the station before anyone could get me arrested. I had a smile on my face as I imagined my mother continuing to act out her part: betrayal and affront – soaking up all the sympathy of customers and lookers-on.

Poor Aunt Auguste. She lived her last year or so with a deal of pain in her back, feeling tired and with swollen feet. I was kept very busy cooking and cleaning for her and helping her to wash and get about the flat. She'd spend her days either in bed or in her armchair, listening to the wireless or looking out at the street from the window. I couldn't leave her for long; so, other than going out to the shops, I had no time to really call my own.

She talked a lot about the old days when she and my grandmother were girls, about life in their village and how my Opa courted my grandmother and how handsome he looked in his hussars' uniform. She also talked about Hanover in the old days when she moved there to be governess for a well-to-do family.

She liked to listen to me play my violin – even when I was practising. She clapped when she saw the improvement and she gave me money to go to the music shop in town to buy sheet music to learn. She also had a gramophone that her late husband had bought.

'Actually, I don't know whether he bought it or not. He often used to come home with nonsense. He was a printer, you know, so had clients in all sorts of businesses. Sometimes things would just take his fancy, and they would throw it in as part of the bill.'

'I thought it was because he was a hoarder.'

'Oh, he was that too. He didn't like to throw things out. But then after he died the things reminded me of him and I couldn't throw them out either – that little pile of junk over by the wall – it's a printing press.'

'It's tiny.'

'Yes – made to be carried in a case – for printing handbills and the like. What use is it to me – it's a dust trap, but throwing it out would be throwing out a part of him – and all his books. I'll never read them, will I? I'm not even convinced he ever read more than half of them. But he liked things more than money. That used to make me so mad. We needed the money to put food on the table, or to pay the bills – and he'd come home with half the money and a parrot cage. What's the use of parrot cage, when you have no food – and no parrot! But the gramophone I didn't mind. He printed posters and advertising for a music shop in Hanover. We'd dance around the apartment to Strauss, or listen to Bach. Wonderful! In your own home! There's a trunk underneath my bed with some of the records in – why don't you have a rummage in there and get them out. We can have a little party. He brought some records back from London too, once; he went there with some of his business cronies in twenty-four to see some big exhibition. They called it a spying mission – said it was all strictly business – to get ideas, but I doubt that very much.

That old trunk was a treasure chest of mementoes – a carving of some deer from the Black Forest, decorative plates, beer mugs from Bavaria. I would have loved to have pulled it all out and gone through it item by item, but that wasn't what I'd been told to do.

I returned with a dozen or so records: American jazz tunes – Gershwin, Al Jolson and others. I played one of these and we danced: my aunt improvising, sitting down. Then I came to an English one with a funny little dog looking inside a gramophone trumpet.

'Auntie, do you know what this means?' I passed it to her.

'Let me see, dear. Where are my spectacles? Yes, I do believe it means "Die Lerche" – The Lark. I have never listened to it – he got it from the music shop not long before he passed away, God rest him. I lost interest in music afterwards. I didn't want to listen to it any more.

'I'm sorry Tante Auguste. We don't need to listen to it.'

'No, let's. I have company now. It's different.'

She passed it back to me. The violinist's name was German: Isolde Menges – that interested me. The Lark Ascending.

When out walking with Jakub we'd look up to the sky on hearing them and try to pick them out in the summer sky – a still speck high up, keeping an eye over the earth below and serenading in a voice distilled from the heavens around it. Its song was one of pure happiness to me.

'What is ascend, Auntie?'

'It is *klettern* I think – like up a mountain.'

'Ah, *Die Lerche Steigtauft* perhaps.'

'*Ja*, that makes more sense.'

I wound the gramophone and got the record out of its cardboard sleeve. As it started playing I felt cords around my chest tighten and my nose tingled and my eyes pricked. I was lying on my back holding Jakub's hand, the warm smell of the heath all round me, staring up at the blue sky and tracking the lark in its aerial vigil. I turned my back on Tante Auguste so that she couldn't see my silly tears. I shut my eyes and absorbed the music. When it finished I wiped my face with the back of my hand.

'I would love to be able to play that, Auntie.'

'No reason why you can't with practice. You have a rare talent.'

Later I got my violin out and tried to play some of it by ear, and next time I went to the music shop I asked him to order the violin score for me.

'You should learn to play German music, Fraulein: Beethoven, Bach, Brahms, Mendelssohn – we have riches of great composers. Why that inferior English fiddle playing?

I DIDN'T KNOW where I was, and it was raining. It looked nothing like London Road, and there were no buses going past, and I didn't have a coat on or my umbrella. I was by a parade of shops that I'd never seen before and I was wearing my carpet slippers for some reason. It didn't make any sense. I was very cold and scared. I felt like a little girl, but I knew I wasn't. I had come here for a reason and it was quite important. What a blasted nuisance it is. A lady took me inside and sat me down in front of all these circular windows going round and round with clothes inside and got me a cup of tea.

Reverend Adamson came and I had a ride in a motor car; not Mr Broadhead's.

'Shall I contact one of your relatives, Mrs Broadhead?'

'Whatever for?'

'I'm just a bit worried about you, that's all.'

'I'm absolutely fine.'

'You were wandering around in your slippers and were distressed.'

'Don't be silly, Vicar. No need for a fuss. Would you like a cup of tea?'

'No, thank you. I can't really stop. Would you like me to put the kettle for you while you go and get dry?'

'Whatever for? I can manage to make a pot of tea, thank you.'

'Of course. Well, I'll pop round and see you tomorrow, and we've got the bazaar on Saturday. Will you be coming?'

'Yes. I always do. I'll be on fancy needlework with Mrs... '

'... Cruickshank?'

'Yes, that's right. Nice young lady. We raised over seventeen pounds eleven shillings last year. Are you sure you won't stop for a cup of tea, Vicar?'

'No, I'd best get back – if you're sure you're all right – I've got a confirmation class at four.'

It was after they took me to hospital with hyp... hyper-thingy that my nephew came over and sorted everything out for me. I'd met up with my friend, Mrs Dobson, who ran the choir, at the cafe in Millhouses Park, and decided I'd walk back, but then on the way through the woods... I thought I'd see if I could find that picnic spot where... oh, I don't know really. It was such a lovely day. A lifetime away. You wonder if these things really happened don't you? So much has changed. Ginger beer and pork pies and piccalilli. And that lovely singing. *People of England! all your valleys call you. High in the rising sun the lark sings clear. Will you dream on, let shameful slumber thrall you? Will you disown your native land so dear? Shall it die unheard – That sweet pleading word? Arise, O England, for the day is here.* All the paths seemed the same, and I think I went round in circles. I never did find the picnic spot. It's probably gone like so many things. I got very sad about it all and a bit panicky when I didn't know which way to go. I was very cold when the lady dog-walker found me.

I couldn't stay in my own home, he said. He said I wasn't looking after myself and that the stairs were too steep, and he worried about me. I'd just had the bedroom decorated as well, and new lino in the bathroom... and a spin dryer. All mod cons. These days they're knocking down perfectly good homes for no other reason than that they don't have indoor bathrooms. Slums they call them. What an insult. I'd never had a bathroom until I married Mr Broadhead. But I've never lived in a slum. They come out of college, still wet behind the ears thinking they know what's best for other folk and break up families and communities as they bring in their bulldozers. We always looked after each other. We knew everyone on the street and kept an eye out for trouble. All mucked in when we needed to. That's what got us through the Great War and the Depression, Hitler's bombs and the shortages.

This place was one of our ideas at the Soroptimists. I can't remember who was behind it. There was Dr Helen Wilson and Lilian Hawson, she was a very good swimmer, and was in the WSPU. There were a few of us militants who went on to become respectable Soroptimist ladies politely applauding the Master Cutler's speeches at annual dinners at the Victoria Hotel, rather than trying to storm and disrupt all the men at the Master Cutler's meetings. Dr Wilson was never a militant, much more at home with polite after-dinner speakers and recitals of WW Gibson poetry. But there you are. We were sisters in search of the best, being polite and always meaning well. Encouraging not attacking.

WE WROTE TO each other regularly – it was nice to have someone to write to, and to get letters back. I sent him postcards of the seaside. He wrote me lovely, thoughtful letters in his beautiful hand. I scrawled like a schoolgirl and wondered what to say sometimes. I don't know what he saw in me. He was much cleverer than me. But he used to tell me off and say it wasn't true, just that he'd not had to pack school in like me.

Then at Christmas he sent me a card with the exciting news that he was coming up again in the New Year and would it be all right for him to pop over to Tynemouth.

It coincided with the opening of the new Carlton Cinema in what was the old Wesley Chapel. It was all converted into a modern design inside, lovely it was: beautiful lighting and chrome fittings, snazzy geometric designs in green, maroon and fawn colours, and a potted palm in the foyer. We went to see Jessie Matthews in *Evergreen*. You remember, the one where she impersonates her famous music hall star mother and reprises all her old roles, and everyone believes the *star* has actually returned. It was, and still probably is, my favourite film – it made me laugh and made me cry. It also made me wonder about the passage of time and disturbed me as the years rolled back to Nineteen Fourteen, and there was that nightmare scene of bombs being made. I was born right in the middle of that terrible war. What was it like? What was my real mother doing? Perhaps she died when the bombs fell, leaving me an orphan. I shivered and grabbed hold of Jack's hand and squeezed it tight.

I left the cinema singing: *Over my shoulder goes one care, over my shoulder goes two cares,* and took off my fur stole, the one that Mrs Forbes gave me, and threw it at Jack.

'Now steady on, miss. We'll have none of that.' He put it back over my shoulders and I grabbed his arm.

'That was wonderful, didn't you think?'

'I did, yes. You have a lovely voice, just like *your* mother I bet: a real Harriet Green. But do you really think someone could pass for their mother?'

'I don't really know.'

'Do you look like your mother?'

I went quiet.

'Jo? Is everything all right? Did I say something?'

'No, it's nothing. Only that... I never knew my real mother.'

'Oh, Jo. I'm sorry. Me and my big mouth. That's why you cried so much when Harriet accompanied the phonograph recording of her mother singing.'

'Yes, wasn't that wonderful. Oh, Jack...' I started sobbing. 'I always loved to sing. My parents – that adopted me – were practically tone deaf. I never understood who I took after. Do you suppose my mother had a lovely voice?'

'If she passed it over to you then, yes, definitely.' He put his arm around me, and I snuggled into his side.

We walked around the block via the seafront. It was a still night and a fret was drifting in off the North Sea, enveloping us, muffling the sounds of a motor car up on Front Street. The world seems to belong to us alone.

'Jo, I've been wanting to ask you something.'

'Yes?'

'I know you're very happy here with the Forbeses and everything. But do you think you could see it in you to come back to Sheffield sometime?'

'What do you mean?'

'To come and live with me, silly. To marry me. I've grown terribly fond of you, and I've been thinking about it a lot. There's no other girl quite like you. You're the bees' knees, the snake's eyebrows, the –'

'Oh do shut up, you silly fool. Come here.' I answered him with a kiss like the one that Harriet gave Tommy when they rehearsed their dance together.

Jack went away to handle all the arrangements for getting married in the spring back home in Sheffield, and on top of that he had his work and the Peace Ballot – or the *National Declaration* as it was officially called. It was all organised through his church; I could imagine the poor boy from his descriptions in his letters trudging from house to house with the ballot papers in the cold, dark, damp February evenings wiping the rain off his spectacles. It was quite some task getting papers back from a hundred and fifty thousand voters in the city. Often as not in the poorer parts of Sharrow he found his time best spent explaining the five questions to people and waiting until they had filled them in – otherwise something else would have cropped up and they never got round to it. In the bigger houses in Nether Edge there was a different problem of the owners refusing to let their servants take part. "The rule of gentlemen, that is what passes for democracy in this country," he told me. "Keep the great unwashed under tight control so that they don't get ideas above themselves – keep them ignorant, only evoke the great deity of democracy when it suits, and play the mob to one's own ends."

I suppose I looked on our forthcoming marriage in a very traditional way. Jack was a clever man and I saw my job as being to support him so that he could carry on doing clever things – and if I could raise clever children, who, if we all survived, might go on to make the world a safer place... That has always felt enough for me – if I had been clever too, full of lots of ideas of my own, or knew what to do with those ideas, then perhaps I would have wanted something different.

When I broke the news to Mr and Mrs Forbes that I would be leaving, they were very pleased for me. All that worry I'd put into finding the right words, and about letting them down, proved pointless. It was the children who were most upset, especially Millie – but she sat on my knee and we talked about what kind of dress I would wear and the flowers I would have, and I promised to write to her and tell her all about it. I wished I could have appeased her by asking her to be a bridesmaid, but it was too far for them to travel.

I had a quandary over who would give me away and where I could stay before the wedding. The only person I could think of to help was Mrs D. I'd stayed in touch and sent her postcards. Did she have any ideas, I asked.

And so it turned out that I was to go back to our street in Darnall for a few days before I started my new life. But first I had some unfinished business in the North East.

I wrote to my aunt and uncle to say I was moving away and could I come and see them on Sunday. A reply came back from

Uncle Eric agreeing, but only for a short visit, since my aunt was not very well.

I got the train into Newcastle then walked down to the river towards the old bridge, the new bridge like a giant towering above me, making me feel a little afraid, though no one else seemed to share my feelings as they trundled their barrows of spring flowers or vegetables, or hurried past to some unknown purpose, or stood gazing at the girls in the street, cigarettes in mouths. A barge went past, belching filthy smoke from its funnel, and the bridge was just swinging closed as I arrived.

I strode purposefully up the hill, and for the mile or so to my aunt's house. I would not be spoken down to by her now. I was an adult and she had no sway over me.

It was the daughter, Alice, who answered the door – no longer lisping and dribbling but growing into a pleasant enough looking young woman; she might even have looked pretty if she could have permitted herself the tiny sin of a smile.

'My father's out with the boys, but mother's expecting you. Do come in.'

'Thank you, Alice. You probably don't remember me: your cousin, Jo.'

'Yes. I know who you are, right enough. Shall I take your coat?'

'Thank you.'

'Mother's not well. If you wait here I'll go and tell her you have arrived.'

She disappeared upstairs. The narrow hallway was dark; what little light there was came through the small fanlight, and the embossed wallpaper below the dado rail was painted a chestnut colour, and it was not much lighter in hue above. The floor was covered in a, now, patternless, linoleum. If my uncle was making any money he certainly wasn't spending it on the house.

'She'll see you now,' said Alice, from the stairs. 'Do come up.'

An equally dingy landing lead to the front bedroom, from which a smell of coal tar emanated – a smell I was familiar with from my father's sickroom. My aunt was sitting up in bed with an old-fashioned cotton bonnet on, and a cream-coloured bed jacket across her shoulders. She had aged much more than the years that had elapsed. She waved her daughter away with a limp gesture.

'I'll be downstairs if you need me, mother. Just bang your stick.'

The room felt stuffy and I would have loved to have been able to throw the window open wide to let some air in – as it was the net curtains only moved slightly from the air that squeezed through the narrow gaps in the sash.

'She's turning into a nice young lady – your Alice.'

Aunt Maud flapped her hand in the direction of a wooden chair next to the bed to indicate I should sit.

'Thank you for seeing me, Aunt Maud. I've come to apologise for any misunderstanding there was between us, and to let you know I am grateful for how everything worked out – I'm going to be married, so I'm moving back to Sheffield.'

She nodded and half closed her eyes as if accepting my apology and taking it as consent that she had been proved right. Well let her. It didn't matter. She kept her eyes on me, studying me, still not speaking. I wondered if she had lost her voice. I spoke again to break the awkward silence.

'There was something I wanted to ask you before I go. Something I need to know. I rummaged in my handbag and pulled out the photograph I'd found in father's biscuit tin. I'd like to know who this is.' I handed it to her.

She gestured towards the bedside table – I passed her the spectacles that rested on the lace square. She stared at the picture for a while. Then she turned her eyes on me again and weakly handed the photograph back – I had to reach forward to take it off her. Still those dull eyes on me.

'I don't know. ' Her voice weak and dry.

'I know I was adopted, Aunt. Just tell me the truth. Please.'

She looked at me again. I didn't think an answer was going to come.

'Aunt Maud, I know you know something. '

'It's Joseph,' she croaked.

'Who was Joseph?'

'He was their son – Joyce and Ernest. He died a few days after this was taken. In his sleep. No reason. Taken by angels in the night.'

'So this is his birth certificate, not mine?'

I passed the document. She looked hard at it. She nodded.

'They wanted a child ever so much. They had tried for a long time and thought their prayers were answered when he arrived. Then they found you.'

'So who am I?'

She shook her head. 'All I know is that she couldn't keep you.'

'Who was she?'

Another shake of the head.

'So my birthday isn't really the twenty six of February?'

She closed her eyes.

'When was I born?'

Those yellowing eyelids flicked open again and she looked at me with something that almost seemed to approach sympathy. 'They got you sometime in June. You were only a tiny baby. They adored you, Josephine. It doesn't mean...'

'I know. I just wish...'

'After your father's... misfortune...'

'What misfortune?'

She closed her eyes. I waited for her to carry on but she was either asleep or pretending to be. That pause, the choice of that word *misfortune*. The words of guilt and blame my parents used in their heated conversations that I overheard whilst lying alone in bed. *Your wrongdoing. You drove me to it.* His months away from us, coinciding with our going down in the world could only have meant one thing.

I took the birth certificate – Joseph's birth certificate off her, tiptoed from the room and downstairs.

Alice heard the stairs creak and came out into the hall.

'She's fallen asleep. I left her. I'll get off. Thank you.' I was gasping for a cup of tea, but there was no such prospect. She lifted my coat off the hook in the hall and passed it to me.

'Goodbye, Alice.'

'Goodbye, Miss Cartwright.'

THAT SUMMER at Nurnberg the national socialists announced that Jews were no longer regarded citizens of Germany. What would the man in the music shop think about Mendelssohn no longer being German? Even raising the German flag was against the law for someone deemed Jewish. I wondered how Herr Doktor Menchel felt about that, wherever he was, or Jakub and his family. Once proud Germans who were now stateless. It made any relationship between Jakub and me illegal, not just frowned upon or taboo. To stop him defiling my German blood and honour.

I thought of him all the time. He was not yet dead. That, at least, is what I interpreted from what my mother told me in her letters – she had received news from the Rosenbaums. But I could not dare to hope he would survive.

What could I do? I nursed my aunt. I learnt to play *die lerche*. I wrote letters to my mother on Uncle's typewriter – to protect her from association with me, from gossiping postmen.

Then one day I received a letter with a King George V stamp on it and a London postmark – so alien and yet the handwriting seemed so familiar.

My dearest Lottchen,

Yes, it is I. I am writing to you from a place called Finsbury Park in London. I am safe, as are my family – all here with me at the house of a friend of a friend of my father's. I was released from Esterwegen – but only on condition that I left the country. My parents have been very traumatised by the whole thing. Perhaps even more than I have. They were not able to settle in the Netherlands so are planning to leave for America once they have arranged passage, visas and the necessary funds. I should go with them – I cannot return to Germany or I will be arrested again. Our arrangement can never come to be. Also how can my parents give their full blessing to something that has brought this about?

I do so miss our walks through the forest and watching the evening stars come out over the heath. I wish I could share more than memories with you, but they will always be with me. Do write back and let me know you are well. I trust that your aunt is being good to you and I know she could have no one better to keep her company.

Your, ever affectionate,

Jakub.

It was a miserable time for me. He seemed clear that he was breaking off with me. He didn't have approval from his parents. He would not go against their wishes, and he was not old enough to marry without their consent. In America I would never see him again. He would meet new friends and would become more and more American as the weeks and months passed. Soon Germany and his Lottchen would become painful memories associated with imprisonment and beatings, just for being who he was. I tried to write several times but what could I say? And I was so down that I could never have found the words even if they existed.

Then my aunt took a turn for the worse – she didn't want to get out of bed and the pain made her cry. Her eyes went all puffy and she complained of itchy skin despite there being nothing to see. The doctor came and gave her some morphine, which took the pain away, but also much of the person that was my aunt – it was one or the other.

'It's her kidneys my dear. There is not much we can do for her except to try to make her comfortable.'

I massaged her limbs with olive oil, played my violin and read to her from an old volume of *Struwwelpeter*, and even managed to make her laugh.

'That's what we need now, Auntie. Agrippa to come along and take Hitler, Göring and Goebbels and dip them and their toys in black ink.'

I wrote to tell my mother that Aunt Auguste was dying and told her about Jakub's letter. I still hadn't replied.

She arranged to come over the following weekend. She closed the shop early on Saturday afternoon – not a small matter in the run-up to Christmas – and caught the train over.

She helped me to get Aunt Auguste comfortable for the night; then we lit candles to make it cosy and sat and ate sausage and kale and opened one of Aunt's bottles of Kirsch.

'How has business been since your Jew-loving, outcast daughter disowned you?'

'It has been better. Back to normal. Everything has settled down.' She smiled. 'You rather overdid it, though: with your acting. People were telling me to go to the Kripo or the Gestapo and report you. I told them I didn't know where you'd gone and didn't very much care.'

'Poor Mama – I'm sorry. But at least it worked. There was nothing else we could have done.'

'No. I suppose not. But there is something else you should know. I couldn't tell you in a letter. The police came to see me asking if it was true what you had said – asking when I had last seen you, wanting to know where you could have gone. Did I know the Rosenbaums? Asking if I knew them to be communists. Or if you were.'

I felt sick. 'I didn't mean to cause you any trouble. Only to help you.'

'I know. I convinced them I knew nothing and they went away. It's all right.'

'They aren't communists. It's ridiculous. The police, they are lunatics.'

She sighed. 'No. But someone has been talking. You should be careful what you say, that's all. Anyway, what did Jakub say in his letter?'

'That he's going to America.'

'What will you do?'

'I don't know. Go to Hamburg and look for work... or Berlin. I'd surely find a job there in a restaurant.'

'Can I see the letter?' She read; her face serious, her eyes sad. 'And you haven't written back?'

'I tried, but what could I say? He won't come back. It is over; he says as much – he says he wishes he had more than memories but that is what he'll have to content himself with.'

Kirsch always made me teary – as if I wasn't already built close enough to water as it was – this bottle was no exception.

'I don't know that you are right. Isn't... isn't there another way to read this – that he wants you to be free to decide, without putting pressure on you? He doesn't say he *will* go with this family – he says: "I *should*." Of course he can't come back, not with the grip the Nazis have. He doesn't want to ask you to leave, though; could that not be it? He cannot ask you to give up everything for him; that must be your choice. You know him better than anyone.'

I took the letter back off her. I had read the letter with my eyes only, not with my heart.

'What can I do, Mama? I can't leave Germany and you.'

'You already shouted in the street that you were never coming back.'

'But there is such a difference between living a few hours away and going where... to America? What should I do?'

'I can't decide that for you. You must be the blacksmith of your own fortune. But you must write to him. I do not think you should live with regrets that you didn't at least try to work something out. In fact you should do it straightaway.'

'But auntie... she... '

'Don't look for excuses *not* to do something, look for reasons to *do* something. We'll find a way. She should probably be in hospital anyway.'

'I can't abandon her now.'

'One thing at a time. Write to him and tell him how you feel.'

I am normally not one for foolish sentimentality but I did kiss that envelope before dropping it into the postbox. It was a long letter, starting off with everything that had happened since that awful day. I told him I still loved him and wanted to be with him. Whatever that was – I told him I didn't just want to be a memory. I wanted to beg him not to go to America because that would surely put him beyond reach forever, but I couldn't make him choose between me and his family, so I hedged around it, said that London wasn't really that far, I couldn't abandon my aunt but if he could delay then perhaps we might yet be able to see each other again, if only to say goodbye properly.

I then had an awful wait for a reply, with not much to distract me except my violin: playing that required so much concentration that my brain had no capacity for anything else. I could lose myself in the mysterious way that something guided my arm and bow, in the way my fingers changed position. The violin took me out of myself; its scent was that of the farm on the moors, of my grandfather's tobacco, the wood resonating with the fields and the rolling clouds over the hills.

The days were short and the evenings cold. I fetched all the blankets from the closet, and made stew with swede, carrot, dumplings and smoked sausage.

My hand trembled when I picked up the letter that eventually came.

My darling Lottchen

You have made me so happy. I thought perhaps you were angry with me, or couldn't love me any more. I have made life most difficult for you. I am sorry. I couldn't take anything for granted, so much seems to have happened – I have seen so much with my own eyes that I could not imagine from fellow human beings. Life has become very complicated. My judgment tainted. They have divided friends and families. There is an evil abroad. It is hard not to hate back. But hatred is poisonous. I have no love left for Germany. If there is a God, then surely he will prevail. I still hope that people will sit up and realise the truth. They would if they opened their eyes to what is being done in their name. There are still many good people who will do their best.

But enough! I will wait here in London until I hear from you again. You have given me hope that it is "au revoir" and not "adieu."

Your devoted, Jakub.

Christmas and New Year were spent quietly: just me and the shadow that was Aunt Auguste. I was glad at least to have made friends with her – I felt I had got to know the real person before she lost her fizz. Now I only saw the glimpses of my aunt that the medication and pain allowed me to see.

'We've run out of margarine and I was going to make pastry – thought I might tempt you with some apple pie. I'm nipping down to the shop, Auntie.'

'You've been so good to me.' She sounded a bit better I thought.

'I'll be back in five minutes.'

She was dead when I returned.

My mother came over on the morning of the funeral and we buried Aunt Auguste on the sort of cold winter's day where gravediggers have to break the top few inches of ground with picks.

There were quite a few people gathered – some of whom my mother knew: cousins and second cousins, great uncles and nephews, and whatever else – names that had arisen once or twice in conversation but which meant little to me in reality. There were also one or two survivors of my aunt's generation – perhaps the "cronies" that my aunt had referred to.

My mother stayed the night and helped me to make plans. I would stay behind to sort out my Aunt's affairs. She would then send me some money to head to London and Jakub to see what the future might hold.

I felt desperately lonely in the flat on my own. I cleaned it top to bottom and started to sort things into piles: clothing, tableware, bedding. I looked through her papers for anything important-looking, and things which could be thrown away.

It was a few days later that I was returning from the furniture shop where I had arranged for the owner to come round to take what he could sell. As I entered the apartment block the old concierge, Herr Goosmann beckoned to me.

'*Komm. Schnell.*'

He was a dear old man – a former teacher and a friend of my auntie. I used to take him a spare piece of cake after I had been baking and he'd always ask after my aunt and say he was praying for her. He cried at the graveside.

Anyway he looked alarmed and hurried me inside his flat and told me to hide in the back room and be quiet.

'Why, whatever is the matter?'

'No. Not now. Please, Fraulein.'

There was fear in his eyes. I did as he asked and climbed into the fusty old wardrobe where I stayed for I don't know how long. How ridiculous: playing hide-and-seek in an old man's wardrobe amongst the mothballs and old clothes. I closed my eyes and may have even snoozed because some voices roused me coming from the next room. Eventually I heard the door open, footsteps and the wardrobe creak open.

'Fraulein, it is now safe.'

'Why what is it? Why… ?'

'Sit down. It was the Gestapo looking for you. Asking questions. I am sorry I had to let them into Auguste's flat. It is a relief she was not there to see it. They asked where you were – I said I didn't know. They said if you returned while they were there I was not to say anything – let you run into the open knife. I could do no such thing.'

'Thank you, Herr Goosmann.'

'Then, a moment ago, they told me to telephone them when you returned.'

I must have gone as pale as chalk.

'Don't be alarmed, Fraulein. They have gone, but they have taken away some things.'

'They have no right.'

'There are no rights any more, Fraulein. Only power. They were asking who had visited the flat – had any men been. Had I seen you with anyone? I said no, of course – that it was all ridiculous. But they seemed sure of themselves.'

'But there is nothing…'

'They have taken away your uncle's old printing press.'

'That old thing? They are mad.'

'And the typewriter. They said it was proof of political subversion.'

'But my aunt… She's not got – she didn't have a bad bone in her body…'

'I know. I know. It is absurd. And you, my dear: look at you – you are not a communist. That I know.'

It was if he was seeking assurance.

'Of course not, Herr Goosman. You know that. But what shall I do?'

'It would be best to leave – if they catch you, they will arrest you. People will confess to detesting their own mother in those cells, or swear an oath that white is black, that vinegar is sweet and sugar sour.'

'What else did they take?'

'I couldn't really tell – a book or two, what looked like letters.'

'Letters?'

'Yes, I noticed something with a blue stamp on it – not a German one, I don't think.'

I was suddenly struck with the thought of how Jakub's words could be interpreted. I had his first letter in my satchel along with all my documents, but the latest one was still in the flat – or now in the possession of the Gestapo. I had been half way through replying and had left it out on the desk. But why had they been round in the first place? Why didn't I burn his letter?

'If I were you, Fraulein, I would go up there and get your things as quick as you can. You never know who they've got on the look out for them.'

'But, I'm supposed to be selling my aunt's things, and there are relatives who... There are some personal things.'

'Why don't you let me deal with all that – you look after yourself. Let me check there's no one in the stairwell for you. Good luck, Fraulein.'

'Thank you, Herr Goosmann.'

I let myself into the flat, afraid that someone might still be there. I went to the desk – everything had been turned upside down – the letter was indeed gone.

Aunt Auguste would forgive me. I took one of her suitcases and quickly filled it with all my clothes. I took what cash there was left and all of her jewellery – some of it very fine. In her wardrobe was a nice coat with a fur collar and wide belt, and a hat that was much nicer than mine: green felt with a turned up brim on one side. She would have wanted me to.

I grabbed the suitcase and my violin case and headed out of the door – I'd been in no more than ten minutes. I looked back into the room one last time, then went back for the silver candlesticks on the mantelpiece and stuffed them inside my coat. I checked the stairwell and left the building, all the time keeping an eye out for plain clothes policeman and spies – my imagination was racing.

There was an antiques dealer on my way to the station and I coolly strode in and presented the candlesticks to him.

'My mother has no need for these any more and she has asked me to sell them – they are unnecessary clutter now that we have electricity she says.'

He offered me twenty-five Reichsmarks for them. I walked out of the shop with thirty-two.

It was a relief when the train pulled away from the station heading west. All through the streets and in the railway station I was trying to damp down the fires of panic in my chest – there were eyes of informers and Gestapo everywhere; and yet I had to stay calm and not look guilty or like a communist and thief or on the run – however it was such people might look.

I relaxed for a while once underway, and there was no one in my carriage who looked like they had the slightest interest in me. I told myself to stop being silly. I couldn't possibly be a priority – they wouldn't be posting my name on every police station wall – and yet, how did they come to be at my aunt's flat? They'd been to see my mother, but that was nothing really, was it? No more than a little outburst in the street. I had taken my role rather too seriously in driving home my point, but this? And no one from home knew I was in Bremen anyway, except my mother, did they? The puzzle went over in my mind. What had happened? Perhaps......? There was that man at the funeral who came weaselling round – Aunt Auguste's nephew: the bald one with glasses – asking whether he could help with my Aunt's affairs, and whether I had located her will.

'I feel I have a duty to my dear old aunt, being her closest remaining heir,' he said. So dear she was to him that he had not been to see her in the six months I had been there, had not written a single letter. It was as clear as the sun what he was after. He thought he was in for a decent payout.

'I do have some experience in these matters,' he said.

I couldn't exactly refuse his help. He was due to come over this week. Hadn't he said he lived in Fallingbostel, a nearby town to ours? He could easily have picked up the local gossip. I probably made him feel guilty and jealous. And if I was out of the way he could do what he liked with Auntie's things – perhaps he thought her investments were still worth something. She said not. He was welcome to whatever he could get his sweaty palms on; though I would have liked to have been able to keep her gramophone and records – it would have reminded me of my aunt when she was happy.

I got as far as Osnabrück that evening. I had thought I could spend the night on the station waiting for my next train but I got scared and went to a small hotel near the station and checked in under the name of Emilia Tischbein. It was the first thing that came into my mind, but it also amused me, and borrowing the name off one of my heroes gave me courage.

The next day was my last in Germany. As the border approached I got more and more nervous, again having to damp down little fires of panic. They would look at my passport and compare my name to their lists, then arrest me and send me to a police station and concentration camp.

The train stopped at the border and from my window seat I could see men in uniform boarding further along. They slowly made their way towards my compartment.

Some people were made to get off the train and their suitcases were opened up and their things gone through – they were Jews, I presumed. How humiliating – undergarments, books, photographs: all being tipped out onto the platform and mauled by unkind hands.

The officers arrived at my compartment and looked at the passports of the ladies opposite. I was to play the role of a nonchalant Aryan girl heading to Amsterdam to visit a relative – that was the destination and story that I had rehearsed in my mind.

I handed my passport over without making eye contact, my heart in my mouth. He glanced at it, looked at me, and looked back at the passport. Then he handed it back. 'Heil Hitler,' he said and left.

I waited for them to come back after making further checks, but they did not and soon the train rolled forward again. We crossed into the Netherlands. I was free. How wonderful that felt. I could no longer be arrested for saying the wrong thing or loving the wrong person. Until you have had that denied you, you can't imagine how it feels.

In Amsterdam I sold some jewellery and bought a ticket for London, and a postcard for mother, which I hurriedly wrote out and placed in an envelope, on which I printed the address.

I got talking to a middle-aged Dutch lady on the ship who spoke very good German. She was interested in my violin case and asked me if I was going to a music school. She too was travelling alone and bought me a coffee. I told her that I was going to see my fiancé – perhaps to stay.

'Then I wish you luck, and hope they let you.'

'What do you mean *let me*?'

'Sometimes they do, sometimes they don't. Everything is not rosy there either, you know. Lots of unemployment. They don't want to add to that, and don't want people taking jobs away from others – usually people can only stay if they have a guaranteed income or a work permit. Have you made plans?'

'I haven't thought that far ahead. I just had to escape Germany.'

'They might just let you stay for a month or so.'

My heart sank. I couldn't go back. My feeling of freedom ran through my hands like sand. Even here the tentacles of Germany reached out for me to pull me back.

'Aunty? They said I'd find you out here.'

'Who is it?'

'It's me, Aunty: Peggy.'

'Peggy?'

'Yes, you know: Mary's daughter.'

'Peggy... yes. Mary's daughter. How is your mother?'

'She's not with us any more Aunty. You remember: Mary Chaplin.'

'Of course I do. Don't be silly. My very dear friend.'

'I brought you some flowers for your room: sweet peas. They put them in a vase for you. May I sit with you for a while? The garden's lovely isn't it? This is a lovely quiet corner. I'll not spoil it – I'll sit here quietly and you can chat if you like.'

Sweet peas. I do like sweet peas. Mr Broadhead was very good with his sweet peas. Very proud of them. She always had a nice face. A warm face. Kind brown eyes and freckles.

'I like your dress, Mary. Very summery. Very modern'

'Thank you. It's Peggy, Aunty.'

Mary went to live in York when the depression hit and Robert lost his job. It worked out well for them. How hard that must have been: flitting with two small children. But people will always want a Robert. He worked his way up to managerial level in the furniture warehouse. They had a lovely house. We spent many a happy time walking around the walls and round the cathedral. Such lovely shops as well – and the tea room. I suppose it must have become repetitive for Mary showing people who visited around every time, but it didn't bother her. For me it was a bit of a holiday, visiting them. We always liked each other's company – caught up with the news and swapped stories about the old days. We'd collect her children from the school, get them their tea. What were they called again? The eldest was a boy, grew up to be just like Robert. Bob. Bobby. Always made me chuckle to myself. A nice young lad. Hard-working. Went off to Leeds University to do engineering. Made Mary and Robert very proud. Spent some time in America. Richard, that was it. And their daughter: very polite and played the clarinet. The image of her mother.

'We had some good times as well as some hard times.'

'Yes, we did.'

'You usually knew what was best. That time we went away to Scarborough. I would never have gone on my own.'

'I don't remember that – you coming with us, Aunty. I must have been too young. I do remember our holidays in Scarborough, though. We spent some happy times there on the beach and in Peasholm Park: on the boats, and Richard sailing his little yacht.'

'There was a lovely concert at the Floral Hall. Is Robert still enjoying his work?'

'Father retired sometime ago, Aunty. He sends his regards – he would have liked to visit you but the poor old dear can't get out very easily these days.'

'Ah, Mrs Pritchard. You found Mrs Broadhead then? Would you like some tea bringing out, Mrs Broadhead? Or perhaps some lemonade since it's so warm? Is everything all right Mrs B?'

'She's fine, aren't you Aunty? Here, I'll walk back with you a little way.'

'She has seemed quite low recently. Not wanting to be with others – spending a lot of time on her own.'

'Don't worry. It's just this time of year. It brings back some painful memories. Especially today. My mother always used to visit her on the fifteenth of June, and I've tried to keep doing it since my mother passed away.'

'She is still very sharp in some ways.'

'Yes, if she is talking about her early life it's still as clear as a bell – it's just other things that get a bit muddled.'

'Yes. Poor Mrs B. It must be hard. She remembers me better from when I was young, but it somehow doesn't seem to join up.'

'You knew her before?'

'Oh, yes…'

It felt so strange to be pulling into Sheffield after all those years – and to be met by Jack, someone associated with the sound of the sea and seagulls and bracing breezes off the North Sea. I'd seen him through the open carriage window before he'd seen me. I'd have rushed at him had it not been for the carefully wrapped, heavy box that I'd been nursing like a newborn all the way. I handed it to him.

'Careful with it, it's a present from Mr and Mrs Forbes: two beautiful, floral Maling vases to remind me of the North East. They were sad they couldn't come.'

We collected my luggage then went for afternoon tea before catching the train to Darnall. Everything seemed so much smaller – the walls, the houses, the hedges. As I walked up our passage, ghosts from the past whirled around me: voices, blurred images and sounds of street games. It was with some trepidation that I knocked on Mrs D's door; fear that everything wouldn't be as I hoped. I needn't have worried. Mrs D opened the door – I swear, looking exactly like she used to – even down to the same housecoat.

'Eee, come here, lass!' She enveloped me in her arms and near squeezed the life out of me. 'Oh, how you've changed – you look just like a film star. Where did that little lass go – all arms and legs you were. And who's this handsome young fella?'

'This is Jack, Mrs D – my fiancé.'

'Well don't stand on ceremony, lad. Come in. Come in. You're a lucky young man.'

'I know that, Mrs Dunstan.'

'Call me Edie. I'll put the kettle on.'

Jack made his excuses shortly after and left us to have a good old natter. She plonked a big pot of tea on the table under a knitted tea cosy, and brought out two plates and a tin from the pantry with *a little something* in it. She updated me on all the comings and goings on the street and I gave her a breakdown of how I met Jack, what I'd been up to, and of my discoveries of my history.

'That explains a lot, I suppose. But I'd never have guessed.'

'Would you not? I didn't look much like either of them, did I?'

'Well, I suppose not, now I think on. But you wouldn't imagine... and it's not so unusual for a child to be a bit of a cuckoo in the nest, is it? Well not round here, leastways.'

'What are you saying, Mrs D?' I pretended to be indignant.

'No, oh, you know what I mean. You were always so bonny...'

I giggled and she gave me a little slap on the wrist. We both laughed.

'Don't tease an old lady.'

'You're not an old lady.'

'I'm afraid I am, dear. Now, would you like another piece of shortbread?'

'Mrs D –?'

'Yes, love.'

'I've no one to give me away and I don't want to go down the aisle on my own. Will you come with me?'

She looked at me. 'Are you sure there's no one?'

I shook my head. 'No one who's related to me. No one I know. No one I want more than you.'

She started crying and got out of her handkerchief.

'Then I'd love to. That'll show 'em, won't it? What modern women we are? I could even see if I've still got my purple, green and white sash somewhere. What do you reckon?'

'Oh, yes Mrs D. You must. So were you a suffragette?'

'Not exactly – I was never one of them to make too much of a fuss. I never chained myself to anything nor broke no windows, but I've always stood up for what's right. And I went on a march in town once, mind.'

If I worried about having no family at the wedding Mrs D made up for it and cried as much as any mother would have done. As well as Mrs D and her Ellen and Evie, there were a few of my old friends from the street who made it over to the Wesleyan Chapel on Ecclesall Road, and Jack's family more than made up for the lack of mine. He'd been christened in that church, been to Boys' Brigade there, and made to suffer many a boring sermon on those hard pews.

Mrs D didn't wear her sash in the end, but settled instead for a discrete ribbon pinned to her lapel.

Jack always said he grinned so much that day that it made his jaw ache.

We moved into a small terraced house in Sharrow – we made it cosy, it was handy for the shops, for walks in the peaceful, lovely, old cemetery and for the Lansdowne Picture Palace at the bottom of the hill – it didn't look much like a palace back then, though: it wasn't until a few years later that it had its fancy pagoda entrance built.

We didn't go on honeymoon – we had to save our holidays for Jack's works' week – but we did have a lovely time. Jack booked a table for dinner at the Grand Hotel and there was a dance band afterwards.

I loved dancing – I'd walk out on Jack's arm with my bright red lipstick and my nails to match, wearing my floral dress. I thought I was quite something and got some very disapproving looks from old Mrs Grundy types. But that just made it more fun. I ran up that dress with some rayon georgette I bought in the sale at T & J's. Mrs D had given me her old sewing machine as a wedding present – I got quite good with it. I wore that dress to quite a few dances – pale blue with a dark pink rose-pattern print. I matched my lipstick to that colour. The sleeves were short and it showed a bit of neckline. I was very proud of it.

Jack was a good dancer and I had learnt a few steps at those Saturday afternoon tea dances at the Plaza that Mr Forbes sometimes took me to if Mrs Forbes was feeling unwell. They had a big ballroom there that they called the Ballroom Fantastique – which sounds quite romantic in French.

It was a wonderful summer – we did such a lot of dancing. There were regular dance bands at the City Hall ballroom and I especially liked the annual works' dance and the feeling of being shown off to all Jack's work mates, having them line-up to take a turn to dance with me. Jack was lucky if he got a look-in.

It was also the summer of the Jubilee. Jack and his friend Norman went for a stroll with their kids, while me and Jean got the picnic together. Then we went over to Norfolk Park to see the twenty-one-gun salute and went pink in the sun listening to the brass band. You could barely move in the park there were so many there. We stayed all afternoon. Someone brought out their banjo and we danced and the children played games. In the evening there were fireworks, the display ending with a picture of the King and Queen in fireworks – really clever. I cuddled into Jack – we could get nowhere near the bonfire to warm up. We looked over the city – searchlights swept the sky from the roof of the City Hall and we could see bonfires on Sky Edge, on Wincobank Hill and a glow in the sky from another bonfire over Ringinglow way.

It was funny when the bonfire was lit – people tried to clamber up the hill and slipped on the grassy bank, tumbling down clutching picnic baskets and clattering into others, sending them flying too. To be honest I think one or two of us had had a barley wine too many.

We did a lot of crazy dancing in those days: copying things we'd seen at the pictures. When it wasn't in the park or on parquet floors it was on the kitchen tiles to the sounds of Roy Fox and his band coming out of the wireless.

My lightness of foot was soon put paid to, however, when little Harriet came along: named Harriet after Harriet Green, of course. Hattie was soon followed by John. So we ended up with a Jack and a Jacky to distinguish them.

It was getting towards evening and going dark when England came in to view – through the rain and clouds. The country of my father; where he still might be in that big village of Sheffield. The country where my Jakub was. Jakub, who didn't even know I was coming.

The Port of Harwich was not at all pretty and presented an especially dreary aspect with low clouds, blending the grey of the skies with those of the sea, so that on the skyline it was hard to see where one ended and the other began. When we docked I lined up with the other passengers to have our papers checked.

It came to my turn and I presented my passport and was met by raised eyebrows.

'Please, sir. I have come to England to meet my fiancé. I hope we will marry here.'

'I see. And is your friend here to meet you? Is he English?'

'No, sir. He is German too. Or rather…not.'

'Well which is it?'

'He is Jewish. He has no State now.'

'Have you filled out an application?'

'Pardon?'

'Have you sought advice from the embassy?'

'No, sir. I… Please, I can't go back. They will arrest me.'

'If you could just stand to one side, miss. We'll deal with you later. Let's get the other passengers through first.'

I stood by and watched the other passengers nodded through one by one – some walked straight through, others were stopped and questioned only briefly.

I tried to work out who the immigration officers were. The one who had spoken to me was serious, with lively eyes, and a well-groomed moustache that twitched when he was thinking. A clever man I thought. He went about his job efficiently, with courtesy, but no warmth. I couldn't quite make him out. His younger colleague was easier to read – not so sharp – someone whose heart wasn't really in it – who did the job then went home – probably to a young wife.

The queue soon dwindled away and I was left.

'Right that's it then,' the younger one said. 'Dinnertime.'

'Oh, damn. There's still her,' the one with the moustache said. He looked at me. 'What are we going to do about you?'

'Come on, let her through, Tony. We'll be missing our soup.'

Yes, Tony, I was thinking, let me through.

'You know we can't. That's not how it's done. We will have dinner first. No point making decisions on an empty stomach. Follow us please, miss.'

'Can you not let me stay? My father's English.'

'Can you prove that?'

'No. I... He... he was a soldier.'

'Come on Tony. I'm starving.'

They sat me on a chair at the edge of their dining room while they joined the table with a dozen other men. I sat and watched as they were waited on. Soup was served from a tureen and empty bottles of wine were replaced by full ones. I was totally ignored until the coffee pot was brought out and chairs were kicked back.

'So, who's your girlfriend then Tony?'

He shook his head. 'Shut your trap, you buffoon. This is not a joking matter.'

The younger immigration officer spoke: 'Just some Hun wanting to come to England – claiming to be half-English. You know how it is.'

'Have a bit of respect will you? I need to speak to her in a bit.'

One of the other men at the table spoke: 'Anyone fancy an after-dinner speech? Why not now? Let's have her story, eh?'

They rapped on the table, clearly enlivened by their wine drinking. I was in a den of hyenas.

'Miss. Please come over and tell us why you should stay,' said Tony.

My knees nearly buckled under me as I stood. Besides anything else I was famished. I only had a couple of bread rolls and a coffee since leaving Amsterdam. All their eyes were on me, some smiling as if in anticipation of a dancing girl. It was an unpleasant atmosphere and I all but crept towards them.

'So, you're going to get married?'

'Yes, sir. I hope so.'

'Who is he?'

'I've known him since I was small. His name is Jakub. He was sent to a concentration camp.'

'He is a criminal?'

'No – except he is Jewish, which in the eyes of the Nazis is the same. I am not. The Nazis – they say that it is criminal for him and me... They come for me too – to arrest me. I escape.'

'What had you done?'

'Nothing. Only fell in love, sir.'

'And you say your father is English.'

'Yes, sir. He was a prisoner in the war. He and my mother... He's from Sheffield.'

'Can he vouch for you?'

'Sorry, what is vouch?'

You know, be a guarantor? Pay your keep. Be responsible for you.'

'No, sir. I don't know where he lives. The war parted them – they took him away. They treat him very badly, the Germans. There was a shaking of heads. I was winning them over, I felt.'

'You see – damned difficult case, isn't it?'

'Could be all just cock and bull though, Tony. She doesn't sound very English.'

'I'll have my cigar first and weigh it up. Thank you. You can sit back down.'

His eyes were still on me as I sat. He was stroking his moustache. 'Is that a violin? Since you're here why don't you play us a tune? Are you any good?'

'Not good, but I play a little.'

'Will you play something for us then?'

There was more rapping on the table. I took my violin out and quickly tuned it. I sensed this man Tony held my fate in his hands – he had tremendous power over me. I tightened my bow and gave it a rub with resin. I stood. The scent of pine trees as a tiny cloud of dust rose when I checked the tuning with the bow across the strings. Blood was pounding against my temples. I closed my eyes and took a deep breath. The scent from the violin's wood was the farmhouse: its wood fire, Opa's pipe smoke, mother's baking and the warm smell of the cows in the byre.

I struck the first notes of The Lark, and stepped out on to the moor. The sky was clear with wispy white clouds, and up there somewhere a little speck of life, of energy, hovering, drawing pure sound from the sky and from the landscape as it kept watch. It soared and wheeled, and then was still again. It spoke to me and my violin picked up its theme. Somewhere Jakub was with me, lying on his back staring at the sky, his hair dishevelled with bits of heather twig.

I stumbled. I'd reached as far into the piece as I could by memory. I stopped, angry with myself for not playing something less of challenge. I'd failed. I'd played for no more than a minute or two. My chin sank to my chest.

'I'm sorry. I've not learnt it very well yet.' But the room was quiet – not a sound.

I looked up. All eyes were on me and the man called Tony was wiping away – was it a tear from under his eye?

'Good God. You do have English blood in you,' he said. He led the men round the table in a short burst of clapping.

He got up and it was as if he shook himself back to the here-and-now.

'Come on. Get your things. Let's get you on your way, miss.'

He took me back through to the disembarkation area.

'Right. I'll sign that for you – as a domestic permit. That means you can do work in service. How does that sound? Normally we would say no work, either paid or unpaid – but this is an exception. Once you arrive you should register as an alien with the local police. Understood?'

'Yes, sir. Thank you.'

'I wish you all the best. And keep up with that violin of yours.'

'Thank you.'

I hurried off the ship before he could change his mind.

The customs hall was empty. All the other passengers being long gone – only a clock-watching official wanting his own dinner.

A porter came to help me with my suitcase – a very polite, respectable-looking family man, I thought.

'You'll be wanting the train to Liverpool Street. You've still got ten minutes, there's no rush. I hope you enjoy your stay.'

I was met with more kindness on the train. I had the compartment to myself to start with; then, at the second or third station, a middle-aged lady got in, dressed head to toe in tweed. Well perhaps that's somewhat of an exaggeration, but it was certainly her textile of choice. For me, she immediately became Miss Marple in my mind, like in the stories my mother used to read. She smiled at me and said: 'How do you do?' Very English.

I replied: 'Very well, thank you,' as I had learnt.

We didn't exactly have a conversation, rather she talked to me a lot, taking each little piece of information I managed to impart as another cue for an exposition of how things were, based on her trip to Baden-Baden before the war. I was given her theories on the war and how she didn't hold it against ordinary Germans. She asked what I thought of Hitler, and, once she had ascertained I was no fan, I got the full discourse on what a horrible little man he was. She was less interested in any insight I might have from my rather better informed knowledge. Still, she was amusing and it was my first real chance to test my English.

She then got out a small parcel wrapped in a tea towel and revealed a neat pile of sandwiches.

'I say, would you like one? It's only potted dog, but you are most welcome.'

'Potted dog?' I said.

'No dear. Don't look so terrified – it's just a little joke we have. It's beef...   At least that's what the butcher claims.' She laughed. 'That was a joke too.'

They were strange sandwiches – soft white bread with no discernible crust, sweet and buttery with a thin meaty layer in the middle. But I was very hungry and very grateful to her. Next she got out a flask and poured a strange brown liquid into the cup that had formed the lid and washed her sandwiches down with it.

'Would you like a cup, dear?' You'll have to use my cup. I don't have another, but I don't mind if you don't. I am not one to stand on ceremony. Here, I'll wipe it for you, first.'

The strange brown liquid was not like the tea I was used to. It wasn't particularly fragrant and didn't have layers of taste: of creaminess and sweetness. It had a strange, bitter, sugary soupiness. But it was warm and felt nourishing, for which I was extremely grateful.

Now, of course, such sandwiches and often rather ropey tea seem part of British life.

As the suburbs of London approached she asked me where I was going and gave me instructions on how to get there.

She shook my hand vigorously when we parted at the station, like she had known me forever. My first encounters with English people left a strong impression on me. Tony, the serious immigration officer with a strong commitment to duty combined with a propensity to drink and melancholy, but above all guided by an innate sense of fair play, and my tweedy Miss Marple: kind-hearted and open, taking people on face value, came to typify two dominant sorts of English person in my mind.

It was getting quite late when I arrived at Finsbury Park. I emerged from the station and looked for some clue as to which way to head, someone to help me find the address – ideally another

Miss Marple, but those people I did see were hurrying home and had their hats pulled down and collars turned up against the rain, or were ploughing a path through the downpour with their umbrellas.

'Horrible night, isn't it, miss?' Before me stood a rather tall, rather broad policeman, his helmet giving him even greater height. A policeman back home was someone to avoid, or be fearful of. But I was incredibly struck by how different this British bobby seemed. 'You seem a bit lost?'

'Yes. Yes, I am. I'm looking for Wilberforce Road and I don't know how to find it.'

'That's easy. I was about to head that way. It's not far. If you want to follow me, miss.'

He didn't walk fast, but he took long, measured strides and was forced to trot to keep up with him. We turned into a high street where trolleybuses, trams and motor taxis competed for space in a completely chaotic and badly thought out way. A beery, smoky smell and the sound of raised voices spilled out of a pub as the door swung open and two men emerged arm in arm, holding each other up, then stopped in their tracks as my policeman friend approached. For a small-town girl raised on a farm it was overwhelming – an assault on my senses. We passed huge glass shop fronts and a theatre that was like a palace to me: bright lights and ornate columns.

The rain bounced off the pavement and ran in rivulets down the sides of the road. My feet were soaked through and my hat no longer provided any resistance to the wet running down my neck. We turned a corner into a more residential street and I managed to catch up with the bobby.

'So? New round here, are you then, miss?'

'Yes. My first time in England.'

'Then take piece of advice from me: invest in a good umbrella. You'll never regret it. No matter how good your oilskins, or the quality of your wool, nothing keeps this English rain out. The worst part of the job.'

'Right here we are. Go up this street and take the first right. Good night, miss. Welcome to sunny London.'

'Goodnight. Thank you.'

The houses were big and solid-looking, some attempting to be even grander than they were with portico entrances. The front gardens were only small, so I could make out the numbers on the doors. When I reached the right one I found it in darkness. Not a single light lit. I feared the intrusion, but what else could I do? I opened the gate, approached the door and reached for the button that invited me to "Press." I waited. Perhaps there was no one in. What would I do then? I was cold, wet and hungry and had no idea where I could go.

I was debating whether to press it again when I heard a noise from within and a light came on.

'What in God's name... At this time of night,' came a voice, as a bolt was pulled back.

The door opened a crack. 'What sort of time do you call this? Waking people up.' A dark-haired man in a dressing gown and silk night cap peered round the door at me.

'I'm sorry. I do beg your pardon. I didn't know... ...'

'I'm sorry to disturb you. My name is Liselottte Heitmann. Is Jakub here? Jakub Rosenbaum? I've come from Germany.'

'Come in. Come in. Out of the cold, child. Look at the state of you. Dear me. The kitchen is warmest. Come through. I'm afraid Jakub has left – two days ago. Take a seat by the stove – it still has some warmth. Let me fetch the housemaid to help you. Wait here a moment.'

Then he left before I could get any more information.

So he had gone to America after all, and left me. And now I had nothing. Stuck in a strange place. Friendless. Unable to go home. I felt too exhausted to cry. Completely undone.

The man returned. 'She's on her way down. I'm sorry I didn't introduce myself. My name is Sanger.' He offered his hand. 'Good grief, you are freezing. The Rosenbaums left for New York last week. Didn't you get the letter?'

'But... ...'

'Young Mr Rosenbaum wrote to you to let you know he'd got work in Nottinghamshire – something he couldn't turn down, he therefore had to leave also.'

'But he said he'd wait... ...'

'Yes. Well, it couldn't be helped, I suppose. I presume he still meant for you to meet him.'

'But I can't go from America. I... ...'

'America? No. He's not in America, he's in Nottinghamshire – up north somewhere – a simple train ride away.'

'Oh, I thought... '

'Ah, here's Emily. Emily, can you get the fire going and get some hot water for our guest: Miss Heitmann? She'll need towels, a bed for the night and whatnot. And can you rustle up a bit of supper too?'

'Yes, of course, Mr Sanger,' she said, rubbing her eyes, her face blank, still half asleep.

I stayed with the Sangers for a couple of days. They were very kind to me – helped me send a telegram to Jakub, got me a good price for some of Tante Auguste's pearls. The telegraphic reply came back within hours: *Can't wait to see you. Come soon. Jakub. X*

'Did you enjoy that, Mrs Broadhead?'

'Yes, dear. It was very nice. The bread was much better than that stuff we usually get.'

'It's the new cook. She's baked it herself. I don't know whether she's just done it for a treat or whether she's planning on doing that more often.'

'Well, tell her it was very nice – just like bread used to be. And the stew was lovely too – I've not had dumplings since... I don't know.'

'I'll tell her. She will be pleased.'

'It makes all the difference, you know, at our age.'

'What's that?'

'Good food, of course. We don't have much to look forward to.'

'Oh. I hope that's not true.'

'It is true. We've lived our lives and are just patiently awaiting the end – and good food is like medicine – it makes things feel better. Makes *you* feel better.'

'Well, that's something at least. And anyway you have lots to look forward to. Your nephew wrote to say he was coming, didn't he?'

'Nephew?'

'Yes. You know: your nephew John. He wrote to say he'd come up at Whit, don't you remember?'

'Oh, yes, of course.'

'He's a very nice man. I met him at Easter. He's the one who teaches in Nottingham, isn't he. It must run in the family – having a skill for teaching, eh? Right let's get this table tidied. Have you finished, Mrs Phillips? Shall I take that away for you? Thank you, Mrs Rogers. I'll take that as well. I'll fetch some coffee in a moment.'

*

'That was another hit. Clean plates.'

'That is good.'

'Mrs B: she liked your apple pie. Said it's the best apple pie she's ever had...'

'That is good too. It is a recipe of my mother, more or less. Have you had your lunch yet?'

'Not yet.'

'Would you like to join me? Angela can carry on here. I'll get us some butter for the bread; we can sit by the window.'

'Nice to take the weight off.'

'Yes. No rest for the godless.'

'You've settled in here, then? And matron treating you well?'

'Yes. Oh, yes. I have everything I need. It's not so pressured as my last job.'

'Where was that?'

'At Tuckwoods – you know, in town.'

'Was that in the kitchen there, too?'

'Yes. Very busy, all the time.'

'Jack and me used to go there for special occasions, but we've not been for a few years now. Have you always been a cook?'

'Yes. It is what I trained as. I have always worked in kitchens.'

'But you're not from Sheffield originally.'

'You can tell I'm not a local? We came here in nineteen forty-five for a clean break. I'm on my own now – kids all grown up. My Michael got married last year when he turned twenty-one. You can't keep them forever can you?'

'No. You can't.'

'You have children?'

'Yes. Grown up too – Hattie has kids of her own.'

'That's nice. I'm going to be a grandmother soon. My Sarah is expecting in October.'

THE NINETEEN THIRTIES were an exceptionally hard time for many in Sheffield but Jack was earning decent money so we avoided the hardship that many faced all around us. The really bad times in the early thirties passed me by while I was up in Tynemouth – people always seem to try to put hard times to one side when they are at the seaside, and I suppose I had no commitments and the naivety of youth on my side.

That sense of impending doom was never far away, though, especially as the decade advanced – I suppose people tried their best to forget about it by having fun when they could. We glided over dance floors as fascists marched across Europe. On Friday nights we put the kids to bed and went to dance classes at the Unity Hall – Jack was a Left Book Club member and they organised things like that, as well as rambling trips. We had an arrangement with Mrs Thornton next door. She'd keep an ear open for Hattie and Jacky on Friday night and we'd do the same with her kids on Saturdays when she and her Derek went out. Almost as soon as we'd moved in she'd asked us – I think it was one of the duties that went with living next door to Mrs Thornton.

'Are you two lovebirds in th' neet? Then you'll not mind keeping half a lug 'ole open for our three upstairs?'

'If you're sure, Dora.'

'Oh, aye. If you 'ear owt – any whining or squabbling – and you will, 'cause them walls is so thin you'd hear a blackclock[1] fart – then just holler at 'em to be quiet.'

'Oh, I wouldn't do that.'

'No, you're too soft. Well, you've got a key if you need it.'

She wasn't half so tough as she made out: Mrs Thornton. No nonsense, but a heart of gold.

Everyone made the best of a bad job – we had to. There didn't seem much we could do about it, especially me with two small children. My greatest hope was that there would still be a world for them to live in. Jack could never accept that he was just one of many bits of straw being blown about by the wind. He tried to do

---

1 cockroach

something to intervene. Like many men he wanted to shape things, exert control. That was why he had jeered at Mosley's car as it drove to the back entrance of the City Hall, and why he and so many others had to be held back by lines of police when the blackshirts from Doncaster and Wakefield were bussed in, that was why he risked being trampled on or arrested as mounted police rushed the crowd.

'We've kept them out of Sheffield, at least,' he'd say. 'Mosley and his henchmen haven't come back. There's not enough support for them here, so they have to bus them in to make a respectable crowd.

He canvassed for the Labour candidate in the council elections in thirty-seven when a fascist stood, and felt a small victory when he polled less than a hundred votes. The blackshirts used to meet by the police box on London Road and poor Jack once got his spectacles knocked off and smashed when he heckled them and a scuffle broke out.

'I wish you wouldn't,' I said to him as I put TCP on the cut on the bridge of his nose. 'Call yourself a pacifist.'

'I have no choice. If you let them spread their lies people start to believe them. People are so susceptible to their easy answers to everything.'

'They have no chance here. People are too sensible.'

'But do you really think the British are so very different to the Germans?'

'I really don't know. Now, will you manage to see well enough with your glasses taped up?'

'I think so. I'll call in at the opticians on the way to work.'

Plans were made for evacuating our big cities and all the talk was of bombing. Air raid shelters were dug in back gardens and air raid wardens recruited; Jack would have signed up to be a warden if he had been old enough. Trenches were dug in our parks to act as shelters and the papers were full of stories about concrete bunkers being constructed under the city, of tunnels and underground car parks. We were all issued with gas masks in the late summer of thirty-eight. Toxic gas, as well as being blown to bits, was to be our fate. We knew what was coming because we had seen the pictures and newsreels of what Franco and his pal Hitler had done to the Basques. And we watched as groups of Basque orphans arrived in

Southampton seeking sanctuary in cities across the country.

This was around the time of Munich and Prime Minister Chamberlain's meetings with Hitler. That Saturday was a beautiful day – one of those early autumn days that carries with it memories of the passing summer, still some warmth in the sun, but tinged with sadness because you know it could be the last such day. Some people were triumphant, celebrating like when their team won that football cup thing a couple of years before. Thoughtful people were wary; some thinking we were giving in to Hitler, others that we were just putting it off until we were in a stronger position. That was Jack's view and he perhaps knew we couldn't yet go to war – he knew how many orders were coming in for parts for machines of war.

Any sense of euphoria that people may have had didn't endure; peace soon started to look like it was a mirage. Nineteen thirty-nine brought news of the defeat of Republican Spain, which deeply troubled Jack. He sat by the fire after tea with his newspapers as I gave the children a flannel wash. He looked ill, I thought.

'The democracies have failed,' he said. 'It will come down to us and France now.'

'I'm sure if Chamberlain can find a way...'

'Bah! Chamberlain...' he muttered, and went back to his newspaper, as if trying to make sense of where the world had become broken, so that he could find a way to fix it.

It was not that I didn't share his unease. I just didn't like to say it out loud – as if somehow saying it made it more likely to happen. Perhaps it did – perhaps we all got so used to the idea of war and bombing that it did become inevitable. It felt like we were on the edge of something for sure, like the ground beneath our feet was trembling, or the winds starting to blow and beat upon our house.

The sense of the old world passing, and us being pitchforked into a future we didn't want is still there in my mind – I can still feel that feeling and it is summed up in several images. For me it was not the events far away that have stayed in my mind: Hitler breaking his promises and taking over the rest of Czechoslovakia seemed too distant and hard to relate to. For me it is symbolic things that I can still see if I shut my eyes: the mourning for King George so soon after the Jubilee, seeing St Paul's Church being demolished on Pinstone Street – not that I'd ever been in, nor that its loss was directly connected with war. It was just... it had always been there – a solid, majestic, part of the city. They broke up and discarded gravestones and shovelled up the remains of great Sheffield citizens, dumped them in a mass grave, and left behind an ugly gaping hole.

Then the same thing happened to the Albert Hall where we had seen Errol Flynn swashbuckling his way into Olivia de Havilland's heart. And where we danced amongst thousands to the Blue Danube. Snow fell as the New Year came in and they started to tear down the walls of the Albert Hall. It was Jack who had called me over when he went to draw the bedroom curtains that night. We could see an orange glow in the sky over the city. He put his arm around me and we shared thoughts of destruction, knowing it was a big fire, and praying that everyone was safe. I don't suppose it could have been saved, but that day I stood for a while, holding Hattie's hand and rocking the pram, watching the workmen high up on the walls swinging their hammers, and mourned the passing of time. There was something in the sight of seeing buildings destroyed like that that troubled me, as if it were some kind of premonition. Foolish of me I know – Jack's fears, based on real understanding of the affairs of men, seemed nobler. I held Hattie and Jacky tight after tea when we got home and settled down to listen to *Children's Hour* on the wireless.

I GOT AN EXPRESS train to Retford and then went a few stops on a local train, all the while looking out of the window: damp fields and hedgerows, grey clouds and church spires in the distance.

Need I describe my meeting with Jakub at the station, other than to say we both cried a lot, then laughed then cried again?

I thought there would be much serious discussions about our future, about America, about practical things. Instead he said: 'So will you stay? I can ask the Marsdens if you can stay. I'm sure they will say yes.'

I just hugged him and said, 'Of course.'

There followed one of the happiest periods of my life. Jakub was working as a dairy hand on a farm: one of the few things an alien could do was agricultural work, and he knew all about cattle.

It was very different to our little farm in Luneberg. The main house was ever so grand, at least from the front – made of lovely red brick with herringbone patterns and red tiles on the roof. A large yard at the back had stables, barns and various outbuildings all around, plus some small cottages nearby for the foreman and gamekeeper and their families.

I was taken on as a general lackey: cleaning and doing laundry, helping in the dairy when they were busy, earning a few shillings a week. I shared a small room up in the roof of the house with a young girl who worked in the kitchen and saw Jakub at mealtimes when those who were attached to house ate together.

We also had some time together on Sundays and went to church together – it was what everyone did. It was expected of us and we wanted to be as English as we could: Jakub especially. Everyone called him Jacob or Jake; he started playing for the village football team and saying things like "old chap" "I say" and "look here." That made me giggle.

As I said, we were very happy – if only time could have stood still. It was almost as if it had, at least for me. But looking back, that time doesn't quite seem real; I wonder if I confuse it with something I read in *Far from the Madding Crowd* or a scene from *The Fox Farm.* I'm not so sure it felt like that for Jakub – for him it was an absence of something, rather than a state of being; it was a time defined by what it was not and what he was running from.

But Germany and its dark shadow would not go away – would not leave us be. We read about what was happening in the newspaper which passed through many hands on the farm and was usually a week old before I got to see it. The Nazis' stranglehold over the country increased. No one voted against them – not that they were offered a choice – in the Reichstag elections on the back of the invasion of the Rhinelands. Jakub said that surely it was now clear to the rest of Europe that they would not stop – surely they could all see that they had to take a stand. But nothing happened. The propaganda machine went full tilt with the Olympics to show what a modern powerful country they were, and everyone tiptoed around them.

We got married that spring. An English country wedding in the church, nothing Jewish or German about it, but that didn't bother us really. The worst part of it was not being able to share it with our families. I missed my mother then more than ever. She sent me some linen that she had beautifully embroidered herself: small tablecloths and mats for dressing tables and so on. She must have been working on them for many months. I held them up to my face, smelt them and kissed them. Jakub had to warn me not to spoil them with tear stains.

But our new friends on the farm put on a party for us in the evening in one of the barns – with much drinking and dancing, and I played *Lustig ist das Zigeunerleben* and Brahms' fifth Hungarian dance on my violin, and the drunken dancing made the floor bounce.

We had tried really hard to fit in and be valued so when we were told by the Marsdens that we could have our own little room at the back of the house overlooking the yard we were overjoyed.

For Jakub's birthday I wanted to surprise him, so I asked cook if I might use the kitchen to make him a dinner to remind him of home. I made a dumpling stew with vegetables and parsley, followed by trout with salt potatoes and asparagus and then a *Welfenspeise* for pudding. I worked at it quietly and carefully in order to not get in cook's way – she kept an interested eye on what I was doing and couldn't resist a taste.

The dinner did not quite have the effect on Jakub I had hoped for. I wanted so much to please him and make him happy, but he did not clap with enthusiasm when I served the stew, like I had imagined he would all the time I was pouring love into making it, and it was as if he had to force the *Welfenspeise* down. I started to cry.

'I wanted to make things perfect for you. Why don't you like it?'

'I do.'

'You don't.'

'Don't cry. It's only that... It reminds me of mother, of home... No. Not home. That is gone – in the past. This is home now – here with you – England. I don't...   I am not German any more, remember?'

'But we were happy there.'

'Yes, Lottchen. Until......'

'I know. Why don't you tell me about it? Maybe it would help.'

'No. It is pointless. It's best to forget.'

That was the last time he called me Lottchen. After that I was always Lottie – the same as everyone else called me.

Not long afterwards, cook had me transferred to the kitchen to work alongside her: no more scrubbing floors and swilling out the dairy.

It was Jakub who suggested the cheese idea. I think he was feeling guilty for appearing ungrateful for the birthday dinner: trying to see things from my point of view, recognising the conflict in me and my homesickness.

'You should make some. Your cheese is far better than anything they have here.'

'No, I couldn't. It takes too long, and anyway it would never come out the same. The cows are different, what they eat is different, the cultures they use here.'

He wouldn't leave it there. He was an expert in buttering up ladies of a certain age, like cook. He was very polite and charming without being a show-off at the same time. He flattered her and begged her to make a bread and butter pudding.

'There's only one thing in this world that tastes as divine as your bread and butter pudding,' he said, leaning against the kitchen door jambe.

'Oh, yes, Master Jacob, and what is that?'

'Lottie's cheese.'

'What cheese is this?'

'It is soft and creamy and melts in your mouth. If only she could be persuaded to make some.' He saw me cast him a look and he smiled.

The seed was sown and cook encouraged me to give it a go.

'The master loves a nice bit of cheese, and complains that the only decent cheese he gets is his Colston Bassett.'

'But I won't know what it will turn out like. It will have a completely different taste to what I'm used to – because of the starters and everything.'

The first few batches were not at all successful.

'You're going to have to help me here, Jakub. I need your best three cows: the ones that produce the finest milk. I'll try three separate batches of buttermilk – one from each. And if that doesn't work, I'll need you to find an untrodden patch of red clover.'

'I say! Roll me over in the clover.'

'Pardon? What do you mean?'

'Nothing, it is only some song some of the boys were singing when we were cutting the hay.'

'Jakub. I'm being serious. It is something my mother mentioned once. Sometimes she used heather flowers, picked first thing in the morning to help her starter. But she said sometimes in the past they used red clover flowers too.'

'Sounds like witchcraft to me.'

After a few more trials I had a cheese ripening that looked and smelt like it was fit for more than the farm hands' lunches. The resulting cheese was not quite like a German cheese, more like a creamy Stilton without the blue veining with a white mould rind and with tiny bubbles like a Tilsit.

Once I had my starter culture I had to keep going. Mr Marsden was impressed and one day called me to his study.

'Come in, Lottie. Take a seat. I've been looking at some figures. We currently sell milk at twelve pence a gallon. The margin is not particularly attractive. If however we were to turn some of our milk production into production of your cheese – a quality product, we could attract a premium. A gallon of milk makes about a pound of cheese, is that right? And a top quality cheese will retail for perhaps two shillings a pound. I think it starts to make sense. What would it take to scale up your cheese production? To let's say fifty or more pounds a week?'

I was taken aback. 'I don't think that's possible, sir.'

'Nonsense. Of course it is. It's simply a matter of getting the right set up. I'd make it worth your while. We'd get you all the equipment you need, and knock the dairy through if needs be. You could run the show – and we'll bring someone in to help.'

'But I couldn't. I... I'm only permitted to do domestic work.'

'Don't worry about that. It would be creating jobs – economic benefit and all that. And what's the point in being a magistrate if I can't oil a few wheels?'

'Well, the milk is certainly good. We've shown what can be done with it.'

'I'll say. Your cheese has a market. I know my cheese. I have no doubt about it. So what are we looking at?'

'I'd need a clean room, warming pans, presses, metal rings for moulds…'

'Excellent. We'll get all that – bring me a list of what you need and we'll make a start in the morning. How does that sound?'

'I don't know what to say. It's… well… exciting.'

'Yes. Yes it is. And we must sort you out with a proper salary.'

No sooner had I written up the list, with Jakub's help – I was being overly cautious he said – than the carpenter was at work making benches and presses. A sheet metal worker arrived and started drawing up plans for vats, warming cupboards and moulds, and a new boiler was being installed and piped up. I then set the carpenter on making a mill for the curds using some parts we found from an old clay mill. I was also given the job of recruiting two staff to help me make the cheese – Maud and Robert – school leavers from the village who were keen, quick learners. I spent several days teaching them about milk hygiene and how the cultures could go wrong if we were careless, and explaining each step of the process. I loved seeing it all come together. That day, when we took our first delivery of milk, I couldn't stop smiling, especially seeing the earnestness with which Maud and Robert approached every task they were given.

We were all kept very busy. Cows don't have days off and nor did we.

When football finished for the winter, the attention of the village sportsmen turned to the exceedingly strange game of cricket. Poor Jakub, he would have so loved to have become the perfect English gentleman, but cricket was beyond him – a step too far. His football friends once put a bat in his hands, but he just got laughed at and they never asked him again. "Stupid sideways-on game," he called it.

We did sometimes watch the local team play in the summer, though; and that summer any excuse for a sit-down on a picnic blanket in the shade of a horse chestnut tree was gladly taken – when I was carrying our Sarah. The name was out of defiance, because the Nazis had ordered all female Jews to take the second name Sarah on their identity papers to mark them out as Jews. I was happy with the name. It is a nice name. We couldn't let the Nazis use it as a badge of shame. The name Israel was never going to work for our son, who came after, however. It had to be something quintessentially English-sounding – he was named after Michael Redgrave who we saw in a film at the picture house in Worksop – *The Lady Vanishes*. As our value as members of staff on the farm grew, we were allowed the occasional evening off.

We started supplying cheese not only to local shops but large stores in Doncaster, Nottingham, Derby and Sheffield – that name cropped up a few times in things I heard people say. It turned out that it was not so far away – the place my father came from. It was some years before I got to visit though.

We were very lucky, I suppose, but Mr Marsden said it was nothing to do with luck. He was certainly right that it didn't need much marketing – it seemed to sell itself somehow, aided no doubt by Mr Marsden enthusing to all his contacts, and sending them samples. Within six months we received our first order from a large London store, famous for its food hall, and Abbey Manor Farmhouse cheese made it onto the best dining tables in the country.

But even this wasn't beyond the dead hand of Hitler – it lasted for a few short years, then we were forced to send all our fresh milk supply to the cities or to the large "efficient" creameries once rationing started.

We kept a worried eye on events in Germany, as did any thinking person back then. But it was different for us. We knew first hand what the Nazis were capable of. We understood them. And, after all, I had once been taken in by their promises. Jakub no longer regarded Germany as home, so he wasn't as torn, but for me it was different – my mother's letters pulled at me and my connection to the land was so strong. I suppose it still is all these years later.

While I was giving birth to Sarah, the Nazis were busy annexing Austria. But still people around us couldn't see what Hitler was doing. What is that game that children play in the street where they slowly creep up on someone? Yes, that's it: What time is it Mr Wolf? Except in this case it was the wolf who was doing the creeping up. The rest of Europe was shouting out "one o'clock" "three o'clock" and they didn't notice how big a stride was being taken until it was too late. They did nothing over the Rhinelands, the Anschluss was not their concern.

There was briefly talk of war that summer, though, and people started to make preparations, but then it was agreed that because the Suedetenlands were already a bit German they didn't really count. As long as you promise, Mr Hitler, that you'll be a good boy from now on and not ask for any more. But then the housekeeper's newspaper showed pictures of Mr Chamberlain and declared that "Great Britain will not be involved in a European war, this year or next year" and most people shrugged and went on with their business. But my mother's words remained in my head – he will never fill his gullet.

It was November of that year that brought about the biggest change in Jakub. At the time I didn't know it, but that was the point at which I started to lose him to a stronger passion. We knew better than anyone what had been unleashed, even as the British newspapers were saying "Looting mobs defy Goebbels," describing synagogues and Jewish shops being looted and burnt. We knew that nothing like that would happen without the Nazis being behind it, orchestrating it. How naïve to think that Goebbels would somehow try to stop it? He and his master were four-square behind it.

It does not take much to lead human beings by the nose, to get them to relinquish free will. It is something the British never really grasped at the time. I'm not sure they ever really have got their heads around the full horror of what came after, or even come near to understanding how a whole nation can be so complicit in evil. But they are not so different. The events of that November were regarded here as rather a fuss, almost something that the Jews had brought on themselves. The British love a saying and instead of "a stitch in time saves nine," the newspaper plumped for "least said, soonest mended" for its headline.

For Jakub it was especially painful – reading of people being rounded up. What had happened to him, repeated one hundred, a thousand-fold. Letters from his father in New Jersey contained details of first-hand accounts from people he knew who had escaped.

'The bastards no longer speak of it in hushed tones. A clear and open pogrom has begun,' he said. 'They will not stop until they have killed every Jew in Europe. Their hatred is lain bare.'

It even happened in our own little town – my mother told me in her letter that the remaining Jewish shopkeepers were driven out, and the long-established Lennhoffs clothing store, such a part of our community, was smashed and looted and the owners taken to the concentration camp.

At first Jakub sought consolation in me and little Sarah – she adored him and was always excited when he came in from work. Dada was her first word. She was crawling about the room by then and lifting her arms up to be picked up by him.

By Christmas she was walking around, though it seemed so strange for someone that small to be walking. If she had spoken to me I shouldn't have been more amazed. I tried to make Christmas that year as cosy and as comforting as I could. I got a small tree for our room and hung it with gingerbread and ribbons tied in bows.

We had some lovely trips to church and the heavens did their best to help by covering the landscape in a white blanket, just in time for Christmas Eve. The message of peace and goodwill was especially meaningful for everyone that year. We hoped for it with all our hearts as we gathered round the table with all the workers on the farm. But as the snow melted soon after Christmas and then nineteen thirty-nine arrived, I felt my hold over Jakub weakening.

He became more angry, more hardened – talked about "bloody Germans" as if he wasn't one, forgetting I was one.

'Jakub, I know she doesn't understand yet, but please don't use that language in front of Sarah. And she mustn't grow up hating a part of herself.'

At that he left the room.

One evening he came back from the pub after a football match and made an announcement.

'I'm going to join the army, Lottie. When the time comes to fight this evil, as is surely inevitable, I have got to be there and ready.'

I was stunned. 'Have you gone mad? That would mean leaving me and... I hadn't yet told him that I suspected I was pregnant again. 'Surely…'

'I don't think it can be avoided. They won't stop until someone stops them. I have to. This will be my fight more than most. You must see that? The head of the snake has to be cut off.'

He wrote to the recruiting office volunteering his services. He was devastated by the response: they were unable to accept non-British volunteers they said.

'That's so short-sighted. I can offer them so much – Germany is my enemy more than theirs. I speak the language. I am motivated, educated.'

I commiserated with him, and tried to hide my relief. I pressed my thumbs and hoped that something would change, that the folly of men would not be repeated.

Mr Marsden did not think it was right that I should work in addition to looking after Sarah, but I persuaded him I could manage, especially since both Maud and Robert were now becoming experts. I could work while Sarah slept and make sure that the list of things that needed doing was managed. In the evenings, after Sarah was put to bed, I could do the books. Getting pregnant again so soon was not quite what I had intended.

It was in the spring that the penny finally dropped with everybody. Poor Mr Chamberlain. I felt sorry for him. We heard him on the wireless after Germany had taken over the whole of Czechoslovakia. There was often a small gathering around the wireless we had in the kitchen for the six o' clock news, or when anything special happened. Some said that he was playing a clever game and that what he had been doing all along was buying time, but I am sure I heard a genuine sense of betrayal in his voice – he now knew that Hitler had all along been sprinkling sand in his eyes. Chamberlain always seemed to speak very precisely. He was easy for us to understand:

Does not the question immediately arise in our minds, if it is so easy to discover good reasons for ignoring assurances so solemnly and so repeatedly given, what reliance can be placed upon any other assurances that come from the same source?

'At last!' Jakub shouted at the wireless.

The prime minister then said there was some justification for uniting Germans into the Reich.

'Nonsense! That's your appeasement again.'

'Be quiet, Jake. We're trying to listen,' someone said.

The events which have taken place this week in complete disregard of the principles laid down by the German government itself seem to fall into a different category, and they must cause us all to be asking ourselves: Is this the end of an old adventure, or is it the beginning of a new?

'It is neither, you old fool – it's one more step. It's what he's been doing all along!'

Is this the last attack upon a small state, or is it to be followed by others? Is this in fact a step in the direction of an attempt to dominate the World by force?'

'Yes!'

As I said, I felt sorry for Chamberlain. I thought he sounded hurt and spent a lot of time trying to justify his actions. But it made Jakub more angry, and he stormed from the room when he said:

I know all individuals will wish to review their own position too, and to consider again if they have done all they can to offer their services to the state.

When my mother's letters arrived I didn't rip them open and read them immediately. I'd keep them in my apron pocket all morning, enjoying the anticipation, waiting for a few minutes to myself with a cup of tea, so that I could read, not the words themselves, but between the rows. I had to *feel* what my mother was writing about, not just read the writing.

She had few friends she could really trust – she had to be very careful not to say anything out of turn since so many things could get someone into trouble. I always checked the letters carefully for signs that they might have been opened, but there were none. I don't know if this was something that the Nazis did but there were few bounds to my paranoia. She told me her news, about changes in the town, of the ducklings she had seen on the river. She wrote of Hitler's fiftieth birthday: how they had all had to get proper flags – and not paper ones, and all the shops displayed portraits of the Fuhrer surrounded by laurel wreaths. "I saw the film of the parade at the cinema. I went with Irene Westermann – you remember her? I was very troubled by it all. I only see black. I fear it can really mean only one thing. All those tanks and guns, and soldiers marching in their thousands. Fearsome aeroplanes in formation. You don't build up an army like that without wanting to use it – and how will the beast be fed? All the talk of 'guns not butter' is no more than that – talk. You cannot sustain a nation on building up an army. They talk about a wonderful future where we all have KdF Wagons and refrigerators, where everyone in the *olksgemeinschaft* gets to go on holiday as a reward for their loyalty. And people believe it – it is as if by the party having said it enough times it becomes true. It's just *Machbarkeitswahn* you know. This future cannot be paid for since all we do is make guns, and borrow money to build factories to make guns, and *autobahns* to trundle them along. Unless that is, you intend to get your resources by expanding the Reich. Oh, Liselotte, I am so glad you are safe away from it all. No one believes that war will not come. Many even relish the idea. They believe it is necessary because Germany is being encircled – that the other European powers just want to keep the country on its knees.

"I hope your cheese is still selling well. I am so proud of you and everything you have achieved. The late summer is a good time to give birth. Hopefully the weather over there will not be too hot for you. I am very excited about the news. Please send another photograph of little Sarah if you get chance. I fear I will wear this one out with kisses."

So, my mother's letters did not reassure me about the prospects for peace, and Jakub was convinced that war was coming. Of course, I understood on one level what was happening, but when you stood back and thought about all that had happened in the Great War and since, it seemed like madness that anyone could even contemplate it again. You couldn't blame Chamberlain for trying to do everything he could to avoid it – it was surely the sanest course.

Jakub wrote to the recruiting office again when he heard about the new conscription law – and received the same response. He got friendly with the gamekeeper and got him to show him how to use a gun, and he'd go out rabbit shooting. He started doing exercises: press ups and swinging from a beam in one of the barns when he had a few spare minutes between jobs. And he started reading the newspaper whenever he could, to improve his English. He was gripped by some sort of mania. He would never discuss his motivation. 'I only want to keep in shape,' he said. 'Blame Cook's puddings.'

Perhaps he didn't really know, himself. He was impotent, as well most ordinary people – this was at least something he could do. So he did it.

The first week in June was beautiful and warm. The English countryside was shown off to its best. I had an excuse for wearing a loose-fitting unfashionable dress as everyone else sweltered. Then in the second week the weather broke and it felt like summer was already over – everyone regretted complaining about feeling too hot the week before. Rain was never far away and we didn't see much of the sun. It seemed to carry on like that for weeks – right through to August. Everybody grumbled. It is one of the things I like about being English – that you can talk to anyone about the weather, and enjoy a good old grumble. Had the weather been warm and sunny it would have been somehow a deceit.

We went to the pictures one Saturday evening; a whole group of us went on the back of a farm truck. It was freezing, though thankfully it didn't rain, and we snuggled under blankets and sang *Summertime* and that old Andrews Sisters' song *Bei Mir Bist du Schoen* – none of them knew the lines were German – not that the way they sang it sounded German anyway, and we weren't about to let on. The picture we saw was *Goodbye Mr Chips* – and it came to epitomise that strange summer in my mind: its quintessential Englishness, Greer Garson's infinite common sense that was lost to the world, the sadness and sense of foreboding, of something gathering, and its hope for continuity. I cried too much – I had become something of a softie ever since I had become a mother. There were no songs on the way home. I held on tight to Jakub's strong arm.

The last letter I got from my mother spoke of the resigned mood in the town. "I sometimes don't know what to believe any more: nothing I read in the newspapers, nothing that people tell me – even what I see with my own eyes I start to doubt. All the talk is of Poles committing atrocities on the Germans in Danzig. Thousands falling victim to bloody terror. Of them refusing to concede to reasonable terms. Everyone goes along with it, but they have been turned into fools, following their master like whimpering dogs."

Inside the letter was a photograph of her, standing outside the shop. "Please show it to Sarah, and tell her how much her Oma Anna loves her and is looking forward to meeting her some day."

Hopes that peace could still prevail were like those of blackbirds whose nest is been discovered by magpies. They keep swooping and twittering because the alternative is too great to contemplate.

Both Jakub and I were born in the War to End All Wars. Its long shadow had touched every aspect of our lives. It now seemed it was the "War that Ended Nothing," the war that just revealed the stupidity of men, the war born from the war before that, the war that begat the next.

As the shadow of one war waned, that of the next grew: like when you walk down a city street at night from lamppost to lamppost, each casts its shadow that grows than cedes to the next. And yet every time the power to kill increases – from sticks and stones, to swords, to guns, to machines and bombs.

That Sunday morning we all went about our business as usual – getting up, seeing to children and animals, going to church, deadheading the roses, sweeping the paths – the Prime Minister's broadcast at a quarter past eleven uppermost in the minds of most.

Jakub woke with a bad head having drank too much at the pub tonight before. He sat with the window flung open, smoking too many cigarettes, as I slowly got breakfast ready. I was very heavy by then, and not doing anything fast. He never used to smoke so much, it's not something I approved of.

I was trembling as the words: *This is London* came over the airwaves. Sarah was playing on the floor with a wooden spoon – I closed my eyes, willing him to speak some words that I could cling to in hope. But instead the words burst and broke like a big wave on a beach:

I have to tell you that no such undertaking has been received, and that consequently this country is at war with Germany.

Tears streamed down my cheeks. I don't remember much else of the speech. Once or twice Jakub smacked his fist into his palm and Sarah tried to clap like her daddy. I stroked her blonde hair.

After the Prime Minister had finished there was a silence that seemed to last forever. Everyone in the kitchen was silent except for Sarah tapping the table leg with her spoon. Church bells started playing over the wireless and people stole glances at each other. What were they thinking of us now? That we were the enemy?

An announcement followed which talked of bombs and poisonous gas and needing to sew an address label onto the clothes of your children in case they... what? Needed to identify their bodies? No one knew what to say afterwards. What was there to say? We all got to our feet and stood for the anthem, then they just went about their business.

I picked Sarah up and cuddled her – she was quite cross with me because the cat had just walked in and she wanted to go after it.

We gathered round the wireless again that evening when the King addressed the country. I always found him very hard to follow – he had a funny way of speaking, and you couldn't tell where his sentences ended, and he used words I could not understand. He used that word "enemy." Perhaps Jakub's vehement anti-Hitler's statements helped dispel any doubts from the minds of our friends. Now if anyone said anything about being German, either in joke or otherwise, he would say: 'I am Jewish, not German. It is not my country. I hate them more than you.'

Hitler had created in him a sense of Jewishness unlike anything he'd had before. His cousin Ephraim in London sent him cuttings from the *Jewish Chronicle*. He was clearly not the only refugee wanting to do his bit for the country that had welcomed him – or to try to defeat the one that had rejected him.

'Look it's been raised in Parliament,' he said.

'They must be coming under awful pressure. And France is not being so short-sighted – refugees are being welcomed into the army there.'

'And Ephraim? Is he wanting to sign up as well?'

'I'll say. He's as keen as mustard.'

He wrote again to the recruiting office and this time did not receive an outright rejection. They said something like: they regret it was not possible at this time but they will keep his letter on file.

Any unease I expressed, or remarks I threw in about needing him, about a young family needing him, were met with: 'But isn't that even more reason to defend our country? To fight for your future, and Sarah's, and the baby's? Can you imagine if they came over here? It would start all over again. They blame international Jews for causing this war. They have to be stopped.'

How could I tell him he was wrong?

I went into labour soon after. Michael had thick dark hair when he was born – Jakub's son, just as Sarah was my daughter.

He finally got the news he wanted, and which I dreaded, in November. He was called before a tribunal, which I have no doubt he brushed aside like an annoying wasp. He had an answer for everything and a desire that was unquenchable.

Within days I was waving him goodbye and trying not to let Sarah see me upset. She was too young to understand anything – she broke my heart, asking after him in her naive way: 'Papa? Kiss. Papa?'

'GOOD MORNING, Mrs Broadhead.'

'Good morning, dear.'

'I've a little surprise for you, if you like. You got me thinking when you said you'd not done any singing. I know you like to sing. And I remember your lovely voice?'

'Do you? Did you go to All Saints?'

'No, Mrs Broadhead. I told you. You were my teacher at Whitby Road.'

'I don't think so. No.'

'I'm Josephine Cartwright – or used to be. Jo Cartwright, you remember?'

'Yes. Yes, of course. Jo Cartwright. I remember your father – poor man. He was a miner, wasn't he?'

'Half the children in the class had miners for fathers. You used to take us up to High Hazels during the strike. Do you remember? And we'd sing songs and do our lessons on the grass.'

'Yes, of course. And you did a play – was it The Water Babies?'

'No, it was Peter Pan.'

'Oh yes. That was wonderful.'

'Anyway I've brought my Dansette in.'

'Pardon? That box?'

'Yes, it's a record player and I found some old records at the jumble sales: hymns. So we could sing along to them.'

'Well I never – how nice.'

'Let me set it up. This one's Fight the Good Fight and I've got Lead us Heavenly Father Lead Us that we used to sing at school in assembly. Do you remember? Mrs Jones used to bash the tunes out on that old piano.'

*

'Is that kettle on, Lottie?'

'Yes – as always.'

'How was the singing?'

'It was fun.'

'And matron doesn't mind?'

'No, as long as I get my work done too.'

'She really came out of herself. I've not seen her smile like that for a while. Music is so powerful don't you think?'

'Oh yes – I used to play the violin. But it always took me back home, and that became too painful. I can't even take it out of its case these days. It was my grandfather's you know.'

'That is sad... I didn't know... It was like I had Miss Oughtershaw back with me.'

'Who is this?'

'That was her name when she was my teacher – she only became Mrs Broadhead some time after the war.'

'I have heard that name before... I don't suppose it can be the same. Ottershore you say?'

'No Oughtershaw. O-U-G-H-T-E-R-S-H-A-W.'

'Ah, it is not the same name, then.'

'What is the name you were thinking of?'

'Ottershore – like the edge of the water and little funny river animals.'

'I've never heard of that as a name. Who was this Ottershore?'

'My father. He was from Sheffield. My mother and he were never married. It was in the war – the first war – a bit scandalous. He was a prisoner of war and was sent to work on my grandfather's farm. My mother was young. Lonely I suppose. And he was very handsome, and kind.'

'What happened to him?'

'She never knew. One day he was taken away and she never saw him again.'

'That's awful.'

'Ach. Maybe. There are worse things.'

'Is that why you came here: to find him?'

'Not really, no. It was simply somewhere to come to look for work – the nearest big place to the village where James and I lived, somewhere I could bring up my kids. But I suppose I always had a notion that I have some roots here. It is true. I feel it. The people are kind and humoristic.'

'Humorous.'

'Ach, yes – humorous. They laugh even when things should not be funny – things that Germans wouldn't find funny – but really are all the ridiculous things that life throws at you. Back in Germany people were always looking over their shoulders, not sure if they were allowed to laugh or poke fun at life. Here you can even call names and joke at

the Prime Minister or the Archbishop. In Sheffield no one expects you
to be something you are not. Odd people are everywhere and no one
minds. They just have a laugh, but also a bit admire them, you know.
Like near me there is a Duke of Darnall, not a real duke of course, but
an eccentric who likes to dress up. But everyone goes along with the
joke and treats him with respect, as if he were really a duke. No one
takes themselves too seriously. They're not allowed to – even if they
did try.'

'They get knocked down a peg or two?'

'A peg? Yes. Like getting someone off their podium, I think'

INGOLDMELLS that summer had been the calm before the storm. We spent a happy week there, on the beach with buckets and spades in the fine drizzle, eating in the dining room without having to trouble about the cooking and washing up, pushing little Hattie on a swing, Jacky giggling as his dad threw him up in the air and caught him in his safe hands, ice cream and candy floss, whelks from the stall and flower beds blooming red and yellow.

After we returned from that all too brief escape from the real world it seemed that the slide into war was inevitable.

Jack took the ARP very seriously – those three letters became as familiar as RAF or BBC – air raid precautions. They became a verb: we ARPed windows or spent weekends ARPing after shopping in Woolies' ARP department. People brought strips of brown paper to paste on their windows or cellophane if you had the money. It became a familiar sight seeing people on their way back from the shops with rolls of black paper under their arms for blacking out their windows.

Jack, being Jack, researched the subject and discussed it at work with engineers and other clever people. He had some chicken wire he'd laid aside the previous year when we thought war was about to start, but then it was "peace in our time," so it got put away.

'Brown paper strips won't stop glass flying given the kinds of pressure that a blast would produce. This government leaflet is next to useless – it's no more than propaganda to stop people getting worried. If they were really bothered about saving lives they'd build underground shelters like we have at work, not expect people to just hide under the stairs.'

So he set to, banging and sawing and creating frames of wire over the windows. He thought of everything. The cellar was fitted out as a shelter: he cemented up cracks around the coal grate and made a thing out of rubber sheeting for sealing it off against gas. We had torches and a hurricane lamp for back up, a spirit kettle, a bunk bed he constructed out of timber and sacking for the children and camp beds for us.

One Saturday he came home with what looked like a pit prop over his shoulder and went about strengthening the cellar ceiling as well. There was probably not another house in Sharrow as well prepared as ours. I just left him to it. It all seemed a bit over the top to me, but I suppose I caught the bug to the extent of laying down supplies. I didn't go mad like some – but for months I'd been buying one plus a spare. So we had tins of potatoes, sardines, SPAM and corned beef. I had jars of various butter substitutes like banana butter and apricot curd and things in mouse-proof, sealed tins on the cellar slab.

At Jack's works they practised an air raid drill and filed down into the shelters.

'You mustn't worry about me, you know – there's nowhere safer. There are concrete tunnels that no bomb could even reach, and they're felt lined to stop any gas.

'But won't the air run out?'

'No way. This bit is genius. There's an air purification plant that draws in gas-free air and so that we're not dependent on power supplies there's this machine that is powered by a bicycle thing and all the chaps were lining up for a turn.'

There was to be an evacuation of school children and that was rehearsed as well – we decided that I should take Hattie and Jacky to safety. It meant leaving Jack behind but we couldn't risk their lives. The only thing that mattered was survival.

That was a horrid day, that first day of September. We had listened to the news that Poland was under attack and Danzig being bombed. Jack had sat back in his chair: 'That's that then,' was all he said.

We expected the air raids to start as soon as war was declared, so getting the children away assumed a new urgency.

We told the kids that mummy was taking them on another holiday but this time to the countryside not the seaside. They were quite excited, even though their daddy wasn't coming too. How do you explain a thing like war to a child? That grown ups want to blast thousands of people to high heaven just because they are greedy? How can you explain the nonsensical?

Jack went off to work as normal that morning and I had to choke back tears and feelings of dread for their sakes.

'Will you manage all right?'

'Of course. Don't worry about me. You concentrate on looking after the little 'uns.'

'I put the extra sugar I put by in the big tin in the cellar.'

'I know. You told me.'

'You sometimes don't pay attention.'

'I do.'

'And there's tins of chicken and ham roll, and braised steak. And there should be enough of that fish pie left for tonight and tomorrow; and perhaps some carrots to go with it.'

'I'll be just fine.'

'You promise me you'll eat properly – buy fresh veg?'

'You're sounding like my mother now. I'll write with a full break down of my diet if you like.'

'Oh, get away with you. Go and draw up plans for some fiendish machine to bash Hitler, or whatever it is you do.'

We kissed on the doorstep not caring who might be passing.

'I'll be late!' And off he dashed down the street.

We weren't allowed to take much with us. I checked and re-checked everything while the children sat on the floor and played with the wooden bricks that Jack had made.

My heart was heavy as I pulled the door to, closing what felt like the peaceful chapter of our lives for good. It was a long walk down to Heeley Station with a toddler on my hip, a small suitcase in my hand and little Hattie trailing along with a parcel of sandwiches swinging across her shoulder, complaining about how far we'd come before we'd even reached London Road. Fortunately, we joined up with a party heading down from Sharrow school, and the teacher got one of the biggest children to help out by giving little Jacky piggybacks. We were swept along by the mood of the excitement. Most of the children had never even left their neighbourhood, so this was a huge adventure and they frequently had to be told to pipe down by the teachers.

Little streams of schoolchildren joined into a river at the bottom of the hill as we approached the station. It was all very efficient as we boarded the trains to take us away from the imminent threat of bombing. I saw Miss Ougthershaw, my old teacher on the platform.

'Miss Oughtershaw?'

She looked at me for a moment, not quite making the connection.

'It's me: Jo Cartwright. Except I'm Jo Burridge now.'

She smiled at me. She was as elegant as ever, even though her dark hair was flecked with grey and her face was lined at the corners of her eyes.

'Jo – how nice to see you! I didn't recognise you. You're all grown up. I've not seen you since... and who's this?' She tickled Jacky's hair and he buried himself further into the collar of my coat.

'This is Jacky. Say hello, Jacky.' But he was having none of it. 'And this is Harriet.'

Miss Oughtershaw bobbed down to her level and shook her hand. 'Lovely to meet you, Harriet.'

'I'm sorry, we're keeping you.'

'No, don't worry. I'll be with you in a minute, Mr Hollins. It's such a responsibility – we don't want to lose any of them.'

'Well, at least they've all got name tags on if they get lost. Are you going with them?'

'Yes. To carry on teaching them at their new school. Are you on the Loughborough train too?'

'Yes, we are.'

'Well, I must go. It was lovely to see you. It's so nice to see one of my old children doing so well. Look after yourselves. Good-bye Harriet.'

'Lovely you to meet you too, Miss Oughtershaw...'

'Who was that nice lady, Mummy?' said Hattie.

'She was my teacher when I was little. She was very kind to me.'

It would have been nice to talk for longer. I felt there was so much I wanted to say to her. I'd not even thanked her – she probably didn't even know how much she had influenced me – I was probably just another former pupil to her.

I saw her again briefly at Loughborough counting heads of children while we are waiting at the station for onward transport.

There was a spirit of a works' outing about the evacuation – it was mostly the children who swept the adults along with them. They did not really understand what war was – and any sign of sadness amongst them was soon snuffed out by their classmates. I can't imagine what their mothers must have felt, though, waving them off to school, not knowing when they'd see them again, with the veil of war hanging heavy over us all.

We were billeted in a small village near Loughborough at the home of a widow called Mrs Unsworth. She was kind and did her best to make us welcome, but I missed Jack terribly and got very bored. She didn't even have a wireless, so we only got to find out that war had finally been declared from what her neighbours said. We went for walks around the village but there wasn't much to see or do, not even a duck pond. I couldn't get very far with the children anyway. Once I'd put them to bed I wrote to Jack or read. Mrs Unsworth was not very talkative and we didn't seem to have much in common. She didn't want to talk about her past or hear any mention of the war and wasn't particularly fond of children. It was as if she had volunteered to have evacuees out of duty, or because the vicar had preached about moral responsibility. That's uncharitable of me, really. She wasn't unkind in any way – I just couldn't see that as being my life. No purpose, no focus other than the children.

I helped around the house and in the kitchen, went to the village shop and back, tried to keep the children clean as well as busy which was hard in the countryside, got them up, put them to bed. I'd never known such monotony.

Evacuation put a strain on village life it seemed. Two women in the shop paused their conversation to look down their noses at me, then carried on complaining.

'I don't know what their mothers were thinking: sending them in that state. Crawling they were: I had to cut their hair short and give them a good scrub and get the nit comb out.'

'The state of their shoes – I've had to give them Alice's old shoes, theirs were so full of holes and with just cardboard patching the soles.'

'I've heard they deliberately sent them in old clothes so as to cadge new ones.'

'No, Reney. I don't think so. The two I've got said they didn't have best clothes and I believe them.'

'Well, it's a crying shame; that's what it is.'

If one good thing came out of the war it was that people were forced into seeing just how poor some of the people in our country were.

In the meantime, bombs had not rained down on Sheffield, nor anywhere else. Jack said that life went on as before and that some children who had been evacuated off our street had already come back home. He said nothing about whether he thought we should, but I'd already made up my mind. Mrs Unsworth took the remaining twenty-five shillings worth of allowance and we caught the train back home. We were not the only Sheffielders on the train heading home that Saturday. At least one mother had come over to take her children back.

I think, looking back, it was mostly the adults who were unhappy. Children are resilient and, if they found good foster parents, leaving the bricks and smoke of Attercliffe or Netherthorpe for the farmyards, trees and fields of rural Leicestershire was not so much of a hardship. They stretched their limbs, climbed trees, lived side by side with nature, and filled their lungs with country air. Their former poor diets were replaced by things grown on the farm, meat rations supplemented by bits on the side and rabbits and pigeons from the fields and woods, and they thrived like they would not have done back home, with parents too busy or too poor even to provide for their basic needs. The only starvation was in the hearts of the grown ups.

I was glad to be back home. It didn't really feel like we were at war. In many ways life went on as before. We tripped and cursed after dark in the blackout and ruined our shoes in unseen puddles, we struggled to find shops selling torch batteries – a new necessity. Butter was scarce, even Stork, and we had to settle for the stuff at sixpence. Before the war we'd easily got through several pounds of butter a week, so being limited to three ounces, even before rationing proper came in, was a nuisance. Other than these inconveniences and seeing more people in uniform there were no outward signs of war.

There were plenty of funny moments in that early blackout before people got used to it and they brought in the new starlight street lighting. People bumped into strangers and friends – quite literally. One evening on his way home from the pub, Mr Armstrong from number fourteen walked straight into our kitchen while I was on my hands and knees polishing the lino. "Ooh, sorry missus. I must have felt my way up the wrong passage by mistake – you can't see your hand in front of your face out there. And I've only had half a mild an' all.'

The fear of air raids passed. Some people thought they would never happen, or at least that is what they said. I think some people couldn't live with the fear, so convinced themselves it was not true.

Rumours were rife: pathetic people trying to appear important by claiming knowledge that London had been bombed and fifteen hundred people killed, or this or that ship having been sunk by submarine. Some people tuned into Hamburg radio to listen to Lord Haw Haw's nonsense – the attraction of the moth to the candle flame. There were going to be disease bombs, children's balloons full of poison gas so that they would pick them up and take them home, and so on. It played to people's gullibility and fears.

But we carried on – Jack had his work, I had the children to look after. We'd tune in to *Bandwaggon* on Saturday night, and saw *Hound of the Baskervilles* at the pictures or Mickey Rooney in the latest Andy Hardy film – lovely heart-warming stuff to take you away from your terror. Jack hated *Bandwaggon* and he wasn't keen on Tommy Handley either: 'They should broadcast that rubbish to Germany on repeat twenty-four hours a day. They would soon surrender. Or at the very least they would resolve never to invade a country so awful as to produce such rot.'

We enjoyed Christmas: roast duck with apple sauce, stuffing and roast potatoes, then plum pudding with brandy. We tuned into the King's speech and winced as he stumbled over his words at the beginning, but once he got going, with the nation straining to will him on, his message was one which seemed to speak for all of us.

It was an awful winter; snow stayed on the ground for weeks, and pipes froze and burst everywhere and influenza took hold. Mrs

Thornton started popping round on Mondays with her washing so that we could do it together and only have to heat one lot of water, bringing a bucket of coal every other week when it was her turn.

'Marjorie from number twenty-two said she had a bit of sole for her tea last night. See if you can guess what she paid for it?'

'I don't know, Dora. I've stopped looking at the fish it's so dear.'

'Three and six. Three and six for a bit of fish!'

'Well, I suppose if you think what the fisherman have got to face to catch it. It would have been bad enough before, risking being drowned, never mind being shot at or torpedoed.'

'I wouldn't buy it even if I could afford it.'

'Why is that?'

'Well, you never know what they've been feeding on – all them dead bodies at the bottom of the sea. I mean fish smells a bit funny at the best of times, but what if, y' know... them dead Jerries.'

'Dora! That's horrid.'

'I've got a tin or two of salmon from before the war though, so I'm all right with that.'

'Should we try hanging the washing out today? It doesn't look too bad.'

'Aye, let's just give it a go – it might dry a bit and then I'll put it over the rack later.'

'Perhaps a touch of warmth in the sun too? Spring is just around the corner.'

'I usually look forward to the spring coming round but I'm so torn this year, Jo.'

'But it will be nice to see a few crocuses and daffodils – a bit of colour.'

'But it could also bring trouble from you know who: Old Nasty. Derek says that's when he'll try to invade. What are we waiting for, that's what I want to know? Why don't we attack him before he gets to us? Send the RAF over. All we've done so far is scatter a few pamphlets over Germany. We need to make them suffer. We should have done it last time: taught them a proper lesson.'

'We're perhaps playing a waiting game, Dora. We've got to catch up with them – they have far more planes and guns than we do.'

'In a way don't you just wish something would happen?'

'There's a lot going on at sea. Maybe we will see the return of peace instead in the spring.'

'Do you really think so?'

'Oh, I don't know – no not really. Perhaps if we were dealing with someone sane, but I'm convinced that Hitler is beyond reason and only hears things that fit his mad view of the world.'

'Mad or bad, if I had him here I'd give him what for.'

'I'm sure you would. Perhaps the RAF should parachute you into Berlin with a broom, Dora?'

'Aye happen they should. I'd give him a right going over.'

IN THE SPRING I was up before a tribunal of my own – like all enemy aliens. The Home Office had to assess me to see how much of a threat I was to security. The room was oak-panelled and I had to sit before these old men. The one who did all the talking did at least have a kind face. He wrote down my details then looked up with his piercing eyes.

'So why are you here?'

'I had to flee Germany, sir.'

'But you are not a Jewess?'

'No.'

'Did you oppose the Nazis, then?'

'No. Not start with.'

He looked down and wrote something on his papers. It was quiet apart from the scratching of his pen. The others stared at me.

'But you did afterwards?'

'Yes, sir.'

'Why? It was a legitimate regime was it not? They were elected?'

'Yes, sir. But then they brainwashed people.'

'I see.' His pen scratched away again.

'You speak very good English.'

'Thank you.'

'Do you have family in Germany?'

'Yes, my mother is there.'

'You are still attached to the country?'

'Yes, sir, but...'

'You would be an ideal spy for the Nazis would you not?'

He was trying to trick me. I got a bit cross, felt my face get hot.

'No. I hate the Nazis. I have been here three and a half years. My children are English. My friends are English. My husband, a German Jew, is joining the British Army. I left Germany because I had no choice.' My vision blurred as tears started to spring up. 'The Nazis shaved my hair to humiliate me and paraded me through the streets of my home town – for no other reason than being seen on the arm of a Jewish man. They took him to a concentration camp...' I dried up. I wanted to cry but fought it back. I felt humiliated enough already.

They put me into category C – the lowest risk.

Jacob was sent to a place called Kitchener camp on the south coast. I kept all his letters from that time – they are in a shoebox in the bottom of my wardrobe. This camp started as a place for Jewish refugees from all over Europe who had fled after Kristallnacht, some just children, sent to safety on their own by parents who were left behind.

"I've got my uniform," he wrote. "You'll not recognise your Jakey when I come on leave – I'll turn a few heads of the village girls I should imagine.

'It was a proud moment to swear allegiance to King George. The NCOs were talking about taking the King's shilling – I thought there'd be an actual shilling that I could keep as souvenir, but that's an old thing apparently. I'll have to be content with my fourteen shillings a week. Have you received your separation allowance yet?

'So anyway, they now call us the King's Most Loyal Enemy Aliens – a bit of a wheeze that. Officially we're the Pioneer Corps under the command of Lord Reading – it's mostly Jews – and he is too, they say. The chaps come from all over – Austria, Germany – we've also got a Pole and a Czech in our hut. We're separate from the main camp where the women, children and older folk are. They're a jolly clever bunch on the whole: musicians, young doctors, engineers, university types. I feel very English next to them – rabbiting on in German all the time. I wish they wouldn't – I'd rather not hear it. They will never learn the language that way.

'I can't see them keeping such skilled people in what is basically a labouring unit, though. They'll want us on the frontline soon, I hope. Once they've got discipline into them. And their English improves. We're all a cut above the English fellows anyway – physically and intellectually – they seem to have sent us a bit of a rough lot. The *Rachitis Kompanie*, they get called – and often, on top of the rickets, they are convicts, and not at all bright.'

I have to admit he did look did look most handsome when he walked into the farmyard on Christmas leave.

Sarah was not quite so impressed and hid from him behind the armchair. He sat in it with a sigh.

'Oh, it's such a shame my little angel's not here. Where is my Sarah?'

He rustled in his knapsack.

'And to think I've bought her some Dolly Mixture, too. Such a shame. It looks like I'll have to eat them myself.'

He pretended to put one in his mouth as her wide eyes peeked round the wings on the chair.

'I like the pink ones best.'

He popped a sweetie on the chair arm and we both giggled as a tiny hand reached up to take it.

He talked a lot about life in the army for the first few days – he seemed more interested in that than in how we'd been fairing without him, talking about the football team, lectures they'd had, and what went on in the NAAFI and the brute of a sergeant major – who I think he actually admired. He seemed to re-acclimatise to the village after a few days and we spent a lovely quiet Christmas, the four of us together – enjoying a warm fire and singing carols. It didn't really feel like there was a war on.

Later on in the New Year he wrote to tell me he was changing his name.

"I suppose that means you will have to as well. I hope you don't mind. I'm going to be known as James Rose from now on. Suits me, don't you think? Sounds rather like a film star, perhaps? As does Lottie Rose. What do you reckon? I thought about it a bit and thought Sarah and Michael Rose had a ring to them too. You see, the thing is, we have been told to make ready to go to France and they don't think it's a good idea if we have Jewish names in case we are captured – not that we will, so don't worry. We are just in support roles, not on the frontline, but still it will be good to do more than just square-bashing."

'How are you, Aunty? You weren't resting were you? I hope I haven't disturbed you.'

'Who are you? I don't want you in my room. Go away. Things have gone missing. Have you taken them?'

'No, Aunty. It's me, John. Your nephew. Tom's son.'

'My nephew? Of course. It's just you can't be too careful these days, can you? Things have been disappearing. Like my alarm clock – you haven't seen it have you?'

'No, Aunty. I'll ask them about it before I go. I expect it is somewhere around. You perhaps put it in your wardrobe or something. Anyway you are looking well.'

'I'm all right. Mustn't grumble. They look after me very well, you know. And my room is lovely and the view of garden is nice, isn't it? Do sit down, you make the place look untidy.'

'Have you had your lunch yet?'

'Yes, dear. We had cottage pie. The food is very good. There's a new cook. It must be costing a lot of money for me to live here.'

'Don't you worry about that, Aunty: you're loaded – after you sold the house and all Mr Broadhead left you. Oh, before I forget: here's a few bars of Pears soap. I know how much you like it. And also a bottle of Yardley lavender that I picked up in Jessops?'

'Thank you.'

'So, what have you been up to?'

'Yes. A very nice lunch. Fresh strawberries and cream for afters.'

'That sounds nice, Aunty.'

'Not as nice as the ones that Mr Forbes used to grow. Can't beat home-grown strawberries, still warm from the sun.'

'Who was Mr Forbes, Aunty?'

'Oh, you know: I stayed with Mr and Mrs Forbes in the war when we were evacuated.'

'Was that in thirty-nine?'

'Yes, that's right, in thirty-nine. We were all very worried about being bombed.'

'I remember. I joined up soon after. What was it like being evacuated?'

'Not everything it was made out to be. I enjoyed the time I spent there, though. A lot of them didn't stay very long. It was a good idea I suppose, at the time. We all expected to be bombed and invaded, but it didn't happen. Not until later did we have bombs, and most of us were back by then. He was a parashot.'

'Who was?'

'Mr Forbes, of course. I told you. Joined the LDV and went out at night looking for signs of Germans landing.'

'And what was the school like?'

'Only small – four classrooms around the hall. A little village school really. Yes.'

'They looked after you well, though – the people you stopped with... ?'

'Oh, yes, very well. Mr and Mrs Forbes they were called. Their son was in the RAF and their daughter was living in Leicester by that time. They grew all sorts of fruit and vegetables. They had chickens too – we were well looked after, yes.'

'So, was it a farm?'

'Was what a farm?'

'Where you were evacuated?'

'No, it was in Frisby-on-the-Wreake – a little place – not far from the countryside.'

'Oh, I see. But they had a big garden – digging for victory and all that?'

'Yes, Mr Forbes had green fingers. Not like me. When we got back to Sheffield we tried planting seeds at school, but I don't think a single radish grew. He had a greenhouse at the bottom where he grew cucumbers and tomatoes. It didn't seem like there was a war on at all. We went about things as normal, but with a nagging sort of feeling – and then you'd remember what it was – there was a war and mad-eyed Germans were waiting to use their jackboots on us. He went out at nights hoping to shoot them down. The parashots they called them.'

'It was a strange time, wasn't it? I was posted in Norfolk at the time and remember how lovely that first springtime was: all the birds singing and the country lanes on the way to the pub as the blackthorn and May blossom came out. It all seemed brighter and more vivid. It was as if either that wasn't real or the war wasn't real. They couldn't both be true. It was a far cry from Burngreave, for sure.'

'Where? What's that about Burngreave?'

'Norfolk – near Thetford, where I was stationed. Not at all like Burngreave.'

'No. Burngreave's not like Norfolk. Tom's son was in the RAF. I think he was in Norfolk.'

'Yes Aunty, that's me. Tom was my father.'

'Oh yes. I remember your mother looking after me once when I was poorly. She was lovely.'

'Yes, she was.'

'Didn't live long after Tom died. She broke her hip and she... '

'Yes, she did.'

'Not many of us old 'uns left are there?'

'No, Aunty. Shall we have a little turn of the garden before I go. Are you up to that, do you think? I don't think you'll need your hat or coat today. Perhaps just a cardigan. I'll pass it to you. It's quite warm. It's not been a bad summer so far has it?'

I SPENT MUCH of that first two years of the war flipping between hope and despair. I almost could believe we were all going to die and yet believe it would soon be over at the same time. At times I hated all Germans, not just Nazis: the whole lot of them for bringing this on us. Someone like Hitler doesn't just pop up from nowhere and take over, he gains in strength because people support him, or at least they allow him to go about unchecked. I looked forward to them being destroyed, and then I'd think perhaps we should seek peace at almost any price because it wasn't worth another life or another ship sunk by torpedo or mine.

I had spells of trying to avoid the news that first year in particular. Those that went about the happiest were the ones whose minds allowed them to ignore it. I don't know, are people like that plain stupid, or shallow, or do they, in fact, have such wisdom that they can live for the moment and enjoy life for what it brings, so long as it goes on?

Jack had to know what was happening. He always listened to the news while he had his tea at six, then again at nine to see if anything had changed. He read the *Sheffield Telegraph* on the bus or tram to and from work.

Every bulletin carried the chance that it would send me into despair or rekindle hope. I don't think Jack ever got the jitters quite like me. He had an inner belief that we would prevail, that even the bad things that happened would fortify us even more and deepen resolve – like homoeopathic medicine where a bit of poison is used to effect a cure.

He was shaken by Stalin's attack on Finland and our feeble attempts to send help to their brave resistance against Russia's overwhelming numbers of soldiers.

'I'm ashamed to think I allowed myself to believe that Russian communism was somehow on the side of good,' he said, when the bulletin ended and the BBC Symphony Orchestra started playing.

'They are showing how anti-democratic they really are – are they really that different from the Nazis after all?'

I tried not to listen and left Jack's question hanging, but it was there in my mind, and what if Stalin and Hitler joined forces to carve up Europe? I took everything out of one of the kitchen cupboards to clean it.

'After this is all over we need some sort of United States of Europe to come about – we failed after the last war. It was nations turning in on themselves and "sod the rest" that brought this on.'

I wiped jars and scrubbed shelves and put the things back tidy.

We stopped believing everything we were told. They said that we were well equipped for fighting in Norway, with French and Canadian alpinists. Our spirits rose when we heard our troops had landed and retaken Bergen and Trondheim, that seven Nazi ships had been scuttled, that we were laying mines to protect Norway and Sweden. Then later we learnt that things were not going so well, that our troops didn't have the guns and aerial support, that they were losing and retreating.

'Bungling idiots – Chamberlain's got to go! We need men of action at the helm, not chair-polishing old men who still get tucked up in bed by nanny with a glass of hot milk at nine-thirty.'

It wasn't long before we stood alone in Europe, with Hitler facing us from across the channel. It all seemed to happen so fast and every day we expected to see parachutists landing. You started seeing people carrying gas masks again in the streets.

Jack took me to the pictures to cheer me up. It was Brian Aherne, one of my favourites, in the *Vigil in the Night*. It did not cheer me up, consisting as it did of various scenes in which children died of meningitis.

It was when the newsreel was shown that I remarked on something that hadn't happened before – people applauded when Churchill was on. It was cause for some hope. As we walked home afterwards Jack said: 'The time has produced the man.' That has always stuck with me.

I decided to stick to Mickey Rooney, Westerns like *Destry Rides Again* and things like the new *Pinocchio* film. In the pub after seeing *Pinocchio*, as we snatched a quick drink, Jack mused: 'Is it possible to fall in love with a cartoon character?'

'What on earth... ?'

'I am sorry to break it to you but I think I have got a crush on the Blue Fairy.'

'Well, at least you're unlikely to run off with her, I suppose. Whereas Errol Flynn is real, so you'd better watch out Mister.'

I regressed a bit at the time: *Pinocchio* and reading *Winnie the Pooh* to my children was a moment of comfort. Those charming little animals, muddling along, full of good intentions and taking joy from the small things in life: a sunny day or snowflakes, with a tendency to lapse into poetry at odd moments, their laziness, their silliness, their love for their friends. How I longed for real life to be like that.

'When's the invasion happening then?' Mrs Thornton bustled in with a pile of ironing. She had taken a liking to using our electric iron that plugged into the light socket rather than her old flat iron.

'Oh, hello, Hattie. Helping your mummy? What a good girl.'

'Yes, Mrs Thornton. We making a pie.'

'Ooh, lovely dear. Where's your brother.'

'He's sleeping – so, no shouting.'

'I promise.'

I got the old blanket out to cover the table for her, then went back to the butterless pastry we were making.

'So you want to know about the invasion? Shall I just give Goering a ring and ask him?'

'Yes, please, if you could sort that out. All this uncertainty is killing me. If Hitler's earmarked the eighteenth of August for his victory parade through London he'll not be wanting to hang about much longer will he?'

'You're ready for when Nazi paratroopers land in the back yard, then?'

'Oh, aye. I won't go down without a fight. He's miscalculated hasn't he? We'll fight to the last man, not surrender like everyone else.'

'What did you reckon to Winston's speech?'

'Proper stirring stuff, wasn't it. He's right though. We'll fight them street by street if we have to. Better dead than living the lives of slaves to the Nazis. They don't understand us British – we refuse to be beat.'

'It looks like we're in for a long haul, though. Jack doesn't think we'll be in a position to attack before nineteen forty-two. Another two years it could last.'

'We can do it. We must.'

'I do worry they're stringing us along though, on the BBC, that they really know we can't win. They say our planes are outnumbered ten to one. They now have the whole continent at their disposal.'

'Now, now. Careless talk and all that. You can get locked up for saying such things.'

'I just hope there's a future for the little ones, Dora.'

'There will be. You'll look back on this time and think what a grand thing it was to be alive today. To see it happen – to be here at the moment when we face our greatest test and we prevail. When victory comes what a moment that will be.'

'My goodness, Dora. Did Churchill consult you on his speech? They should put you on the wireless.'

'What a good idea. Now speaking of which why don't you pop it on. There might be a bit of an orchestra or a theatre organ to cheer us up. Hattie, perhaps you would like to draw me a picture when you've washed your hands? What if I go and fetch some of that blackout paper and some chalks?'

'Yes please, Mrs Thornton. I'll draw you a cat. I like cats. Do you like cats?'

She did indeed like cats, so much so that she kept bringing them home, and I'd have to shoo them out of the yard.

SARAH WAS having her afternoon nap and Michael was asleep in the pram. I sat on the village green where the crocuses were starting to emerge and read his letter telling me they were off to France. He couldn't say where they were going or when they'd be back.

Every day after that I worried about whether we'd see him again. On the wireless they talked of Holland and Belgium falling. British troops arrived back from Dunkirk and there was still no news of Jakub, or James as I was now supposed to call him. All I'd had was a postcard or two from a place called Harfleur.

Soon the swastika was flying over Paris. There was still no news.

It wasn't until June that I received a letter posted in Portsmouth saying they had arrived back safely. He then spent some time at Alexandra Palace before he was allowed on leave again. He hadn't wanted to tell me anything about what had happened in France – he played it all down and said it had been as boring as Kent.

It was only later that I learnt from one of his comrades, Walter – a refugee from Breslau, gentle with dark curly hair and brown eyes – who I met in town in forty-six, just how hard things had been for them, and that he had not earned his first stripe just by heaving sandbags and crates about.

They were in Le Havre loading freight in the docks as the Dunkirk evacuation was taking place up the coast and stuck at it despite being bombed by the Luftwaffe. James showed his strength of character under pressure, and his ability to command his men. One night, some time after midnight, they were ordered to leave and take only essentials before boarding lorries to take them away to where they did not know. They soon realised from the position of the stars that they were heading east to the front line. They were given orders to fight side by side with the other soldiers, and were armed for the first time and given basic instructions in how to use their guns and even man a field gun. None of them had ever even held a rifle before.

All the time the Germans were closing in. They must have been scared what would happen if they got captured by the Nazis – men and boys who had experienced Kristallnacht and Dachau. Fortunately the German army turned away and swept on towards Paris.

The Pioneers pulled back towards Rennes where they spent a few horrible weeks digging trenches, then retreating as the sound of gunfire got closer and closer. The French turned against them when they saw themselves being abandoned. As they retreated towards St Malo, the villagers lined the streets to jeer at them and call them every name under the sun – even hurling clods of muck at them.

Before they left they had to destroy anything useful they could not take. They pushed vehicles that had not even been brought into service off cliffs, made bonfires of brand new uniforms, and set fire to fuel depots.

They feared they had been abandoned by the army at one point, when all the officers disappeared and there was no sign of any movement. Soldiers from various other regiments seemed to be just wandering about aimlessly, or drunk, having got separated from their units. And all the time they could hear the sound of heavy gunfire in the distance.

When the convoy of lorries arrived for them they were greatly relieved. At least they made it back, which was more than some did, falling victim to German dive-bombers over the Channel.

James then went all round the country – on the south coast building defences and gun emplacements, felling trees in Wales for pit props, labouring at docks, all the while getting more frustrated that he wasn't in a fighting role.

'Why don't they trust us?'

'I'm sure they do.'

'Just not very much. It's such a waste of skills. I'm sick of working alongside old men and wasters.'

'At least they're not sending you to an internment camp.'

'I know. The whole of the south coast is on alert for an invasion – some of the lads got picked up by the local police. Someone had reported overhearing some German spies disguised as British soldiers. Even their army paybooks were taken to be good forgeries to start with. It wasn't until they phoned up the company commander that they got released. Even some of our own troops don't trust us. "Just because you're wearing a British uniform, that doesn't make you British," they say.'

'How horrid of them.'

When the Blitz started he was moved to London to assist the fire wardens, and the people of London. He helped pull people from the bombed buildings and knock down unstable structures after the raids: solitary chimneys and staircases left standing amongst the rubble of people's lives.

The war never directly touched our village. Young men went away of course. Robert went not long after James, but the cheese business soon had to close anyway as milk supplies were rationed. But apart from that, and things like the lovely old way-markers being removed from the crossroads, blackout blinds, and the occasional army vehicle passing through, outward signs of war were scarce. We often heard planes overhead at night-time and we knew they were on their way to cause destruction and massacre in the big Northern towns: Manchester, Liverpool, Sheffield and Glasgow.

I started to help out with the farm work – getting up early to milk the cows and helping supervise the work of the two land girls Addie and Kath who were billeted at our farm.

Of course I was now cut off from my mother – all we had were thoughts and prayers. I could not even tell her that she now had a grandson. I was grateful to be so busy. I had little time for melancholy. I'd worry about my mother and James but then Sarah would cover me in sloppy kisses or do something to make me laugh. Or Michael would fall over and need his pain and tears blowing away; you couldn't be like mimosa growing up on a farm.

I was never sure that James missed us as much as I missed him. The only frustration he seemed to have was that he was not wielding a gun. He'd come back on his eight days leave and would be irritable. It seemed to take him a few days to adjust back to our way of life – where your time of waking was governed by the needs of children and animals, not by military discipline, where he went from NCO in charge of a group of men to being a father and husband in charge of just himself. He'd nitpick at things we did and I'd accuse him of wanting us to stand by our beds whilst he inspected our boots. And then I'd get sad that we were wasting our precious time together bickering and he'd storm off to the pub and drink like a soldier.

We'd then have two or three days were everyone was happy and then he'd have to go off again.

Army life suited him too much – everything regulated, entertainment in the evenings from the camp band, football matches against the Royal Engineers and other regiments, the camaraderie.

He gained another stripe and was sent on weapons training in Devon, much to his satisfaction. He wrote of his success on assault courses and his accuracy statistics. His letters were full of it all. It made my letters about Michael's first steps holding onto Sarah's skirt, of the birth of new calves, or the difficulties the weather was presenting for the harvest, seem boring. He told me off for always writing "I have nothing much to tell you." He said he wanted to know that everything was the same. That was why he was doing his duty: to preserve all that, he said.

It's been a filthy day out there hasn't it?'

'It has, dear, yes.'

'I'll leave your Ovaltine on the table for you. Don't forget it will you now?'

'No, dear. Of course not. Have you remembered to lock the front door?'

'We'll not forget. Don't you go worrying.'

'Well, there's been things going missing. There must be a burglar getting in.'

'You're not still on about your alarm clock are you? We put it away in the suitcase because it kept going off in the middle of the night, you remember?'

'But I like to see what time it is in the night.'

'Your nephew, John, said he'd get you a clock without an alarm on, so that you can't set the alarm by mistake.'

'But what about my Waterford crystal vase? Someone has stolen it from the windowsill. It had sweetpeas in.'

'It fell off and broke a while ago. We'll find you a new one. So no more fretting.'

'Well, best lock that door.'

'Of course.'

'Don't forget.'

'Right. I'll pop and check if you need anything else before bedtime.'

'Thank you. Could you turn that blasted thing off on your way out.'

'People on the news making you cross again?'

'Bless her, she's left me some Ovaltine. It's dark now. And quiet now that man has shut up: that American on the wireless. The one they all go on about. But I don't trust him. You can tell by the tone of his voice. Thinks he's right. Full of himself. No better than that Stalin. These men, they're dangerous, puffed up and have no one to tell them they're wrong: no one who dares. They even start to think that God is guiding their arm. All this talk of cold wars and invasions, attacking little countries rather than letting them get on with it. How many times? How many times? This ship we're all in, twice it's been through seas so rough that it has threatened to smash the ship, and these men are seriously contemplating steering straight towards another even bigger storm. They're not men though – that's the trouble. They are no more than scaled-up boys – they never mature – not the ones who lust for power. They just want to have things their own way; lots of things in their collection – acquiring things and money, thinking that is success – they confuse idolatry with love. It is sad and dangerous. They don't know the value of life like women – women who understand caring for others, who grow life inside them then nurture it. These men, these presidents, these warlords – just immature boys. Is it any surprise that all the obsessive collectors – of art, of stamps, of coins, of birds' eggs, of butterflies, are all men? They will raid the nest of a beautiful bird, then destroy the life in their eggs and display them like trophies. They kill butterflies, pin them out on boards – destroying life in the process of trying to tame it, they kill animals and mount their heads on walls.

If women were in charge, it would be life itself that would be valued. I always tried to teach kindness and respect to my boys, but felt I was struggling against something stronger – even at the age of ten some of those boys, sons of labourers who had cardboard in their shoes to patch the holes, looked down on me, like I was a servant, had been taught arrogance by the world around them. Arrogant little boys become arrogant big boys, and the ones with birth right are pushed to the top, pushed ahead of those who are brought up to be kind and gentle, ahead of those who understand life and people.

Do you remember at the beginning of the war, we tuned into Priestley's broadcasts on Sunday night? He came across as a different kind of man. He was not lecturing us or telling us from a position of power what we should do, how we should behave, how we should feel. It was none of the: "listen to me and my words of wisdom – I am an important person" stuff. He spoke to us all as friends and shared his feelings and did what every good writer should do: expressed in words what people were feeling – thoughts that many of us had, if only vague and unformed. He once talked of women with real understanding. That grotesque blimp that says that a woman's place is in the home and that only the masculine mind can deal with the cut and thrust of political and financial life: he just stuck a pin in and the whole thing deflated – pthhhh! Men had no right to talk when they had made such a mess of things. He talked of the common sense of women and, when he said: "the sooner some of our communal and national affairs are managed by women the better," I gave a little cheer. I took it up and used it many a time.

It was one of the themes of his broadcasts – the need for something better to be built on the other side of the war to stop the drunken pursuit of power, and instead value creation: shaping a better world from ruins, not just looking to go back to what we had before. That's what happened after the first war. Once the cheering and flag-waving stopped the heroes who returned were pushed aside or shut away. Don't embarrass us by talking about what you claim to have happened, it's beastly. Don't show your scars and your deformed faces, your missing limbs. Stiff upper lip and all that; there's a good chap. Perhaps Smith was spared an even worse fate – a long, drawn-out decline like so many others of those boys, who came back ancient-looking in their twenties, and were homeless, humiliated, trudging around for work or queuing up for a pittance on the dole while black-marketeers drank champagne and did the Charleston or whiled away their leisure *Puttin' on the Ritz*. The old guard – those who had stayed behind while the best of men were butchered – the money men, gentry and swindlers got their hands back on the tiller and through their stupidity plunged us back into despair and nationalism. That's why they took Priestley off the air. Ideas like his were too powerful for the stuffed-shirts. It served them well to have some honest, trusted northerner rallying spirits after Dunkirk and in our darkest hour, but once he started putting ideas and thoughts into the heads of the masses, well that really wouldn't do. He was a genie they had unwittingly released and had to be stuffed back in his bottle. Good god, the man's making out that this is some kind of struggle for democracy or redistribution of wealth! Get on the blower to Reith and sort it out – the man's a bloody menace. Just rally behind the flag, by jingo! Sing a bit of *Tipperary* and we'll all get back to our weekends in the country playing lawn tennis and sipping Pimm's just like before. Party before country, what?

We followed the news of the Battle of Britain and listened in awe to the BBC commentary of a German attack on a convoy in the Channel and Spitfires chasing the Junkers and dog fights with Messerschmitts. It gave us hope that our boys were doing a grand job. That our planes were better than theirs.

All the predicted dates for the invasion came and went. The end of the world was not quite so nigh. Instead of Hitler parading through London in August he tried to bomb it to hell. But people woke up the next morning, cleared up the mess and carried on with their lives; shop-girls with their neat little handbags, civil servants with their newspapers under their arms, and labourers with their snap tins, heading for the tube or bus every morning, stepping round the piles of rubble being swept to one side. We started to feel he had done his worst and his worst wasn't enough.

It was in August that we had our first experience of air raids in Sheffield when we were woken in the night by sirens. We scooped the children up and took them to the cellar. They knew nothing of it and were excited when they woke up in the cellar in the morning. I, on the other hand, didn't get back to sleep all night, though I might have dozed a little towards dawn. I lay awake straining my ears for sounds, thoughts of what was about to happen rushing around my head.

The same thing went on for a few nights and on some occasions I had heard a distant sound of an exploding bomb.

I started to regret my selfishness in bringing myself and the kids back home. Should we have stayed in Leicestershire? Some people had sent their children far away to Canada or Australia – there was talk about the Princesses Elizabeth and Margaret being sent to Canada too. There were too many responsibilities. My worries fed off each other. It was crushing. I forced myself to think of other things.

Mrs Thornton was far more stoical than me. She got fed up with it all and after the first couple of nights said she wasn't going to bother any more.

'I can't be doing with all that traipsing up and down and trying to shake Derek awake. That man will sleep through owt. And as soon as he's lying down he's snoring, keeping me awake.'

'What about the kids?'

'I'll maybe just put them to bed in the cellar and take my chances upstairs. They do say if a bomb's got your name on it... But, I can't be doing with it – I'll die of exhaustion first. That's what they're doing – trying to break our will – making us lose sleep and cower in our cellars. Well, I'm done with it.'

'I suppose you are right.'

'A brave person dies only once, a coward over and over, or summat like that.'

'Is that in one of your speeches you've been writing for Churchill?'

'Nay, lass. It were someone clever on t' wireless.'

They weren't really air raids in those early days – there was damage to the odd building here and there, and a couple of people killed by a chance direct hit. So being in your Anderson shelter or your cellar wouldn't have done you much good anyway.

We now know of course that these isolated attacks were probably just practice runs. We read about the devastation of Coventry and Birmingham with mass bombing raids lighting up the night sky, of ongoing attacks on London. Perhaps Sheffield was protected by her hills – perhaps we were hard to find.

We prepared for our second Christmas of the war. I'd saved some pre-war currants and candied peel for a plum pudding and still had a bit of treacle in a tin, and had put aside a little bit of the sugar ration each week. Some people use the same recipe as their mother and their grandmother, stir in it the exact same silver sixpence – often with the young queen's head on. What did I have? Nothing. Even from the Cartwrights, all I had were a few old papers and the photograph of the child I replaced. How I envied those women who knew who they were, who felt the weight of the branches and the trunk of the tree supporting them. Me and Hattie and Jacky were starting afresh. This shiny George V sixpence was in its fifth year. Perhaps in twenty years time I'll be copying this recipe into a book for Hattie and giving her the sixpence.

'Right. Have we put everything in?'

'Yes, Mummy – there's nothing left on the table.'

'We need to give it a good stir then.'

'Right who's turn next? Jacky here you are. Now go steady lad.' I always had to scrape bits off the table to put back in the bowl with Jacky. 'Now you've to make a wish.'

'I wish I can have a dog.'

Hattie laughed at him. 'You're not supposed to tell anyone, Jacky. It doesn't work if it's not secret.'

Jacky looked upset.

'It's all right, Jacky. You have another go and don't tell anyone this time.'

Hattie stirred with her eyes shut and such an earnest expression on her face. I wondered if she was wishing for the war to end as I was.

'Go and fetch Daddy, Jacky. He has to do it too.'

We made some paper chains with cut-up strips of painted newspaper and hung them over the fireplace.

Jack was working long hours – sometimes putting in a double shift. The poor boy was exhausted – don't ever let anyone tell you that those in reserved occupations had an easy time of it.

The children were in their pyjamas and playing together nicely on the bedroom floor so I did a few quick jobs. I was on my own that evening, doing my usual juggling act. I knocked the ashes out of the fire in the living room, swept the hearth into the ash pan, and took it outside into the yard to empty it, switching off the light before opening the door as we'd got into the habit of doing. The temperature had dropped; my breath rose into the night air – clear and crisp, no clouds and a bright moon above. Before the war, walking home arm in arm from a dance, we would have regarded it as a beautiful night, but in nineteen forty we all longed for thick blankets of cloud to conceal us.

The sirens started their wailing. I quickly emptied the ashes into the dustbin and went to gather up the children to take them down to the cellar. I tucked them in their little beds and got the Mother Goose out to read to them and sang A Frog he Would A-wooing Go – such a lovely nonsensical song. Maisie used to sing it to me and I had retained a vague recollection of a tune she sang it to, and had made up the rest of it. It was one of Hattie's and Jacky's favourites, and had become a regular bedtime thing.

The siren stopped and Jacky was soon asleep. How I envied his ability to just close his eyes and fall asleep. Hattie too closed her eyes and I lit the hurricane lamp hung from the wire that fixed to a beam and turned off the cellar light. It was so quiet. I picked up my Georgette Heyer library book. I read a few lines but its power wasn't sufficient to drag me back to the heather moors, highwaymen and turnpike roads. I heard some footsteps hurrying past the coal grate. I stroked Hattie's hair away from her eyes; she was asleep too.

My ears strained for the drone of Heinkels and Dorniers. People reckoned they could even tell by the sound of them whether they were loaded with bombs or not – often the sirens went off accompanied by the occasional firing of an ack-ack as planes went overhead on their way to other targets or returning before the Spitfires could pick them off in daylight.

The first thing I heard that night was the boom of big guns and the bark of ack-acks followed by explosions. Then a huge bang as one landed nearby and the ground shook. The hurricane lamp rattled and dust shook out from the cracks in the floorboards above. Harriet sat up in bed and looked at me, her face confused. Almost straightaway another almighty explosion. She started crying and reached out for me. Then came a high-pitched whistling sound, followed by an even bigger blast that shook the whole house, and the sound of breaking glass and rumbling noises as something nearby fell to the ground, perhaps even parts of our house. Jacky woke too and started crying.

I picked up the Mother Goose and sang to them again. There was the sound of running feet outside and shouting.

'So off he set with his opera hat, Heigh-ho, says Rowley. And on the road he met with the cat.' It seemed like bombs were coming down all around as. I had both children on my knee and rocked them backwards and forwards. 'With a roly-poly, gammon and spinach, Heigh-ho says Anthony Rowley.'

'Bang, mummy.'

'Yes, don't worry about it. We're safe here. A cat and her kittens came tumbling in, with a roly-poly...'

It went on and on all around us and I carried on singing gently and softly as if all were well, trying to be calm for their sakes, when I was fit to scream myself. One explosion sounded like it was right above us, and shortly after I heard shouting: 'Jo, are you there? Quickly.'

'Look after Jacky for a minute, Hattie.'

As I reached the top of the steps there was an orange glow – my back door had gone and fire was burning in the kitchen.

'It's an incendiary, Jo.' It was Derek from next-door, just outside, throwing sand from a bucket onto it.

I grabbed the kettle and poured its contents over and rushed to the sink to soak a towel to throw over it. We put the fire out and Derek fetched a broom to push it all outside.

'That was lucky. They sometimes explode. Are you all right?'

'Yes, are you? Dora?'

'Down the cellar with the kids. She'd made me pop up to get the bread out of the oven and I saw this land. Hitler or no Hitler she'd not have her bread ruined. You'd better get back down too... The bastards. Pardon my French.'

There were three waves of attack that awful night. After the first when things seemed to have quietened down, I went back up to check there were no more fires in the house. Then I got the children to sleep again before going back to check the rest of the house. We had broken windows, but that was it. Jack's wire mesh window guards had stopped the glass from flying in at least. I put my coat on and went outside to see if anyone needed help. The Arnold's house over the road was ablaze and a bucket chain was in operation. Up the street curtains were sticking out through broken glass and there were chimney pots and slates strewn around on the pavements. There was nothing I could do to help. I had to be with the children in case anything happened.

The second wave was if anything more intense than the first: I suppose by now the city was burning bright and made an even better target than it had with just the moonlight reflecting back off frosted rooftops. It was said afterwards that they were able to follow railway tracks and rivers in the moonlight to guide them to the city. I spent the night praying that we would not take a direct hit, and that Jack was safe. I hoped he had still been at work when it started and not out in the open. That those shelters he'd talked about were as good as he'd claimed. I imagined all the scenarios, most of them bad, that long, exhausting night. I listened for the whistle of bombs and braced myself for the impact. How could this be happening? What could be going through the minds of those young men up there in the sky knowing they were killing children, women and old people by releasing their deadly payloads. What does anyone gain from this? From hatred built upon hatred until the whole thing topples down?

I sat on the chair next to their bed; both of them cuddled together on the bottom bunk and held their hands, more for my benefit than theirs. They somehow slept through the rest of the night with only the occasional murmur. The sleep of innocence.

The all clear eventually came in the early hours of the morning as the cowardly, deadly machines fled back to their bases across the Channel before dawn. I went to make a cup of tea and to nip across the yard while the kettle boiled. The sky glowed orange as if dawn had broken several hours too early and the air was thick with smoke; there was no longer that chill in the air. I sat by candlelight because the electricity had gone off and sipped my tea, shivering in the kitchen with cold December entering from where the remains of my backdoor was propped up in the doorway, before going back to the cellar to lie down and close my eyes, to rest if not sleep.

I heard Jack's voice and rushed up to see him before he could take fright at the state of the kitchen. He looked ghostly pale in the thin, early morning light.

'Thank God you're all right. We're all safe.'

'Thank God. When I saw... It is awful out there. I hate to think... I had to walk all the way – the streets are barely passable even on foot. Haymarket, Angel Street, High Street. There's nothing left. And the Moor... There are twisted tracks and carcasses of blazing trams. So much... It's unreal, Jo. Like a scene from Hell.'

I eventually released myself from his arms and put the kettle on – there was no longer any gas. I'll get the fire going instead. You sit down.

'Hattie and Jacky?'

'Still asleep downstairs.'

'I'll go and see them.'

I pushed the pram down to the shops the following morning. People had started to sweep up the mess – broken glass and bits and masonry and roof slate. I stopped and chatted to some of those who were out.

'Ooh, what a nuisance that Mr Hitler is, eh Hattie?'

'Did you look after your little brother last night?'

'Yes. I didn't like it very much.'

'But you are brave, eh? We keep smiling don't we? They won't break us that easily.'

'How are the Arnolds?'

There was a little shake of the head.

'And you've heard from your Muriel?'

'Yes, she called in on her way to work this morning. She set off early because the roads are blocked. Ooh, it makes you mad doesn't it?'

On the way down to London Road there were houses here and there still smouldering, and some completely gone: rubble-filled gaps where previously there had been a family home. The air was like on Bonfire Night.

The block where the bank was, opposite the Co-op, had taken a direct hit but the Co-op itself was largely unaffected. Smoke was still rising from inside the building. Looking over to my left I didn't recognise the city – the skyline had changed. The Moor looked terrible and further up London Road near the picture palace was the twisted metal frame of what had once been a tram. I felt for those poor devils who had been caught up outside when it happened.

On the Saturday we heard planes flying overhead. 'No doubt checking what damage they've done,' said Jack. Then on the Sunday night it happened again, but at least that time I had Jack with me. It was not so bad as the first night, at least not over us – the bombs seemed to be further over on the other side of the city – no doubt they were after the steelworks they had missed the first time.

The gas, water and electricity came back on. "Business as usual" signs went up on boarded-out shops. Flattened areas of rubble slowly replaced the hideous burnt out stacks of teetering masonry, creating extra playgrounds for the kids. Some of them stayed for years. Jack fixed the back door and the damage to the kitchen floor was not so bad, thanks to Dora's loaf tins and Derek's quick action; a rug covered up the burnt lino. The broken windows were boarded up and we still enjoyed a proper family Christmas. There was a joke going round that Father Christmas wouldn't be coming that year as he had been called up to the Swiss Navy, but for some homes it was no joke and he wouldn't be visiting that year – ones that were uninhabitable or where the parents couldn't afford a Christmas. Many people spent their Christmas sleeping on the floors of relatives' living rooms or in church halls.

Those days were the low point. Hitler had done his worst and we had come through it. There were one or two small raids later on but nothing to compare; although one in the spring destroyed a few houses around us and I was again down the cellar reliving the fear of that earlier raid. Our city will never ever be the same again, but life went on. Then in September Hattie started school. I was very proud of how grown up she had become.

Instead of the dictators joining forces to carve Europe up, Hitler turned his attention to fighting his old ally Stalin. He really was off his rocker. Then later that year the Americans joined the war at last. I'm not surprised they caused a stir in many a young, and not so young, girl's heart. They were smart in their uniforms and had a certain style, a swagger, that we weren't used to. Jack did not approve when one of them asked me to dance at the Grand Hotel. Had it been not been for Jack I would have gladly danced with him; it was all rather thrilling. I was one of the first to wear the red jacket with the black skirt that became all the fashion that year. I would have been disappointed if I hadn't turned a few GI eyes. Poor Jack! Concerts of the Hallé at the City Hall with Barbirolli conducting was safer ground for him. We holidayed at home and enjoyed the entertainment put on in the parks – even the awful comic duets which were more funny for the poor quality of the singing than the humour of the lyrics. We dabbed chicken pox with calamine and warmed tins of coal tar for whooping cough, bathed grazed knees in Dettol and kissed bumps better.

Two years after Hattie started school I waved my big girl and my little boy off as they walked hand in hand down the street together. I walked back up the passage and into the kitchen and stood there feeling bereft. How silly of me. That's one of the things that stands out for me about the war – how I entered it as the mother of two little tots and by the time it had ended they were big kids, no longer being read to at night and reading not just comics but quite grown up books, stopping out until nearly dark, roaming the streets and getting into goodness knows what scrapes with all the other kids.

I knew the war was nearly over when Hattie came home one Saturday teatime bursting to tell us her news – she and her friend Vera had bought a real Wall's ice cream. 'It was lovely, Mummy? Have you ever had one?' What was she? nearly nine-years-old and that was her first memory of ice-cream.

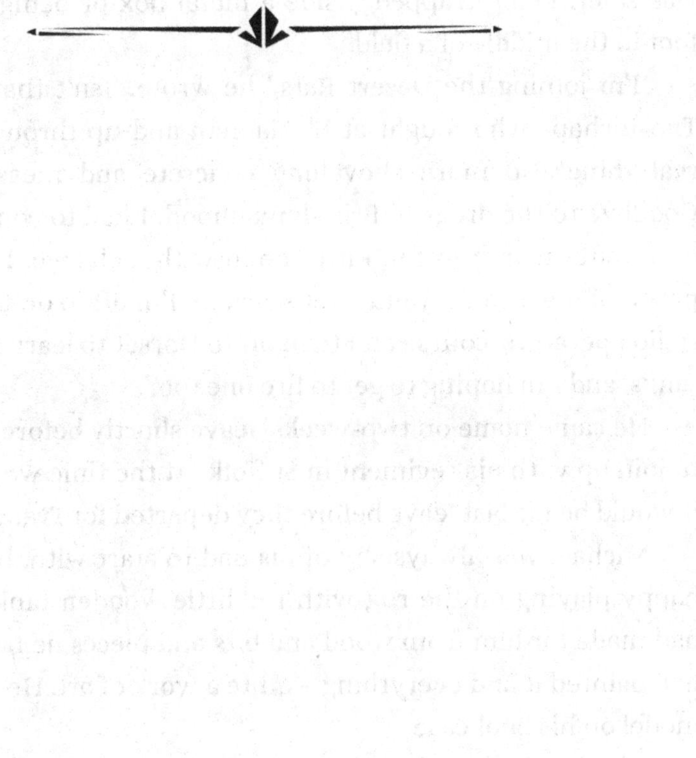

One day there seemed to be Americans everywhere, even in our little village shop. The darkest days seemed over as the talk shifted from "could we survive" to "when we would invade?" The army dropped its reluctance to include aliens in the fighting forces as necessity prevailed. Of course at the earliest opportunity James left the Royal Pioneer Corps and applied for where he could find the biggest guns – the Tank Regiment. I wasn't sure whether which was safer: being trapped inside a metal box or being exposed on foot in the middle of a field.

'I'm joining the Desert Rats,' he wrote. 'Isn't that incredible? Those chaps who fought at El Alamein and up through Italy. The real thing! No more shovelling concrete and measuring bolts. Goodbye to the dregs of British manhood. I had to complete a ten-mile route march in full kit to be in with a chance. I hope you're proud of me. I can't wait to get stuck in. I'm off to do the advanced radio operators' course and then off to Dorset to learn all about the tanks, and I'm hoping to get to fire one too.'

He came home on two-weeks' leave shortly before he travelled to join up with his regiment in Suffolk. At the time we didn't know it would be his last leave before they departed for France.

Michael was always shy of his dad to start with, but was soon happy playing on the rug with the little wooden tank that James had made for him from wood and bits and pieces he had found. He had painted it and everything – quite a work of art. He still has that model on his bookcase.

'That's a Cromwell tank, Micky. Like the one Daddy will be in: showing the Jerries what for.'

'Daddy drive a tank.'

'No – I'll be the radio operator, but I know how to use the guns too. It's a really fast tank, the Cromwell – it can do thirty-five miles an hour. It's got a Rolls Royce Merlin engine just like the Spitfire.'

For Sarah he had some American chocolate – a whole big bar to herself. It gave her daddy the status of a magician to be able to conjure up such a rare luxury. He gave me a pair of nylon stockings he had traded from one of his American chums. He was excited but I could also sense his nervousness. I sat next to him as he quietly smoked his cigarette and stared at the dying fire in the hearth.

'I hope I can prove myself, Lottie.'

'You've nothing to prove to us. We only want you to stay safe.'

He picked up the poker and sent sparks up the chimney.

'These chaps, though: they've seen it all. They're real heroes. They drink like there's no tomorrow, they get into fights for fun. If they are scared they never show it on their faces. They've been together overseas for four years. They've lost good comrades and then the likes of me come along to fill their places.'

'You should be yourself. You're a hero to us. They can't fail to like you for yourself. You'll see.'

His first letter reassured us that all was well.

You were right. The chaps have been most welcoming, but I shall never keep up with them. They have brought their awareness of tactics to the front of things here in the middle of nowhere: they have scoured the area for miles and miles and mapped out with precision every pub, all the dance halls, fish and chip shops, and WAAF stations. They know how to have a good time and they are always getting into scrapes – with the locals, or the RAF chaps or the Canadians. Last night I turned in at gone one in the morning and most of them were still going strong. They have also knocked up a theatre nearby for ENSA concerts where we can cheer the dancing girls, boo the rotten comedians, sing along to all the favourites and get forty winks when they recite Shakespeare.

You'll never believe who came to see us on Saturday! Monty himself! What a man. Some of the chaps were in a bad sorts about their leave – they had slopped "NO LEAVE – NO SECOND FRONT" on some tanks in white paint. You must bear in mind they have been away for four years. There was a frightful stink because they was no time to clean it off before Monty arrived. We had been bashed into square formation by the bawling sergeant majors, but Monty, after he had inspected the ranks, he went and climbed onto the bonnet of his Jeep, showing off all his medals on his battledress. There was a big cheer. He quietened everyone down: "All right boys. Close in a bit. You can break ranks. I want to talk to you. It is good to see you all again and I am proud to be fighting the Boche with you back in Europe." He said he sympathised about the leave but he took it head on: "you won't be getting that," he said, "but you will be getting a second front." He is not one of those lofty general types – spinning us a yarn – but one of us. "Good luck boys," he said. "I will see you over there."

We're off up to Scotland to do some practising with the tanks before we go.

James wrote letters from France. From what he told me it was all very plain sailing.

My darling Lottie,

All is well here – tickety-boo, as they say.

The show already had been going quite well by the time we got to the beaches. We had sailed all the way round from Felixstowe, having waited on board for two days before we set sail. The flotilla heading to sort out the Jerries was quite some sight. It was a bit choppy and many of us failed to hang onto our breakfast. We were two days and a night at sea – remind me never to join the navy! We landed a bit behind the schedule and most of the fun was already finished – the beach was already under control. The Spitfires and Lightnings were in charge of the sky and there was no sign of the Luftwaffe. It was lovely to see the houses on the cliffs already flying the tricolor.

We are now leaguered up a few miles inland. We have done our chores, got washed and shaved, had our tea. Boy they feed us well. We are now sitting about, smoking a gasper or a Lucky Strike: we did some trades with an American division over to our side. We've got more Brits and Canadians on the other. We've been through Bayeux today – it is not too badly damaged. The folks were out to greet us and glad it is over for them – much better than that last time I saw Froggies, no lumps of horse dung this time, only flowers. We didn't get to see the tapestry though. Have to save that for another day. I will write some more tomorrow.

Been here a couple of days now. I get to hear what is going on elsewhere over the wireless – we have got them on the run now. We have had a day of laziness again today playing cards, making tea and a bit of blanket drill (sleeping). On our tank is Ginger the tank commander. He is no redhead but is called Rogers, Niblick is the "driver," (that is a joke too – it is a golf club apparently) Dinger is the co-driver because he is Bell, Smudge is the gunner and then there is me: Stink. Not because I do particularly – no more than anyone else after days in a hot tank, but because roses smell. Everyone has to have a nickname.

We have also got a tank mascot now: a chicken called Betsy who one of the chaps found wandering about – she lives in a crate and seems quite happy with her new mates. We have got a rota set up for any eggs she will lay – worked out after a round or two of rummy. Spoils of war!

We have not had a to-do with an enemy tank yet. The only brew-up we had was an abandoned Tiger. But it was frightfully good fun as target practice. See! There is nothing to it this war lark. I shall get this posted now. Keep your ears stiff!

Kisses to Sarah and Mickey.

I wasn't fooled by his upbeat letters. I knew there was a lot he wasn't telling me, and I suppose he couldn't say too much anyway without risking censorship. That first letter took a while to arrive. I can't imagine the chaos there was – remarkable even that the post would arrive at all.

After that I tracked his progress across France from his letters, arriving only few days after he'd put them in the Green Envelope.

The town of Caen was a terrible mess, he said. Those poor people – to see war brought to their doorstep then march right in the front door, then have it all completely destroyed in order to set you free. So many lives lost. What madness. What a terrible species humans are.

He wrote a lot about Betsy and I always asked about her in my letters. It was somehow nice that he had female company to watch over him. When they stopped for the night, they would let her out for a scratch around and to find bugs to eat. The boys used to sleep on the ground when they weren't put up in a farmhouse, but Betsy always used to hop back onto the tank at night to sleep inside in her crate. He also described some nights which they had to spend in the tank when heavy rain came, and being bitten all over by mosquitoes by morning. If Betsy was out and about and heard the engine start up, she'd come running in order that she wasn't left behind. I grew very fond of her. One of James's letters enclosed one of her black and white mottled feathers and a photograph of her and James in front of the tank. She was a very pretty hen and he looks all happy in the picture: his teeth flashing a smile contrasting with his bronzed face – they seemed to spend more time sunbathing than fighting, if you believe the contents of the letters. Only occasionally did he mention that they had had "a bit of a bust up" or had to "ginger up" some Germans who were hiding in a wood or "they stood on top of the tank to get a better view of the good hiding that the bombers were giving to an enemy position."

My Darling Lottie

Your letter arrived in today's post. It is hard to believe that Micky is about to start in his second year in infants. Tell him I shall keep his letter with the lovely drawing of a tank in my pocket. Sarah's handwriting is very neat, much neater than mine. What a clever girl she is. I love her little painting of a rose – she is as pretty as her name in the photograph you sent me.

We have crossed the Seine and next full speed to Belgium. Hardly a bridge was left at all. The Jerries have blown them up so we crossed on Bailey bridges. Those boys in the engineers can replace a bridge double quick and onwards we go like that. The remaining Germans have fled Paris and have been sorted out good and proper. We've seen our first few prisoners. I was asked to go and speak to two of them – officers they were – to see if I could find anything out quickly before they were sent back for proper interrogation. They were very confused to hear a British soldier speaking their language! The looks on their faces!

The mademoiselles have all been out in their best clothes giving flowers to the soldiers, wine and cognac. Last night we found a small cafe which had a good supply of calvados. Some Canadians then joined us and we made a made quite a night of it. There were a few sore heads in the morning.

We met a Welshman earlier who has become a bit of a celebrity. He was shot down in 44 and has been hiding in a farmhouse ever since, waiting for us to arrive so he can get stuck in again. These little things cheer us up a lot.

We went to see George Formby while we were resting near Aunay. He is terribly funny and we had a good laugh and a bit of a sing-along. They also have laid on cinema and all sorts to keep morale up. Another funny thing – we were lying on our backs the other day topping up our suntans when we saw a doodlebug up in the sky – but it wasn't heading for England. Instead of that flying south. Sammy – who replaced Ginger as our driver after a bit of a skirmish at Villers – he said it couldn't be going south – but after we put him straight on that we all agreed it was. Smudge said that is because there are Spitfires who have broomsticks who intercept them over the channel and nudge at them back round the way they came.

By September they were in Belgium. I think they were the first in Ghent and the streets were full. Everybody was out: old and young, cheering and patting them on the backs and kissing them. They were treated like film stars and signed their autographs on books and flags and anything else to hand. They got used to people lining the streets and offering them beer, eggs, cognac and apples. They were heroes after all. In Eindhoven they parked their tanks, or leaguered them, or whatever it was they call it, in the public park and played football with some local boys.

They reached a place called Nistelrode and then they got stuck as autumn and winter came on. James got bored and frustrated, and even organised games of football against other regiments didn't stop him getting depressed. He just wanted to get it over with: cross the Rhine, sort Hitler out, and then get back home.

He had leave in Brussels and Antwerp over Christmas and New Year and no doubt they were treated well, but it's not home is it?

In the last letter I got from him he had crossed the Rhine and was full of hope that it would be soon over.

It was in April that I learnt that James, my Jakub, had been lost in battle. The telegram was so stark – "deeply regret to inform you that on 10 April your husband corporal James Rose has been killed on active service. Letter follows shortly."

The letter which arrived from the Ministry in London was a bit more personal, but not much. Typed by some secretary who knew nothing about Jakub or what had happened. It spoke of his bravery and hope that that would be of some comfort to me. Then it hit me. The letter said that he was buried in a military cemetery only a few miles from our little town in Germany. He had died there – where he was born.

I got another letter, postmarked Berlin, a few months later, this time hand-written, from a Lieutenant Richards who James had served under. It was hard to read through my tears.

He wrote: "I thought you would perhaps like to know what had happened. To put your mind at rest and so that you know what a stout fellow James was....

"I smoked a cigarette and shared some cognac with his crew the night before. He was in good spirits and telling us about the region. His knowledge had been put to good use earlier in the day when he had been called in by the major to a conference with the troop commanders to go over the maps and tactics for the next stage. He told us a few funny stories from his youth and talked of happy times there with you and of the walks you made on the heath.

"We were pushing on towards Bremen and each squadron was allocated to a different infantry battalion as they advanced and flushed out any remaining enemy. James was riding in the lead tank of a squadron heading towards a town called Retham, carrying infantrymen on the tanks in the advance on the town. The woods had already been patrolled that morning so it was assumed they were clear. They were ambushed by some marines – a group of, largely young, Nazi fanatics who were hell-bent on fighting to the death, even though they knew defeat was inevitable. James' tank was hit by a bazooka it seemed, and they all bailed out and were involved in a fierce fight in which all of the crew perished. He took a bullet in the heart and died instantly. He did not suffer.

"His body was recovered and he was buried by his pals. He was a decent man, a brave man. He died in honour, fighting for everything that is good in the world. You can be proud of the part he played in defeating evil. His cause was just and he was determined to see right prevail. I am sure his only regret would have been not being there for you and your children. I know his pals debated whether to return the letter you wrote to him and the photos and drawings he always carried in his pocket, but in the end they decided to let him keep them where he rested. I enclose a photograph of his grave.'

It is hard for me to recount what happened. Rethem was a name I knew well. It was only a few miles down the road. Jakub would have known it well from travelling with his father's business. Had he lived he would have experienced the satisfaction of occupying our town, not long after – satisfaction and vindication, of seeing the faces of those who had turned away when they saw us mistreated. But it would also have been a moment of grief.

When the war was over, some normality returned and the postal service resumed, I was able to write to my mother. I sent her a photograph of her grandchildren and asked her to put some flowers on Jakub's grave – and explained that she needed to look for Lance Corporal James Rose of the Tank Regiment.

I had a long nervous wait for a reply, and when it came a few weeks later it was not in my mother's hand.

Dear Liselotte

I am so sorry to have to be the one to send you bad news. Your mother was killed on the 15th April, a few hours before the British arrived. We knew that the Allied troops were approaching – we had heard the guns getting progressively closer. It was so clearly lost. We all knew it. We wanted no more death or bombing. We did not want our town to be shelled and reduced to rubble in a last ditch battle. We women implored the Wehrmacht commander to leave. To not make us a target. We met at the Town Hall and they tried to make us disperse but we shouted at the soldiers. They threatened to report us to the Gestapo, called us traitors.

The remaining soldiers decided to leave and as the British came nearer we hung sheets as white flags from our windows. To most it was an act of sanity, of acceptance of the truth, for people like me and your mother it was much more – an act of friendship from people who had always seen through the lies. Some, however, saw it as an act of treason. A young Nazi ran through the town as he fled the approaching troops and started shooting at people he saw as traitors. Your mother was hit and died soon after. I'm sorry, Liselotte. She was a good woman and did not deserve to die by a coward's bullet. She loved you and the children very much: I have taken their photo to her graveside. They are beautiful and Jakub must have been so proud of you all. I will look after some of her possessions for you, should you ever be able to send for them.

I have placed some roses on Jakub's grave for you. I hope you don't mind that I read your letter. He was a lovely young man. I was ashamed of what happened, how he was treated.

There have been some awful things. You have probably read the news. You will recognise the name Bergen. Had you already left when they started building the military base there? Afterwards the camps that housed construction workers were turned into prisoner of war camps. It will forever be a stain over our district what came after – we never knew the real truth. We suspected it was not good, but what is said happened is beyond comprehension. We were all so powerless. I'm sure you understand that better than most and will not judge us too harshly. Would any human being have acted so differently?

We have all lost so much – my Gunter never made it back from the East. I hope we can now build a new world. Look after yourself and those darling children.

With friendly greetings,

Irene Westermann

Both my husband and my mother died within a few hours of each other, and only a few miles apart. I don't really know how I got through that time – but for Sarah and Michael keeping me busy I am not sure that I would have.

I stayed on at the farm for a few months but it became too much to bear. I had to get away and start again – to somewhere I wouldn't keep expecting Jakub to come round the corner. I kept seeing him in the way someone walked, in a voice I heard across the yard, in a shout that drifted over from the football field. It was too much. The Greens were sad to see us leave. They tried hard to persuade me to stay; to re-start the business, but I would have choked on German farm cheese. They had grown very fond of the children and had become something like surrogate grandparents to them, but I could not see my life stretching out there, depending so much on other people.

So we set off on an adventure from our little village to the nearest town – to the biggest village in England. To the home of my father – Sheffield. I had stayed in touch with Adela and Kathleen, the landgirls who were billeted at our farm. Addie was getting married now that her fiancé had been demobbed. She was moving out and leaving her widowed mother on her own in a big house and suggested that I could move in with the children – it would cheer her up to have little ones around, give her a focus, stop her moping about. Her mother could help out with the children while I went out to work – she said someone who could cook like me would easily find work.

So it was we found ourselves on a train clanking along the tracks on the approach to the city.

'Hattie! Hadn't you best be getting off in a minute to be back for when the kids finish school?'

'I'll be down in a minute. Just going for a wee.'

'What were you shouting?'

'Just saying it's nearly time for the bell – you don't want to be late back.'

'I'm all right for a couple of minutes.'

'Well, don't dawdle, Harriet. They won't like it if you're not there.'

'Oh, mother. They'll be fine. Dot's very sensible and looks after her brother.'

'She's a lot like you were, it's true. Thank you for helping out today – it was a great help having someone else to shepherd the old dears around the gardens.'

'I enjoyed it – it's ages since I've been to Whirlow – not since Stan and me were courting.'

'I hated you going off on that motorbike... I think the gardens are at their best at this time of the year with the roses out. Can you just reach up and get me that packet of semolina down? Thanks. You seemed to be getting on well with Mrs Broadhead.'

'Yes, we had a nice little chat about the olden days. We got on really well – like we've met before. She was telling me all about the suffragettes. I can't remember how we got onto politics – I must have said something about campaigning for Vera in the election. I bet you didn't know she had set fire to postboxes did you?'

'Never! What Mrs Broadhead?'

'Yes. She had a real twinkle in her eye when she was telling me; you wouldn't think she had it in her would you? But when you get her on that stuff you realise just how feisty she is. I like that.'

'*You* would. You have met her before you know.'

'Have I?'

'Yes. Once in the war when we were being evacuated. She was with her class taking them away too. She stopped to chat to you at the station.'

'I'm not sure I remember. I was only four I suppose. There's something a bit sad about her though, don't you think? I asked her about her husband – she'd said something about having to give up teaching and that was one of the things that made her support the Suffragettes. I asked her what Mr Broadhead had thought about that, and she went a bit quiet. She married twice, you know.'

'I knew she was Oughtershaw before the war, but we always called her *Miss*. You don't ever imagine your teachers having private lives do you?'

'Her first husband died after the war – the First World War.'

'I didn't know.'

'He had an odd name too, her husband: Smith – as a Christian name not a surname... What is it, Mum?'

'Oh, nothing. I just thought I'd heard that before somewhere. It is odd.'

'I also asked if she'd had any children.'

'You Nosey Parker, Harriet Meacher.'

'I'm not. Just interested in people and their stories. Anyway, she didn't say. She just asked me about Dot and Stuart. But I couldn't help thinking... Like she was changing the subject. I bet her story would be fascinating – I bet you could write a book about it. I just got that feeling, you know.'

'Yes, still waters run deep. I'm just pleased that I can help make her time at Prior Bank pleasant, poor dear. She seems happy enough most of the time, though. The only completely happy ones are the bonkers ones who think they're little girls still. Mrs B's the one I told you about, who used to be my teacher.'

'Oh, that makes sense now. You said she was kind. Is she the one who went to your father's funeral?'

'Yes, that's her.'

'I often wonder who my real grandfather and grandmother were.'

'I know. But you were lucky to have Nanny and Grandpa Burridge. They spoilt you rotten... and Jackie.'

'I never seemed to leave theirs without a silver sixpence in my pocket, did I? And a toffee or something.'

'I'm surprised your teeth aren't falling out.'

'Mackintosh's toffees still remind me of granny... '

'That tin of hers never seemed to run out. I think it was a magic tin.'

'... that and the vanillary smell of Grandpa's pipe smoke.'

'He was very particular about his tobacco. '

'I still feel I missed out though, not knowing my other grandparents.'

'Yes, it's a version of what I feel, I suppose – not quite knowing.'

'I didn't mean... I'm sorry. It is so much harder for you. I'm very grateful. I know where I'm from and have the best parents in the world.'

'And if you don't want to be the worst parent in the world you'd better get your skates on, my girl.'

'Okay, I'm off then. I'll be round Thursday.'

'And are you going to come to the garden party on Sunday to celebrate the Prior Bank anniversary? You could carry on your interrogation into the lives of our esteemed residents.'

'I'll see if Oliver will take the kids to the park? Then they can collect me on their way back. Will they be allowed to pop in for a few minutes?'

'If they are on their best behaviour. I'll ask Matron. The Lady Mayoress is coming and various other bigwigs. The old dears like to see well-presented children, though. It always cheers them up.'

'Okay. I'd best dash.'

Was it Priestley who played with the ideas of time in his plays: its permanence and whether those things that happened exist any less than we do here and now? We panic, imagining fragility, the clock and our lives ticking away, destroying everything. Those other parts of our lives exist just as much – the whole landscape is still there and... that was it: time just moves us on from one peephole to the next. Those echoes of the past are always with us and are passed through the generations.

'Hello, Elsie. Mum said I'd find you here. Are you going to get ready to come down to the garden party? Everyone's arriving. There is home-made lemonade and cucumber sandwiches.'

'I don't know, dear.'

'Come on. We can't have you sitting by the window all afternoon.'

'Are you my niece?'

'No, Elsie. I'm Hattie – Mrs Burridge's daughter. You know, Mrs Burridge who works here.'

'Oh yes. I thought I recognised you. Something about your eyes...'

'We had a lovely chat the other week when we went to Whirlow. Do you remember? You were telling me about the WSPU.'

'I was thinking about those times when you came in.'

'Why don't you tell me some more at a garden party. I like to hear about it – did you ever meet the Pankhursts?'

'Yes, I knew Adela, and heard the others speak. I liked Sylvia especially.'

'Will you tell me all about it when we get outside? Shall we get you in your glad rags? What have you got in your wardrobe? We can't have you meeting the Lady Mayoress in that old cardy.'

'There's nothing wrong with this cardigan.'

'No, Elsie there isn't, but we want to impress the Lady Mayoress don't we? This nice jacket is just the thing. I'll brush some of this lavender into your hair and we'll rouge your cheeks. Put you a bit of my lippy on.'

'We never had make-up when I was young. It was frowned on. Only loose women and actresses ever painted their faces. We just nipped our cheeks to make them a bit pinker.'

'Well, I'm glad you weren't a loose woman. Now, don't worry, I'll not overdo it – no one will even know except you and me. There – you look lovely. Now we need some jewels. What have we got in this box? What about this? This is lovely. Is it gold?'

'No – not that. I don't wear that any more.'

'Why ever not? It is so pretty.'

'It is subversive you know.'

'How can a necklace be subversive?'

'The stones are green white and violet: Give Women Votes.'

'Oh, how wonderful. You should wear it.'

'I can't. Would you like it?'

'Oh no. I couldn't.'

'I'd like you to have it. I don't want them to just be given to a junk shop when I'm gone. I know you will look after it.'

'No. Really, I couldn't.'

'It was given to me by someone very special. Now would you put it on, please.'

'Are you sure you wouldn't like to wear it?'

'No. I've never worn it – not since... Let me look at you, dear. He would have liked you.'

'Who was he? Your husband? I'm sorry – my mother calls me nosey, but I'm just interested in people. That's my excuse. Thank you, Elsie. I will treasure it. Really. And I'll think of you every time I look at it.'

'That makes me very happy.'

'Look, what about these pearls then? Are they real?'

'I don't know. Mr Broadhead gave them to me for my birthday once. He said they were real, but he was easily taken in.'

'Well, they are pretty, too. Look at us – don't we look nice? I'll just sort your hair out a bit, then we'll go down and see if we can't find a sherry or two and get sloshed shall we?'

*

'Oh, what a day! What can I get you to drink, Lottie?'

'Campari and soda, please.'

'There's a table by the window over there. Go and bagsy it and I'll bring the drinks over.'

'Bagsy? What is bagsy?'

'Oh, it just means get the table for us, that's all.'

'There: two large Campari and sodas, or is it Camparis and soda? Just shut me up prattling.'

'What was it you wanted to talk to me about?'

'It's something Mrs B said.'

'Poor Mrs Broadhead. How was the service?'

'It was lovely. Her nephew spoke very well. She had a full life. Such a strong woman.'

'You will miss her, I think.'

'Yes, I became very fond of her.'

'It was quite sudden? I didn't even know about it until the next day. I was so busy with the food and drinks then tidying away afterwards.'

'She was having such a lovely time; laughing and joking with Hattie and just took a little turn. Poor Hattie was very upset. We got her up to her room and called for the doctor. He just made her comfortable and said he thought moving her to the hospital would only make things worse, distress her more.'

'Were you with her, then?'

'Yes. She wouldn't let go of my hand so I stayed until the end. She was very peaceful. She drifted away quite slowly and it was like she was talking to people; to me, but others as well. All a bit muddled. I think she knew – even before the doctor came. She made me fetch her biscuit tin from the wardrobe and gave me strict instructions not to let anyone in her family have it.'

'Biscuit tin?'

'Where she kept things: letters and whatnot. She said I should take it away and burn it.'

'And did you?'

'No. Not yet anyway. I'll see. It seems a shame. I haven't looked in it yet – it seems a bit, y'know… There was a photo of a handsome young man in uniform. She was holding it in her hand when she passed away. I brought it to show you.'

'He is handsome isn't he?'

'The thing is…'

'What?'

'The other week, my daughter, Hattie. She could have been in the Ges... well she's very inquisitive, you know, with how she wheedles information out of people.'

'Wheedles?'

'Yes. People tell here everything, you know. And she found out that Mrs Broadhead's first husband was called Smith, and he died after the war, the First World War. I checked today with her nephew.'

'You mean…'

'You know you told me he was Ottershore, well that must be Oughtershaw. There is no such name as Ottershore.'

'That is what everyone says.'

'And there are thousands of Smiths, but not as a Christian name.'

'He made it back here then. That is good. My mother, she would… Do you think... could this be him?'

'I don't know. I meant to tell you before, and now she's gone and you can't talk to her. She was holding this picture when she passed. I'm sorry.'

'Don't be sorry.'

'You could talk to her nephew – he might know a bit more. I did ask him today but he says he doesn't remember her husband – he was only little.'

'No. There is no need. It wouldn't help. I don't need to know any more. I sort of know enough already – from inside me. And to know he made it home... My mother said my father called Sheffield the biggest village in England. When I arrived here I thought that was nonsense – it was so big. But I came to understand. I understand now. I feel I know him well enough. I am home too.'

Dear reader

If you thought this book was at least half decent, it would be really appreciated if you could do a quick review on Amazon, Goodreads or other online sites you use. Just a word or two would be great. 1889 Books is a small-scale undertaking so word of mouth is vital to letting readers know about it.

You can sign up for news and offers at www.1889books.co.uk, such as a free e-book of my first novel *The Evergreen in Red and White* set in Sheffield in 1897/98 (see below).

Acknowledgements

Sheffield Local Studies Library and staff. An invaluable resource that should be cherished.

Also to Stephan Heinemann for putting me in touch with somewhere I could held hold of his book *Zwischen Demokratie und Diktatur.* Thanks Stephan, for the correspondence and advice which prevented me from making a pretty serious historical error. And to Anke von Fintel at Landkreis Heidekreis for sorting the book out for me.

Carmel for her early encouragement.

The "sort-of" prequel to *The Winds Blew.*

Elsie has two feet in the 20th century. Smith has one foot in the 19th. Their marriage, founded on physical attraction, is built on sand as all around them the earth of Europe also starts to quake. Prised apart by emotional conflict and the loss of two children they are flung apart by the most violent physical conflict in human history. The question is whether they can survive, together or at all.

Rab they call me. Or the "little gypsy." Lucky parentage they say. If only! Irrepressible – whatever that means. Happy-go-lucky. Hah! Like they know. I wonder who the hell I really am. Coal miner, footballer, husband, father, lover, fighter? Always being defined by others. Anyhow, that 1897/98 season were a belter. We were top of the league. I were playing my best. Selina, the missus, got pregnant. Then I met Ada. Oops! Then there were bloody Sunderland. And then the wheels fell off.

"Thoroughly enjoyed the book… minutely observed and well-depicted background of Sheffield" – Graham Phythian, author of *Colossus the true story of William Foulke* and *Shooting Stars the brief and glorious history of Blackburn Olympic*

"A lost treasure of a footballer from the first golden age of the game. Researched and told with love and genuine care, a truly fascinating piece of work" – John Garrett, Sheffield United FC Supporter Liaison Officer and Historian, co-author of *Sheffield United FC The Biography* and author of *Blades Folklore and Fables*

"A poignant love story set in the gritty streets of Sheffield at the turn of the century. Meticulously researched, this is a must for local history enthusiasts and anyone who loves a good read" – Cheryl Bailey, Senior Archivist, Sheffield Archives

"A meticulous novel that brings social and football history to life in the form of a truly unique character from football folklore" – Scott McCabe, Sheffield United

"An engaging, compelling, read, with finely drawn characters and a fascinating background. Highly recommended." – Historical Novel Society

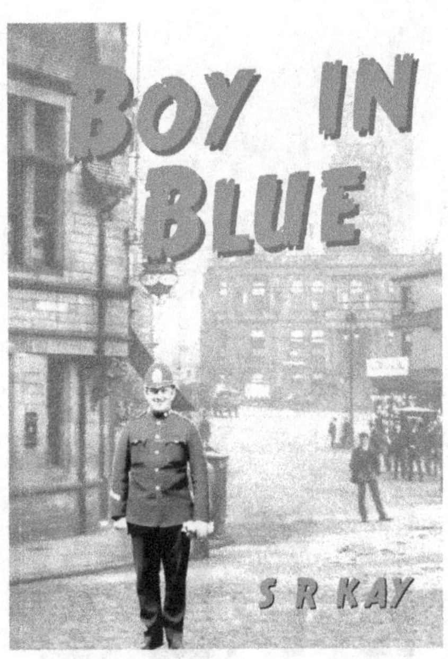

Based on the true story of PC John Higgins - a "pretty policeman" whose evidence convicted twelve ordinary men for what was a victimless crime. He gained their trust and was invited to their private party. On Higgin's evidence they felt the full weight of the law and were treated worse than murderers.

But was he really undercover, or was it just a cover-up? To bury deep and shameful desires and protect the Police's reputation? This is a carefully researched tale of love, temptation and betrayal in Victorian England, told from the point of view of Higgins, his wife Annie, and of his close friend Bill Kilroy, who spent the rest of his life in a lunatic asylum. It is gritty, lyrical and moving.

What would happen if a left-wing, Labour leader remained popular despite every smear and lie the establishment and their media chums threw at them? What if, as the election approached, he started to gain traction because of a serious downturn in the economy, unrest in the country and corruption revealed at the highest levels? What if the electorate started seeing him as an answer to their problems? How vicious would the right-wing and ultra capitalist reaction be?

Finding himself at the heart of a conspiracy is 30-year-old Health and Safety Inspector, Mitch Miller who falls in love with someone he shouldn't and gets into very hot water. A modern day Romeo and Juliet, facing car chases through the streets of Sheffield, murder, betrayal, kidnap and the odd explosion.